THE BLOOD TREE

BOOK 1

LYNDELL CASELLA

THE GREATER GOOD TRILOGY

Queensland, Australia

Cover design by Judith San Nicolas
Typeset in Devangari 18/36 pt and Goudy Old Style 9/12pt
Printed and bound in Australia by IngramSpark
Prepared for publication by Dr Juliette Lachemeier @ The Erudite Pen: theeruditepen.com

A catalogue record for this book is available from the National Library of Australia

The Blood Tree: Greater Good Trilogy – Book One – 1st ed.
ISBN 9780645280401 (Paperback)
ISBN 9780645280418 (Ebook)

Dedication

To my late mother and my readers,
this book comes from my heart to yours. I give it to you in the spirit of
sharing a story. It is my own arrangement of words, created with love.
Wherever you are now, Mum, I hope you know that
this small treasure is also for you.

Book One

Prologue

November, 1978

Racing down the concrete steps of the Melbourne City Library and turning right towards Flinders Street Station, Scarlett Jones joined the rush of commuters leaving the city. She merged into the crowd that resembled a human river sweeping along the pavement.

It was Tuesday, the day before her final exams, and she was feverishly anticipating the finish line. Exhausted from skipping meals and sleep for longer than she could remember, finally the end was here. After tomorrow, it was surreal to think she was actually going to be a doctor. Well, almost. She still had to complete an internship and then residency at St. Vincent's Hospital, where the real work would begin.

All day she had sat under the library study lamp, hunched over her text books, expanding her brain while shrinking every other muscle in her body. Tired and cramped, Scarlett longed for a hot bath and then sleep. But fate had other plans.

Dashing along the footpath towards her bus, Scarlett waved her arms to alert the driver, but instead of waiting, he closed the hissing doors and pulled out into the congested traffic. Nobody had hailed the bus to wait, nobody came to her aid, nobody cared. There was just a cluster of indifferent faces staring down at her from their prized seats.

With no choice but to wait in the bus shelter, Scarlett took a seat then leaned back to close her eyes and ease a thumping headache. Other commuters gradually filled the bench seat until they resembled chickens roosting for the night. The shelter was a haven that provided little protection when a late afternoon storm broke. Wrathful black clouds flung rain at them in a spiteful slant until the creeping cold numbed the hands and feet of all those pressed together in common misery.

After an overcrowded bus ride home, the sky was dark when it finally stopped at her street. Scarlett shivered in her damp clothes as she stepped out into the chilly breeze. The storm had stripped leaves and branches from trees and strewn them like confetti across the pathway. They crackled ominously like brittle bones under her wet shoes.

Just as her hand reached for the gate latch, she was snatched from behind. Like a bat swooping from the sky, he was there without warning. In the hush of the suburban night, a strong arm grabbed hold of her tightly. For one small second, she thought it was a friend playing a prank until a dirty sock was jammed past her teeth and halfway down her throat. Gagging as the sock's smell of vomit and blood assaulted her senses, it was this offence that broke her dreamlike state. Twisting towards her assailant, she reached up to rake her nails over his eyes, but he was ready. Smashing his fist into the side of her head, Scarlett was plunged into a world of darkness.

Unconscious for most of the time it took to travel from the safety of her home into the unknown, she groggily lifted her head off the floor of what seemed to be a van. Her breath was short and sharp, hissing through her nostrils, even drowning out the road noise. She hyperventilated until her head spun. *Calm yourself,* her medical mind ordered, so she slowed her breathing until the dizziness abated. Scanning the space in the dark, she lay there on her belly, arms tied firmly behind her back.

Her mind was frantic. She needed to get out of here now. Groaning, she rolled over onto her bound hands, waiting a moment for the pain to ease. Slowly, using her feet, she pushed across the floor until her shoulders bumped into a panel. Now to find the door to escape.

Sliding along the length of the van, her hands searched for the framework of the door and located the handle. With numb fingers, she fiddled furiously with it, slipping time and time again. If she could just get the door to slide open, she wouldn't hesitate to tumble out. It would surely be better to die quickly than face what was to come. Finally, she got a firm enough hold to pull as hard as she could, only to find it was locked. At this moment, the van turned sharply, toppling Scarlett over and bashing her shoulder into the unforgiving floor. The van raced around corner after corner, and with nowhere to hold on, she slid from one side of the van to the other throughout the wild ride. Scarlett whimpered in distress. The gag was hot and heavy in her mouth, and now full of her own saliva. Fear coursed through her. Tears ran down her cheeks and blocked her nose, making it even more difficult to breathe.

Who was this person? What did he plan to do? Was he going to rape and kill her in some isolated place, where nobody would hear her screams? Panic threatened to overwhelm her senses, so she closed her eyes a moment to shut out the reality of her situation. Eventually, she managed to slow her heart and regain some measure of control. Trying not to focus on the odious tastes coming from the gag, she slithered across to the far panel to support her back. Where they were going, she didn't know.

The ride seemed to last forever, but then when she thought of the destination, it would never be long enough. She didn't know how long she had been unconscious. It could have been an hour or only fifteen minutes. Peering through the van's side windows, she noticed there were no lights from passing cars, so they must have moved beyond the city limits. Dreading what lay ahead when they did stop, Scarlett prepared herself to escape as soon as that door slid open.

The feared moment came when the van slammed to a stop, throwing Scarlett forward. She heard the door unlock. It slid back with a crash, and she was dragged out, grunting through the gag as her feet hit the ground. Scarlett took in her abductor, trying to see if it could possibly be someone she knew. Or was this a case of mistaken identity? Did he think she was a person he knew? It still didn't seem possible that this was a violent, random attack, and her mind sought a reason for this insanity. In the dark, it was hard to discern any features, but she could make out that he was tall and thin, wearing a dark jacket and jeans, with a pack slung over his shoulders. *What was in that pack?* Something sinister, she feared.

She tried to pull away from him, but his hands punishingly gripped her shoulders, his fingers digging deep and bruising the tender flesh. Twisting her body, she desperately turned to kick at him, but he held her at arm's length. Choking with frustration, she launched herself at him, hoping he would lose his footing and fall backwards, but instead she slammed into the taut muscles of his chest and abdomen. He pushed her away and took one handful of her hair. Clamping the other hand on her shoulder, he shoved her ahead of him across an uneven rocky surface until they found a narrow path through the forest. Keen and close, the branches scratched viciously at her face. She was briefly distracted by a trickle of warm blood that ran down the side of her cheek to drip off her jaw and paint the front of her t-shirt in a sorry portrait.

Her mind was frantic as he shoved her along, but it struggled to catch up with her sudden change in reality. Still it yearned to dwell on the familiar fear of failing her exams.

I must survive this monster, she resolved. There was nobody here to save her, so it was now or never. Looking left and right, it was so dark that she couldn't even see the path ahead. The trees pressed close with no chance to dart to the side, and with her arms bound, it would be impossible to outrun him. Scarlett prayed for a break in the trees so she could run off and maybe find somewhere to hide in the bush until the sun came up.

Taking stock of her injuries, apart from a bruised and scratched face, possibly a ruptured eardrum and aching shoulder, she would still be able to make a run for it. Within about ten strides, her prayers were answered. The trees thinned, so as quick as a fox she slipped out of his grasp and off to the side, ripping out a handful of hair as she bolted. But that pain would be insignificant compared to the loss of her life. The branches did even more damage to her face, but she ignored the pain and blood. Fighting to stay upright, she sprinted away.

At first, she heard nothing but the sound of her own breath. Was he taunting her with a head start? Pushing even harder, her heart pumped like a steam engine with little oxygen, yet she didn't dare slow down, half believing she might make it. Until she was tackled from behind.

'No, no, no, I don't want to die, not yet!' her mind screamed as she hit the ground with him on top of her. The impact cracked several of her ribs as they slammed into the unyielding ground, and no matter how hard she tried, her lungs remained closed. Like a fish taken from the water, she lay there gasping yet dying all the same. Blood oozed over her lips, and instinctively she tried to mop up the mess with her tongue, but compressed by the gag, it leaked into her mouth instead.

Without uttering a sound, he dragged her back along the path until they got to a timber shack that was seemingly abandoned and cleverly hidden from any passing traffic. Pushing open the door with his shoulder, he shoved her into the dark interior. The gloom pressed in upon her misery as Scarlett was forced to her knees while he secured her bound hands tight against a rough pole. The only sound was Scarlett's short, painful gasps.

Once he knew she couldn't escape, he lit several lanterns that cast a soft glow around the wooden walls. The shack's construction was basic, with large timber posts holding up the tin roof over a dirt floor. There was no furniture apart from an old wooden work bench.

Bringing a lantern closer, he squatted on his haunches in front of her, studying every detail. Scarlett shrank from him in terror, her eyes so wide with shock and pain they seemed to fill her face.

He looked up and spoke into the dimness above, 'Let's see what trophy we have this time.'

Trophy! To think her suffering was for some kind of sport! Frothing with fury, snot streaming out of her nose and over her chin, she slid to the ground to strain against the ropes and kick out at him with her feet. If released, she would have fought for her life, doing whatever it took to destroy the understated monster before her.

Not reacting at all to her state of distress, he calmly took hold of her ankles and shushed her like a small child while he restrained them with a short, rough rope. 'Don't fight now, little one. Let me see you.' He squatted again and stared at her.

'Not bad at all, considering I plucked you out of the dark. A lovely black beauty.' He smiled as he stroked her long, glossy black hair, gently disentangling twigs and leaves until it sat smoothly again.

With her chest heaving, she studied him. He was maybe in his late thirties, shaved head, no beard. Then she looked at his eyes. They were a soft brown but vacant as if he wasn't even home, like something else lived in this body. He seemed more possessive than sexually aroused, like he had discovered a treasure for a prized collection. She recoiled from his touch.

When he was happy with her hair, he pulled a pocket knife from his pocket, flicked open the blade and held it to the light. 'Keep still and I won't cut you.' It was an order.

Starting at her top, he began to cut her clothes off. Every small piece was removed and neatly placed into a little pile, except for her shoes and socks. Her shirt and bra straps were sliced open, and each piece was peeled away. He cut her skirt and pulled it from her under her body, then slipped the knife through the side seam of her panties and drew the soft material away. She noticed there was not one slip of the blade. The only blood was from the branch scratches on her legs and arms. The fight in her faded as quickly as it came, and now humiliation flowed through her in a river of blush. Such an intimate experience should not be shared with a heartless abductor.

Gently he laid his hand on her pubic bone, staring at her nakedness with very little reaction. He didn't stroke and touch her in a sexual way. Her female anatomy seemed to intrigue him more than arouse him. Turning away from her garbled pleas for mercy, he began to unpack his rucksack. Once it was emptied, he placed the pieces of her clothing into the pack. Scarlett saw this as an ominous sign. She wasn't going home. She was going to die in this godforsaken place.

The knowledge that all the experiences of her life had led to this moment was unbearable. The love of her parents, and her younger brother Joel, these treasured people would never even know what happened. Never finding her body and the not knowing what happened to her would break her father's heart. Choked sobs, raw with desolation, ripped from her broken chest while the gag filled with fresh tears and swelled even larger within her mouth.

Her outburst of despair didn't even cause him to glance her way. Instead, with great ceremony and concentration, he began setting out a line of knives on the work bench, from a small paring knife to a huge cleaver that could cut cleanly through bone.

There was enough light to reflect off the steel, which seemed shiny and eager to begin its unholy ritual. As her eyes roamed over the sharp instruments, her stomach clenched with terror and her bowels wanted to empty, knowing these blades were going to be used on her body. Scarlett had never felt so afraid nor so alone. Sweat began to run in small rivers along her bare skin, and embarrassingly, her bladder emptied in a puddle on the floor beneath her.

Dread filled her soul, and even though she knew he couldn't hear her, she called out in her mind to the one person who had always been her rock. 'Dad, please come save me, please. I don't want to die like this. Dad, please save me!'

Her face now resembled a fierce tribal warrior. The pattern of blood, dirt and tears made a frightening mask that totally misrepresented the hopelessness of her true state.

Oh God, please save me from this monster. Heaven above, can anybody hear me?

However, no matter how much she prayed, Heaven remained mute. Scarlett reached deep inside her core, trying to draw strength for what was to come. Remembering the past and trying to picture the future, she searched for courage where there wasn't any.

No matter what happens, I must stay alive for me and my family. Taking a painful breath, she held it in her cracked chest as she drilled her resolve.

After arranging his tools in the precise order, her abductor turned around to face her, seeming puzzled by her presence. Almost as if this frightened young woman had stumbled into a waking dream and now he wasn't sure what to do with her. The two personalities in him warred with each other: one a killer and the other not.

For a long time, he stood there, seemingly uncertain and confused, almost until she dared to hope he might change his mind. Doing her best not to ruin this slight chance of reprieve, she sucked in her sobs and prayed under her breath for salvation.

The suspense ended suddenly for her when the killer won, and his tortured mind dropped into gear. With one last glance towards the ceiling, he chose his weapon, selecting a short knife with a curved blade, one that sliced deeply if turned at the right angle. No longer uncertain, his eyes hardened and focused on her as he came close to whisper softly into her dirty, blood-streaked face.

'Don't be frightened, little fish. I have done this many times before, and the pain is only bad at first. Once shock sets in, it will be easier to accept. Hate me only a little, for I live with this demon inside me every day, and as much as I fight the voice within, eventually he always wins. It's always the same, just a different face each and every time.'

There was a hint of peppermint on his breath as the eyes of the confused man begged solemnly for understanding. But no matter how much he pleaded, she couldn't forgive what he was about to do. After a quick glance at his face, she turned away so that he couldn't see the fear in her eyes. Yet no amount of will-power could hold back the whimper of horror that slipped from her dry, choked throat. It was the thought of all those other victims that made her shake with sorrow. How many had suffered here before? How many innocent lives had perished in this hell on earth? When he was finished with her, would he dump her bones into the same grave where the other souls lay trapped?

Once again, her heart pleaded for mercy and cried out for a miracle. Close now, his breath shivered through her fringe as he gently traced the curve of her cheek, lovingly cupping the side of her face, and with just the tip of his finger he followed the sweet innocence of her upturned nose. Gently, he tugged her bottom lip away from the wet gag, running his finger along its soft pink interior. During this exploration, she kept her eyes tightly closed, not daring to open them and see him so close.

'So lovely,' he whispered huskily. 'Where shall I begin?'

Without volition, her eyes popped open again to plead with him. She whimpered and shook her head wildly, hoping he would show her mercy.

His eyes hardened. 'Shush, I can't stop now. Don't you see we have to dance with death until the music stops.'

There was no way to break free, and before she could cry out, he bent over slightly to take his first slice from the top of her leg. The flesh slid off easily under the sharpened blade, abandoning her body and submissively becoming his to possess. Shrieking into the gag, she arched her back in agony as she tried to twist out of the restraints that held her captive. Scarlett could no longer pretend this was just a bad dream, or that there was a way out. He was going to cut her up, piece by piece, until she bled out.

The room was filled with Scarlett's painful, choked cries as her mind called out again in desperation. 'Mum. Dad. Come save me. Stop the pain, please, please. I beg you.'

She turned her face away in revulsion when he took the first bite. But even with her eyes closed she could see her blood all over his chin as he chewed and swallowed. The open wound on her leg oozed slick and heavy, and when he moved closer again, his breath smelled of her death. Her body waste had turned the dirt floor to a sticky mud as she lay there like a butchered beast, without the relief of a quick end.

Deep slices of flesh came away from all of her limbs. Her upper legs and arms were now covered in gaping wounds, and blood loss gave the room a dreamy quality. Unconsciousness was not far away. Whimpering with dread and shivering with shock, Scarlett waited for him to strike again. It was only the disgusting sock gag that stopped her teeth from biting off her dry tongue. *Oh, God. Would he slice at her face next?*

He moved to the bench to select his next tool, picking up a long, straight blade, one that wouldn't falter to work under pressure. Smiling ever so slightly, he tilted his eyes towards the ceiling as if to acknowledge unseen spectators.

Scarlett closed her eyes tightly, even when he came to crouch behind her head. It was the longest moment of her life. The waiting seemed to intensify the terror of uncertainty. Knowing another cut was coming, her nostrils flared when he took a fistful of her long black hair and pulled it tight, almost like a clumsy father about to tie it up in a high ponytail. But this was no tender loving parent. It was a madman intent on his own gratification, and nothing could prepare her for the next insult.

Whispering softly, he explained what he was about to do. 'It's time now to take a trophy as a keepsake of your passing through my doorway to join the world beyond. If you look up to the rafters, you will see the others who made the journey before you.'

Slowly pulling her head back towards the shadows, he made her look up. She choked in horror when she saw the quantity of clumps of hair hanging from the timber beams. Some were quite fresh, and the others; well, only dusty tufts remained.

The knowledge that her own glossy locks would soon join the grisly parade made her shake with terror. She didn't want to become another victim of his. She wanted to live, to find love, to have children, to heal the sick. This devil was a thief of all of her dreams, and she used the last of her strength to protest this bitter end. Scarlett pulled on the restraints until the ropes cut their own wounds into her skin. She clamped down on the wet gag, and in her mind, roared her hatred for what was happening. In the depths of her being, she bellowed at God for not caring enough to save her. She was a good person and didn't deserve to die like this. The room echoed with her despair, and the emotional energy surging from within bounced from the walls to the rafters. The creatures in the forest scuttled away in fear. Hers was a cry so full of rage that surely the heavens trembled with her fury.

'You could lift the roof with your screeching, but there is no one to hear even your muffled cries. No one can save you now.' He smiled devilishly up at his other victims.

'Now that I've feasted on your flesh, I am going to pop open your skull to enjoy your greatest treasure: your brain. Soon your suffering will be over. Just a little longer, and I will let you join your sisters.'

The shrieks caught in her throat when he began to slice along the edge of her dark hair, tugging the skin as his silver blade separated it from her skull. The pain was excruciating, far worse than the open wounds.

This abomination was so great that her second muffled cry was involuntarily for liberation. As the blood flowed down her forehead and across her eyes, it clumped her lashes together and blurred her vision until the world became red and ruled by terror.

No longer afraid to die, fear became friends with her will to live and together they walked away. To end this suffering was all that mattered now. The future no longer held any allure; exams and careers were all trifles of life. Her world became consumed with a burning pain that blinded all other coherent thought, blotting out memories of happiness and love.

In her mind, Scarlett cried out to the universe. 'No more pain. Please God, just let me go!' The end nudged a little closer as she waited for unconsciousness, welcoming the freedom from pain, the promise of oblivion. The lines blurred between reality and strange visions.

The slippery, soiled surface of the floor became distant, and the smell of blood and shat no longer offended her senses. The air took on a dreamlike quality, and faces began to drift before her eyes. The lost souls offered comfort and encouraged her not to give up.

Was she already amongst them? Nothing seemed real anymore. Scarlett imagined she saw the rustic timber wall begin to shimmer and ripple, like a veil was being torn open. The hallucination became more unreal when an illumined creature in a shimmering robe with huge white-folded wings stepped through the wall.

Her butcher was so intent on removing her hair for his trophy that he jumped with undiluted disbelief when the angel appeared in front of him. Jerking his blade back, he stood up, tall and threatening, to challenge the intruder. As Scarlett watched, his whole face began to change, and his voice became lower and harsher than a human tone. His features, which had seemed so normal before, now twisted grotesquely, and Scarlett got a glimpse of what lay within. The human guise was superseded by the possessor, with gnarly, veined purplish skin and sharp fangs that pulled back the taut line of his lip. His red eyes were so filled with hate that it was palpable.

'How dare you, Fallon!' he hissed at the intruder with recognition. 'You have no right!' It was a guttural snarl.

'Jinn, I've been searching everywhere for you and now see how far you have fallen from grace,' the angel countered.

'I have no appetite for grace. Instead, I hunger for human flesh.' Jinn spat at her perfection.

'You need to leave this one now. Enough damage has been done.' It was a command.

'Just who do you think you are? We're no longer content to remain in obscurity. You cannot hold us prisoners any longer. This world is ours, and these people are now ours to do with what we please.' His coarse, rasping voice filled the shack.

Keeping out of his reach, her saviour dismissed his taunts. 'You may have broken out of your bonds, broken your word, and even broken the treaty, but I won't let you take this life. Now is not her time to die.' Her green-eyed gaze was steely.

'No, Fallon, even you can't stop me. She's mine!' he screamed, lunging at her with the bloody knife.

Scarlett watched in a daze while the angel held the still-hungry blade as it quivered near her face, her green eyes glazing with contempt and disgust as she easily held her captor at bay.

'How, Jinn? How did you fall so far? To think you were once a creature of glory, a messenger of light.' Dismay echoed throughout her voice.

Scowling, he twisted his hand out of hers and lunged again to slice at her gleaming white robe.

Knocking the knife out of his hand, the angel stood taller and opened her vast wings. The edges were tipped with gold, and she filled the small cabin with her glory. It was such a wondrous sight that Scarlett momentarily forgot the pain of her wounds.

The man–demon took a step back and eyed her warily. Stepping forward, she grasped him by the throat, and with one hand, held him off the ground.

'Your time here is done, demon. Go back to the shadows, back to where you belong,' she whispered into his furious yet determined face.

Reaching out, he couldn't prise her hand off his throat, so instead he grasped the shimmering red star worn around her neck.

'Get your hands off that,' she ordered.

Instead of releasing it, the demon held it tight until it cracked and tumbled into the shadows and blood.

'You should not have done that, Jinn.' The celestial green eyes glowed with a burning anger.

'Crushing this small trinket is nothing compared with what we will take from you,' he said between gasps of air. 'You will be sorry for this intrusion. One day soon, Fallon, I will be your master, and you will be my eternal slave. Even if you stop me this night, you are losing this war. Our strength is growing stronger every day.'

'You play games and use innocents to fulfil your vile desires.' She spat into his face in disgust.

'Our kind no longer suffers from being cast out of the light. For not much longer will we dwell in the shadows. When we take back the City of Angels, we'll place Lucifer on the throne, and he will rule all of the realms.'

The angel scoffed. 'You lost everything, brother, when you cast your lot with that usurper. There is now nothing left for you but dirt, loneliness and darkness.'

Scarlett squinted through the blood to try and understand what was happening. She now understood that the man who abducted her was gone, and in his place was the monster he carried within.

His legs dangled while long, curved fingernails reached out to scratch at the angel's face. As she squeezed his throat a little tighter, he let out a wheezy laugh. Without blinking, she squeezed again, and his laugh was cut short. His eyes bulged until he coughed a small puff of grey smoke, and then to Scarlett's astonishment, the now-smoking body collapsed to the ground and lay smouldering at the angel's feet, once again resembling the human form and not the monster.

Moving gracefully to Scarlett, her rescuer released the restraints and helped her to sit up against the timber pole. Using her robe, the angel gently wiped the blood from the young woman's eyes and removed the revolting gag.

Scarlett's split and bloody lips could barely form a whisper. 'Have I died?'

The splendorous vision in white smiled gently at her, the green eyes shining with love. 'No, Scarlett, it's not yet your time to pass into the next realm. That day is many years from now.'

Next, her healing fingertips lightly touched the grievous wounds to stop the bleeding and dull the pain.

'How did you get here? How did you find me?' Scarlett feared the rescue was only a dream.

'I heard your cry. I think most of Heaven felt your anguish.' The celestial being cradled Scarlett's face between her tender hands.

'Are you an angel?'

'Yes, Scarlett. But some call me a messenger. Even though I'm more of a warrior for the light.'

'I never believed such things existed.' Scarlett still feared she was hallucinating from the blood loss.

'There are many things hidden to the human eye, but that doesn't stop them being true.' The angel smiled again.

'So if you're an angel, was he a devil?'

'At first, he was just a man, until he became intrigued with evil. Then he was possessed and consumed by the very power he sought.'

Scarlett looked at the slumped form and began to shake with dread that he would awaken to continue his unholy assault on her. Turning to the one who had stopped him, she begged, 'Please don't leave me here with that monster. Take me with you.' Scarlett caught hold of her rescuer's hand in desperation. 'How will I get out of here?'

'Scarlett, I cannot take you where I go, but I promise he can't hurt you anymore. He has forfeited his life to evil, and for him there is no escape. Soon someone will come to liberate you. Rest now, child, as you have suffered enough this day,' the angel soothed as she brushed her fingers lightly over Scarlett's suddenly heavy eyes.

'What is your name? How can I ever thank you?' Scarlett whispered as her lids slowly closed.

'You may call me Fallon. And you can thank me by living your best life, Scarlett. Don't waste a day,' she whispered back. 'One day we will meet again.'

Fallon searched for her treasured pendant that the demon had broken with his insolence. Nowhere on the blood-soaked floor could she see the beautiful red star. After accepting it was lost to her, she stood for a moment to honour the spirits of the gruesome trophies hoarded in the ceiling. Guilt gnawed at her. They were losing this war, and humanity was suffering for it.

Turning away, she looked down at the now-resting Scarlett one last time before blazing white and stepping once again through the rippling timber wall.

Fallon now stood on the top of gruesome shack, easily balancing on the tin roof. Stretching her wings open, she reached for the power source deep within and began to beam a brilliant flood of pulsating white light, pushing it from within and into the night sky.

It was impossible not to stop in wonder at the sight, and many vehicles pulled off Forest and Windemere Roads to turn into the Serendip Wetlands to investigate. A few cars followed each other as they nervously drove towards what they thought might be an alien spacecraft beaming a light from the bushland. The small cavalcade followed the road until it stopped at a dead end in the forest. Getting out of their cars, the soon-to-be rescuers stood around in the clearing, fearfully discussing who would go towards the light pulsing in the night sky.

Eventually, several men took up the lead through the rough path, torches in hand in case darkness closed in again. The two in the front had palpitating hearts, unsure of what lay ahead. The others jostled closely behind, whispering their excitement to each other until they turned the corner to find an abandoned shack with an open front door. Tentatively walking towards it, they halted in their tracks as the light suddenly stopped and instead began winking from within the walls. Standing close together to bolster their courage, they walked one by one through the doorway just as the light vanished.

Their torches clicked on to expose the grisly scene within. A male body in burnt clothes lay on the floor, and a bloodied naked girl seemingly dead or unconscious was propped up against a wooden post.

Reeling in shock, they quickly checked each body for signs of life. The man on the floor was dead, but the young woman was breathing. One of them rushed back to the cars to call an ambulance while the other men took off their jackets to cover her wounds, which strangely were open but not oozing blood. They couldn't believe what they had found or the injuries sustained in this bushland hideaway. Nervously they kept their torches beaming into the trees in case the perpetrator was still skulking close by.

Nobody would believe Scarlett's explanation that an angel had saved her from certain death. The medical staff said it was disorientation caused by blood loss, and that her memories would be distorted by trauma. However, the police had no explanation for the pulsing light that had drawn her rescuers on that fateful night.

It was eventually dismissed as an unexplained, rare light phenomenon.

Scarlett knew better than to argue as she could hardly believe the miracle herself. Only her initial rescuers felt the same sense of wonder as they had never experienced anything like it before either.

One of these men visited her in hospital a week later, bringing a gift. 'Scarlett, I stumbled over this in the shack that night, after the ambulance had left. It seems to be broken but I thought it might be yours.'

Scarlett took the red metal shard out of his hand. It was half of a star, snapped down the middle. Closing her eyes for a moment, she remembered the demon's grip breaking it that night. She also remembered how upset Fallon had been at the time.

She clasped it tightly in her hands. 'Thank you so much. This pendant is very special to me. You didn't happen to find the other piece, did you?'

He shook his head. 'Sorry, Scarlett. I found it on the night, but now the place is a crime scene with forensics crawling all over it.'

Scarlett shivered at the thought of how close she had been to joining all those lost souls whose scalped hair hung from the ceiling of that shack.

'Thank you, anyway. At least I still have a piece of it.' She clutched the gleaming red metal piece close to her heart.

'I'm sure the police will find the other piece when they clean the mess away,' he tried to reassure her.

Scarlett would never forget the mess.

She never told anyone about the pendant, the shimmering broken star. It was cool to the touch and glimmered in the light. This small treasure she would keep as a memory of the worst and the most wondrous night of her life.

She had many surgical procedures to repair the knife damage to her body, including skin grafts and plastic surgery. However, the one scar she wanted to keep was the hairline cut that had almost taken her scalp and shiny black locks. It was a reminder to hold a constant prayer for those who had not been as lucky as she had.

A year later, she sat and passed her medical exams. When the university chancellor put the degree in her hands, she paused on the auditorium stage to raise her eyes heavenward and say thank you to the one who had saved her life, promising to dedicate herself to healing the sick and living her best life.

One

Normally Fallon was fascinated with blood, but today it burned into her skin like acid, a stain of evil that refused to wash away. Kneeling down in the remote bushland of the Grampians, she took handfuls of the coarse river sand and scrubbed and scrubbed, doing her best to wash the traces away. Fallon wished Scarlett could have had the same luxury, to bathe in a river of forgiveness and step out to feel clean and new again. After tonight, the nightmares would haunt Scarlett for many years to come. The flesh wounds would leave nasty scars but Fallon knew it was her mind that would suffer the most.

The angel took a moment to absorb the peaceful setting, hoping it could take away some of her own night terrors, and to remind herself that Scarlett didn't suffer a violent end. Her intervention had given the young woman the chance to live, and maybe this experience would allow Scarlett to help others.

The natural surroundings of the bushland were idyllic, from the trees to the little tufts of green grass that grew right to the edge of the river. The water bubbled over colourful rocks and brushed the delicate ferns like the tresses of a forest fairy. But no matter how much she tried, the tranquillity was lost on her heart, which was unable to forget the scene in that bloody shack.

What did that fallen brother mean about coming to retake what was theirs? The council would never allow the rebels to return to the City of Angels, the Silver City.

Sighing at her thoughts, Fallon longed to file a report and renew her strength in the light, so standing tall she stretched her wingspan. The early morning breeze ruffled her gold-tipped feathers, and for one sweet moment, like a butterfly, her slender body was dwarfed by their glory.

Eyes closed, she reached for the morning sunshine as gradually her image began to disappear, first the tips of her fingers, then down her arms, the top of her golden head and down her torso until each perfectly formed foot faded from view.

Just as the scene became ordinary again, the quiet morning was shattered by the snap of wings as she launched off the sand and into the weightlessness of a very different dimension.

Every homecoming was a sweet reward for the messengers of light. It was pure delight to look up at the mighty gates that shimmered in divine splendour, and to inhale the potent cocktail of hope and joy. This sight was exactly the remedy Josiel had longed for, where there was no more deception and lies, no more skulking in the shadows. For here the incandescent light cast out all darkness. To savour the moment, she set her feet on the ground and let her immense wings draw close to sit high at her shoulders. Standing there, she gazed up at the golden sculpture of thousands of angels all bound together with arms and wings intertwined, a mighty shield protecting the front wall of the city.

'To serve is to conquer; to conquer is to serve,' Josiel whispered their creed.

She paused for another brief moment of indulgence to soak in the spectre of colour and sound that caressed her senses. The light of the Silver City was dawn and sunset intertwined. This this deep purple, pink and coral backdrop made for an exquisite setting for the crystal gates and golden towers that sparkled in the soft light, the glint off the rooftops stretching as far as she could see.

Her essence had darkened from being away from the light for so long, but now it rejoiced in her return. The light was always an intoxicating elixir to cure the travel-weary. Josiel strode through the entrance with a spring in her step. The excitement of also seeing her friends again and to have time for rejuvenation made her want to skip with joy.

The reunion would have to wait a little longer though, for as soon as the register was signed, she was summoned before the council. The angelic council comprised three of the most eminent angels, voted from the vast number of messengers for their wisdom, strength and power.

Turning away from the busy corridors, she moved out of the shadows and towards a radiance that got brighter and brighter as she ascended the wide stone stairs. By the time she arrived at the vast chamber, her face glowed brightly and a golden halo of light shimmered above her head.

The council watched in silence as Josiel bowed reverently. This messenger was not the most beautiful angel, and though quiet and slow to speak, they had learnt not to underestimate her bravery and unique wisdom. Josiel was one of their most valued spies. She knew where to locate their enemies, how to camouflage and how to disappear. There was no other who could provide a better interpretation of events, and none present were too proud to listen to her counsel.

'Rise, Josiel. We have long awaited your return from the realms of our enemies and the depths of the earth. We understand how draining it is to be far from the light for so long, and thank you for postponing your rejuvenation long enough for us to hear your report.'

It was Remiel who had addressed her. He had been voted onto the council for his intuition. He had also drawn up the treaty that banned Lucifer and one-third of the angels from ever returning home.

Saraquel was voted in for his wisdom. He seemed harsh and unbending but knew more than anyone about the history of the realms and the laws that had built the foundations of the universe. He was the oldest of the three and had been one of the first messengers created to serve the light, having been there at first creation, and sometimes the weight of time sat heavily upon him.

Zinnia was voted in for her power. No other angel had more victories in battle, and her strength was legendary. She had once stood at Lucifer's shoulder as a sister before she knew him to be a traitor to their kind.

Taking a moment, Josiel looked earnestly at each face. There was Remiel, his large head crowned with thick white hair. He was her favourite of the three, always with a twinkle in his kind eyes. Beside him sat Zinnia, whose appearance was different from all other messengers, with bright yellow feline eyes and black skin that rippled when she moved. Nobody knew why she was created so, but the aura of light around her seemed limitless. With many victories over the ages and such courage, this had earned her a place beside two very powerful allies. Finally, Josiel cast her gaze over Saraquel, whose harsh features looked set in stone. No smile softened the frown that permanently sat upon his wide forehead. On his face were all the cares of the worlds.

'I fear to disappoint you, my wise leaders. I know how crucial this scouting mission was to the council. But all I have gathered is a lot of speculation with little proof. In his kingdom, Lucifer hides himself well. During my time in his domain, all I could discover were whispers and innuendos of unrest.'

'Tell us anyway, Josiel,' Remiel encouraged. 'We want to know what is spoken beyond the gates and in their camps.'

'My lords, as our scouts have already reported, the exiled angels are moving freely from the astral jail they were imprisoned in many aeons ago. No longer do they remain in the bowels of the earthly astral realm. Instead, bolder than ever before, they roam amongst men. But a new development is that they boast their agents have found a way through the Eye of God.'

'That is impossible! They would never be able to locate the portal entry. It was hidden from those who live in darkness,' Saraquel huffed in anger.

'The Eye of God would never sanction them a safe passage.' Zinnia slammed her fist upon the shimmering surface of their high bench, causing the others to jump. Pacing out from behind the barrier, she stood glaring at Josiel.

Josiel stood as still as stone, not wanting to cause affront. Zinnia's presence was so intense it overshadowed all other distractions in the vast space. This warrior angel was a manifestation of magnificence.

Remiel intervened to restore some calm amongst the frustration and anger swirling amongst them. 'The Eye of God was created as a portal for messengers of the light, not those who choose the shadows.' He nodded his head at Josiel for her to continue.

Josiel took a deep breath and spoke again. 'As I advised earlier, these are just rumours for now; however, I heard the same story time and time again. Like you, my lords, I cannot imagine how the demons could locate the portal or find safe passage.'

'It is our responsibility to hold the borders to keep the demons from returning.' Saraquel looked gravely at his fellow counsellors as he spoke.

'I am afraid there is yet more troubling news to report.' Josiel dropped her voice to a husky whisper.

'Pray speak, child, be not be afraid of our outrage, for it is not directed towards you.' Remiel again encouraged her to go on.

'There is talk that Lucifer has found a new source of power and is planning to attack us and rule as he once aspired.'

Saraquel squared his shoulders in denial, while his eyes communicated his outrage. 'That will never happen! The usurpers will at no time be allowed to re-enter our city. I swore Lucifer would never again walk through these gates.'

Zinnia moved closer to stand in front of Josiel, causing her to take a step back and stand very still. The scales on Zinnia's skin shimmered like a black cobra, and her eyes looked deep into the soul, probing all the time.

Like a cat, she twitched with fury. 'Lucifer was not always so repulsive, quite the opposite in fact. I remember his beauty as if it were only a moment ago. The most magnificent angel ever created, music was made by him and for him. His golden hair was worn like a crown, and his smile could soften the hardest of hearts. Everyone loved him. I loved him. Like brother and sister, we were inseparable, sharing the same name day and ordained to be close from the beginning. Every experience and dream were shared. Until I realised my beloved brother had changed into someone I no longer recognised. Instead of serving life, he chafed to become as powerful as the light, to become the light itself.

'Lucifer tried so hard to convince me of his right to ascend. Instead, I chose to join the ranks of the army that stood against him and the angelic hosts who rebelled against their own kind. We fought fiercely to stop them taking this city for their own and to push our former friends into exile, never again to rejuvenate their strength in the light.' All eyes gazed intently at Zinnia as she spoke.

'It broke me to stand against my brothers and sisters, and since that time our lives have changed forever. Instead of one mighty force, our ranks are split in two and this never-ending battle began.'

Meeting the councillors' gazes in turn, she continued. 'My brothers, we cannot let his thirst for power cause more division. Already he has broken the treaty, and already he has broken the astral bonds that bound him. How far do we let him trespass before we stop his madness?'

Remiel inclined his head at Zinnia. 'Zinnia, I agree there is much for us to discuss, but now it is time to release Josiel. I see that she is trembling with exhaustion and desperately needs to renew her strength. Go, child, you have earned your rest and the opportunity to see your friends again.'

Zinnia nodded her understanding and came to stand before the weary angel. Placing her hands on the sides of her face, she leaned forward to touch her brow against Josiel's and whispered softly, 'I know you have returned from this assignment quite exhausted, so I want to give you some of my light to bolster your reserves.'

Josiel shuddered as warmth spread from the contact and moved through her whole being. It was so strong she had to stand on her tip toes to contain the infusion of power.

Wide-eyed, shaking and thrilled all at the same time, she gasped, 'Thank you, wise one.'

'Thank you for your service.' Smiling, Zinnia held on to her arms as Josiel swayed before her.

Taking a deep breath to steady her equilibrium, and after acknowledging each member of the council with a bow of respect, Josiel turned to descend the long flight of stone stairs with renewed vigour.

Walking the familiar and loved pathways that wove between the high arched halls and sparkling white buildings, Josiel scanned the assemblies, looking for Fallon's blonde head.

She couldn't see her deliberating in the Stratagem antechamber, where the constant movement between virtues, messengers and guides generated organised chaos. Here in the Strategem, the elders received orders from the wise ones and assigned duties to the guides and messengers.

From the towering ornate gold ceiling that adorned the foyer, many corridors branched off into a myriad of chambers, some busy with war councils, some with units bound to maintaining peace, and many others set aside for the general maintenance of creation.

From the shadows, Josiel scanned the prostrated forms that filled the sanctum, careful not to disturb their meditations. The heavenly choir breathed music. Their sweet gentle notes filled the vaulted space and swept through those worshipping, washing away all weariness and filling them with light and love. This was where her heart longed to be, to throw herself on the ground and absorb the power of sound, letting it wash around and through her. Music was their link to the light. It pulsated with energy and renewed their strength and purpose.

The last hall she checked was the collective, the noisiest part of the city. This was the messengers' base, where many of the hosts could take some respite from their duties, to sit, laugh, cry and share stories. When Josiel entered the bright, cheerful room that shimmered with sunlight, many of her friends and comrades called out greetings to welcome her home. She was overjoyed to see them.

'Have you seen Fallon?' she called out to a group.

'We saw her walking towards the Blood Tree not too long ago, so you should find her either under the branches or maybe near the top, where she is apt to sit.'

Josiel thanked them and headed to the most ancient, mysterious area of the Silver City. Upon arriving, she walked across the soft grass and stepped under the tree's branches. This was a favourite place for messengers, especially Fallon. The breathtaking tree's gnarly roots entwined at the base in a perpetual embrace while massive branches swathed with star-shaped blood-red leaves reached high to embrace the twilight firmament.

Josiel peered up in to the branches, looking for Fallon. Her sister and her closest friend, they shared a name day, which linked them for eternity. There she was, her blonde head just discernible at the very top of the tree.

'Josiel, is it really you?' The exclamation of surprise could be heard even from this distance.

Leaping through the life-giving branches and almost falling into Josiel's embrace, they stood holding on to each other. Fallon, tall and willowy with bright green eyes, while Josiel was shorter in stature with dark hair and solemn grey eyes. Grey eyes that now gazed anxiously into Fallon's green tear-washed ones.

'Josiel, I can hardly believe my eyes. I have missed you so much.' Fallon hugged her sister tightly.

Inhaling Josiel's goodness made all Fallon's worries, which were so troubling only moments ago, fall away in her presence.

'Heart of my heart, it brings me great joy to see you again.' Josiel held her close then let her go to join her sister on a lower branch of the ancient tree. Together they sat in companionship, catching up on each other's news until Josiel exclaimed in surprise, 'Where is your pendant?'

Immediately Fallon's hands fluttered to where it usually hung at the front of her robe.

'I'm so sorry, Josiel. It was torn off my neck by Jinn, one of our fallen brothers, during my last assignment. You know how much it meant to me. Can you forgive me?'

'Of course, dear sister. But there is nothing to forgive. I imagine you do miss it though.' Josiel placed her hand over Fallon's heart where the blood-red pendant used to sit.

'Very much, and this may be why my spirits are so low. If the tree approves, would you make me another?' Fallon's green eyes pleaded with Josiel's grey ones.

'Of course I will. It shall be done.' Josiel made her pledge to Fallon.

During her journeys, Josiel had collected the seventeen rare earth metals to forge the pendant in the same star shape as a Blood Tree leaf. With the tree's permission, she had harvested a small handful of leaves. She had then placed these leaves into the hot metal, and the colour turned a bright blood-red. Using her powers to fashion the metal into the shape of the tree's star leaves, she had then allowed it to cool. Immediately upon placing it around her neck, Fallon had felt a sustaining link to the tree, and its strength had become hers. But now this treasure had been lost.

Taking her hand, Josiel looked at Fallon quizzically. 'Is your missing pendant the only reason you are feeling low?'

Fallon shook her head. 'I feel weary of company, sister, and I need time to reflect.'

'What troubles you so? Are you still with Gadriel's squad?'

'Yes, I'm still with him. He is now in charge of the messengers and warriors. He has us moving between the realms as often as we can maintain our strength, but I fear we are losing ground, Josiel. For every fallen brother that I shut down, two more rise up. We need more warriors in our unit because we can no longer control the violence. Lucifer and his ilk are freely moving amongst the sons of men, spreading an epidemic of evil.'

'Your efforts are not in vain.' Josiel tried to bolster Fallon's downtrodden spirits.

'I am so worried about the people who call Earth their home. Lucifer and his followers were meant to be bound in an astral prison of our making, but now this boundary has been breached, and still we do almost nothing.'

Rubbing her hands over her own world-weary eyes, Josiel took her sister's hand and said, 'Fallon, you think too much. Or maybe you feel too much. It is not for us to question the laws of the universe. We must have faith in our superiors. Their power and wisdom are certain, even against the Morning Star and his twisted legions of demons.'

'That is what Gadriel, my unit leader, keeps telling me. But what I see is a war that we cannot win, for surely it is impossible to stop a force like us, one that is immortal.'

'Fallon, the only comfort I can give you is that our leaders, the wisest and strongest among us, are fully aware of the transgressions and activities of the rebellious brothers and sisters we once loved.'

Fallon's expression remained unconvinced. 'Our enemies no longer resemble any of their former glory or intend to abide by the treaty. We need to stop them before they've destroyed all the realms. Before it's too late.' Fallon's words sailed on a sigh of frustration that came from deep within.

'My heart feels the weight of yours, and as you say, our conflict will be ongoing for some time to come. Now my most pressing need is to renew my strength. I have been far from the light for too long.' Josiel now leaned against Fallon for support.

'If you wait one moment, I will accompany you to the sanctum.' Fallon took Josiel's hand in her hers.

Looking down at Fallon's blood-stained hand, she said, 'This is still your favourite place in all the realms, isn't it?' Josiel smiled fondly at her sister's quirks.

'Of course it is. I love the tree, and it loves me.' Fallon simplified their connection with a shrug.

Josiel just raised her dark brows.

'I know it defies explanation, but it has always been this way.' Fallon hugged her sister with affection.

'Is it the blood that you still find fascinating?'

Fallon took a moment before replying. 'Yes, I love to ponder its power, for surely blood is the miracle of life, but it's more than that. The tree speaks to me and makes me stronger.' Fallon stared in wonder at the red star-shaped leaves she held in her hand.

'It is curious that it only speaks to you, but then again, maybe not, Fallon. There is something about you that sets you apart from all of us. There is a strength in you that not all of us possess.' Josiel's eyes held hers.

'What do you mean, sister? All immortals are made the same, apart from the wise one, Zinnia,' Fallon parried back.

'I cannot explain this suspicion I have always harboured about you. It's just the belief that you are unique and will one day bring about a revolution,' Josiel revealed.

'Me? Ha, I cannot even convince Gadriel to send more warriors. How could I ever bring about significant change?' Fallon laughed at Josiel's folly.

'We'll see,' was Josiel's only reaction to her sister's humour.

'Anyway, we must get you to the light, but first give me a moment to return these leaves to my ancient friend.'

Josiel pondered this as Fallon walked closer to the lowest branches. *Fallon, if only you knew just how special you really are. The blood calls to you, sets you apart for something grand, something none of us can even imagine. You may not have blood within your veins, but the power of the Blood Tree is going to use you as its instrument.* Josiel didn't know how she knew this, but she just did.

Two

As Fallon meandered around the vast tree, she tilted her head to see the light flickering through its far-reaching branches. This tree had been here since the light began. Before the rebellion, before her name day, this mighty giant had born witness to so much joy. Now it also bore witness to sorrow and treachery. The tree had blood flowing through every leaf and branch, down to the roots that reached deep beneath the ground. Blood was the proof of life in many creatures, unlike angels, who were immortal. For without blood, they lived forever.

There was once another Blood Tree on Earth, a sister to this one, until mankind became consumed with superstition and mistrust. Believing the tree to be a vessel of evil, they came in hoards with their axes and torches to chop and burn each and every branch. The tree had screamed with agony during the onslaught, and its life-giving blood had flowed like a river around the knees of the malevolent men. The destruction didn't stop until only a torched circle on the ground remained to mark the place of the ancient monolith. Fallon remembered the pain of that day. She had sat here in this very place as the Blood Tree mourned for the loss of its other half. Writhing in agony, Fallon had shared the tree's torment. It had lost many leaves in the time afterwards, and some feared their mythical tree would perish as well, until slowly the light nurtured it back to its original splendour.

All messengers admired and respected the magnificent tree, but for Fallon, it was more than a symbol of the everlasting. She strangely felt a special bond with it. From the first time she had stood under its branches, the Blood Tree had spoken to her heart. It whispered stories of times long ago and seemed to feed some part deep within her core. It was her place for dreaming, and if she was away from the Silver City for too long, it called her home, begging for her to come and commune with it again. The tree's strength was somehow woven into the very fabric of her being. She needed the tree and somehow the tree needed her. It was a mysterious connection that could not be denied.

Reverently, Fallon approached the great tree and placed each red star leaf back to where it belonged. Immediately, they were reclaimed, bright red blood breathing life back into the fine leafy network until they were once again sparkling and vibrant.

'Thank you, my old friend,' she whispered humbly.

Together, they walked to the sanctum. Josiel embraced Fallon before going inside to further renew her strength and purpose. From the sanctum, Fallon walked over to watch the life bearers. A line of angels moved past her to a platform, where they were entrusted with a precious cargo. Fallon looked at the silver orbs placed in line along the shiny bench and felt such a surge of protectiveness towards these precious new souls ready for life.

This is what it was all about, the continuance of life. And to serve that life was their creed: To be there at the start of life, to walk in the human souls' dreams throughout life, and to be present at the end of life.

New souls, sweet and innocent, were so full of potential for the journey ahead. Being a life bearer was a rewarding duty, especially when compared with her orders, which were to search for and destroy darkness.

Each life-bearer messenger eagerly accepted their charge, and as soon as the iridescent sphere swirling with the soul's lifeforce was placed into their arms, they unfolded their wings and sped away in anticipation. Fallon watched them depart, and in her heart, wished them safe travels.

The last remaining sphere was waiting for its turn. The life force was strong within, and the movement was captivating to watch. Fallon could see the soul and knew it was eager for its birth day, but alas, no one came forward to claim it. Fallon hesitated, curious to see who would take this assignment.

With consternation, the elder who commanded this contingent frowned at Fallon and checked his list. Once he realised she was not there to report for duty, he returned to his chambers to reorganise this last mission. She could not tear her eyes away from the soul within the orb. It seemed to be whispering softly to her heart, 'I'm waiting for you, take me now.' And even though this was not her duty, she felt compelled to respond.

'What could be the harm?' she reasoned. It would be a treat to be a messenger of good news instead of obstructing demons, and she could be back before Gadriel even knew that she had left.

Tossing all doubts to the wind, she deftly snatched up the glistening ball of light and hugged it close as she spread her glorious wings and took flight. As soon as the orb touched her heart, she knew where to take this tiny life to meet its birth day.

No one was there to see the elder march stiff-backed to the high bench, or to witness his expression of confusion to see it empty. He looked this way and that until ruefully shaking his head. Then he began to clear the shimmering crystal surface in preparation for the next consignment.

The atmosphere was clear and starry as Fallon moved silently into the outer etheric shield that cradled Planet Earth. Like a womb, the shield was designed to protect it from being swallowed by deep space. *How many times over the millennia have I set this course, looking for the portal, the Eye of God, and seeking entry to the world of men?*

However, this night, before she had time to locate the entry, a crash exploded in the hushed void. Without warning, a fiery force swirling with darkness struck Fallon, causing her to spiral out of control. Protectively, she wrapped her arms and wings around the soul she carried as they fell towards Earth.

Demons were excluded from this realm, and the Eye of God was created to keep them apart, yet here they are! How did this happen? Her mind whirred as she fought to regain her trajectory.

Another fiery demon attached itself to her and tried to snatch the orb out of her arms. Unable to fly any faster, she did the opposite, and used all of her strength to stop suddenly. This caught her foes by surprise, especially when their own descent drew them swiftly away. It would only be a momentary reprieve, so with no time to dwell on her own capture, she hurried back to find the entrance. *Where was the Eye of God?*

Flooding with relief, she saw the portal. It never stayed in the same location, and like a snow hurricane it swirled within itself, creating an energy force that pushed the messengers from one dimension to another. A messenger would never be able to sustain this level of energy to move between realms; hence, they needed the portal's power to transport them. She flew as fast as she could towards the familiar purplish haze that hid their angelic realm. Once she entered, a golden light energised her through, and the sides of the void moved constantly, so she had to trust the light to get to the other side.

Once she was safely through, her mind became dizzy with confusion. Did the council know of this trespass?

With the enemy in pursuit, Fallon had little time left to consider the consequences or the disparity of what was happening. She had to lose them fast and get this soul delivered in time. To the naked eye, the ethereal visitors would have appeared to be falling stars spinning through the black night, descending through the atmosphere and burning brighter than the sun. Determined to throw them off the scent, Fallon flew through the most challenging landscapes she could find.

Travelling straight to a massive sun-soaked rock sitting in the middle of the red desert, she went around it a little slower until the two fallen brethren narrowed the gap. Once she knew they were locked in on her scent, she dived down the cliff face and along the rocky, barren river beds, darting and diving through a eucalypt forest until slipping into the mist of a favourite waterfall, where she hid behind the towering curtain of tumbling water and waited.

She saw them rush past, then come back again trying to pick up the chase. One even hovered at other side of the screen of water and seemed to look straight at her, and for one heartstopping moment she thought she had been discovered. However, after some heated arguments, these hounds of hell sped off in the direction they had come and disappeared. Fallon waited as long as she dared and then cautiously made her way to her original destination.

Finally arriving at the appointed place, it was with a sinking heart she saw that the life she had fought so hard to save had already begun to fade.

'No, please don't die now. We're here. Look, there is your new mother and father, waiting to love you.' Placing her hands around the capsule, she willed light and love into it, speaking words in the spirit tongue, asking the light to renew this soul.

Refusing to give up, she begged over and over again, but no matter how hard she prayed, it would not glow. With disbelief, she saw the light flicker out entirely. The soul in its orb now sat dark and still in her hands. Tears filled her bright green eyes, and even though she had eluded capture, because of evil, this fragile life had missed its birth day. Tonight, she had become a messenger of sorrow instead of joy, a truth that weighed heavy on her heart and bowed her blonde head in shame

Grief overwhelmed all reason, and shaking with remorse, she dropped to her knees and prayed that the parents could forgive her.

Three

Thirty-three-year-old Kathleen Harrison was only faintly aware that the sheets had slipped down to tangle around her ankles as another wave of pain approached, washing relentlessly round her cringing form, as regular as the waves that crashed upon the sand. The contraction tightened and drew her tired, protesting muscles tight across the protruding bulge of her abdomen. On and on it went, no matter how much it hurt. It had not seemed this difficult with the boys, although the youngest, Thomas, was born four years ago. Maybe time and the joy of a new baby had lessened her memory of the pain, or maybe it was because she had been younger then.

Tears of exhaustion seeped out of the sides of her scrunched eyes. Whimpering, she turned to her husband. 'Frank, I'm so tired. I can't take it anymore.'

'Honey, just one more time. Come on, we'll work together. I'm going to stand behind you and support your shoulders, and I want you to push against me with everything you've got. You've done this with the boys, now one more time for this little one.' He brushed the soft brown curls off her sweaty brow and encouraged her to not give up.

Clenching her teeth with determination, Kathleen pushed back against him and bore down, her womb feeling the vice-like compression with the mass of the baby now moving through her pelvis.

Frank cringed with helpless pity, feeling useless as she strained to deliver.

'Come on, Kathleen. I know you're exhausted but we all want to see this baby. With this next push you are going to deliver.' The tall doctor leaned forward to look into her eyes, warmly encouraging her to push even harder.

Knowing the end was almost here, she tried again, grasping the sides of the bed to hold steady. The pressure grew tighter and tighter, so taut that her eyes bulged and she felt the fine membranes pop to bloom red like a crushed flower.

'It's burning. Oh my God, Frank, it's burning so bad.' She gasped with shock as the doctor stretched her perineum over the baby's head.

'Steady now, Kathleen, just focus on your breathing and don't push too hard. We need to ease this little one out,' he coached while he gently turned the infant's head to smooth the last transition.

The room was silent apart from Kathleen's breath rushing air in and out, trying not to push when all of her instincts screamed to get the infant out. She cried out with relief when the baby's head presented, and thankfully the shoulders turned to slip through without resistance.

Rich red blood squirted across the white sheets when the umbilical cord was cut, and the nurse scooped up the limp purple-hued baby and quickly moved to a small examination table. One that had bright lights and a suction hose to clear mucous from the airways, doing everything possible to help the baby take its first breath.

'Oh, sweet mother, thank God it's over.' Kathleen lay back against the pillows, exhausted and now feeling strangely empty. In spite of her relief, the silence stretched out to worry her. Why wasn't the baby crying?

'What's happening with my baby,' she called out in alarm.

'Kathleen, we have a little girl and just need a moment to get her going,' the doctor reassured her.

Suddenly, the quiet weighed heavily upon the sterile hospital delivery room. The clock ticking seemed to boom around the silent room. This wasn't normal, and Kathleen held her breath as she waited for those anticipated cries of outrage.

But this baby remained mute, and no matter what the medical staff did to resuscitate, there was no response. After several minutes, the infant was sadly wrapped up and passed back to the shocked, disbelieving parents.

'I am so sorry, Kathleen and Frank, but she never took a breath. I'm afraid the infant is stillborn.' The doctor's eyes were bleak and tear-filled to deliver such a heartbreaking result. He stood there awkwardly with slumped shoulders. Medical school could never fully prepare anyone for these tragic situations.

'Nooooooo! No, this isn't true. You're lying! She can't be dead. Look at her, she's perfect. You have to get her breathing. For God's sake don't give up on her, do something, anything but this, not this.' Her cries were so loud they could be heard in the empty corridors as she tried to pass the infant back to the doctor or the nurse.

'We're so sorry, Kathleen and Frank. We've tried to resuscitate, but she never took her first breath.' The nurse came to stand at Frank's shoulder, and she too had tears streaming down her face.

Kathleen opened the blanket to look at her daughter's closed eyes and perfectly formed features. Frank came and sat on the side of the bed. Leaning forward, he placed his head close to the daughter he would never take home to love. His shoulders shook with sobs as sorrow and disappointment crushed him.

Kathleen wound her hand through his thick hair, holding him and the baby close.

She was still unable to comprehend this was really happening. How would they tell the boys their baby sister didn't make it? The whole family was excited to welcome a new baby, and now this news would tear them apart.

The sense of loss and intense grief was more than she could bear. The nurse drew up a chair and sat on the other side of the bed, explaining through her tears what would happen next in this tragic event.

'The doctor will come back after you have had some time together, and we will organise a grief counsellor for you both and the boys,' she said as she squeezed Kathleen's shoulder and then sadly moved out of the room to give them time.

With just the three of them there, the room seemed overbearingly gloomy.

'Frank, how could this happen to us?' Kathleen choked. 'We've never hurt a soul, and we're good parents. Why has God punished us? I just don't understand.' Kathleen cried out against the injustice. 'I should have pushed harder. It's my fault. I took too long to deliver her, and now she'll never come home in our arms, never smile or laugh.' In her anguish, tears had combined with mucous to run over her chin and drip on the baby blanket.

'Kathleen, I don't think God works like that. Why would he punish this little one? It's not your fault either. You were amazing. Nobody could have tried harder or endured more to see her get here any faster. It's just a tragic event that doesn't make any sense.' Frank gently placed his large hand protectively over his baby's head as his own tears streaked down his drawn face.

Frozen with grief and hunched protectively over the unmoving bundle of cloth, there was not a sign of life as the tiny infant lay there bathed in their tears of sorrow. They stared at her delicate face, so perfect and frozen, her eyes closed as if she were only sleeping.

Kathleen held one little finger and examined the miniature oval fingernail that was formed so precisely. If only she could turn back time and see her baby being born again. Somehow, she had failed this precious child. She should have tried harder and not let the labour draw out so long. It all felt like her fault, and the tears of guilt just wouldn't stop.

'I am so sorry, my darling girl,' she kept whispering over and over again.

'My love, stop blaming yourself, please,' Frank begged.

'I have to blame someone,' she said, crying even harder.

Clinging to her daughter, with drenched cheeks and jerky sobs, Kathleen refused to accept that her baby wasn't going to get better. With her pressed close against her chest, her daughter stayed warm, and pressing her nose against the soft downy hair, she smelled the sweet perfume of innocence.

'Help me, Frank, my heart is breaking.'

'My darling, nothing I can do or say will make this better.' Frank stood and began to pace the room, his jaw clenched and eyes shadowed from the long delivery. He liked to make things better, to fix things, but no words of comfort could change this. He couldn't fix it.

Unseen by human eyes, there was another witness standing beside them, one who bore the full burden of their blame. How could she make it up to them? Never actually assigned to this duty, did she dare make it worse? Guilt clouded her judgement, and all she could see and feel was their pain and tears. Prudence urged her to turn away, to go home and face the condemnation of her peers, yet responsibility and remorse held her frozen in the moment.

Staring down at the dark orb, now dull and lifeless, she tried to weigh up the consequences of the frantic plan that was forming in her mind. Would Heaven forgive her for breaking the rules? Would they even try to understand her motives? Did she dare, or did she accept failure and return to report the hostilities she had encountered?

Stay or go? Whatever her choice, she would have to act quickly to halt the chill of death that was already creeping through the tiny form. She chose to take the leap and clear her debt and make reparation to this family. Throwing caution to the wind, Fallon took a deep breath and blew it into the baby's shrunken lungs, and the static heart began to move with the rhythm of angel's wings. As the angel merged with the tiny body, it was an exchange so seamless that nobody in the room noticed that the baby's dull grey eyes had changed colour, or that the downy hair now softly gleamed with silver strands of blonde.

It was such a quiet, gentle transition as she stepped away from the angelic realm and into the human.

When the doctor and nurse slipped quietly back inside, Kathleen worried that their time was almost up, so she held her baby fiercely close to cherish these last few precious moments.

'Kathleen and Frank, there is no need to worry. You can spend as much time as you want with her.' The doctor hastened to reassure them.

Reluctant to let her baby go, Kathleen unwound the blanket and bent closer to inhale her baby's scent, locking it into her memory forever. She never wanted to forget these moments with her tiny daughter. However, as she looked closer, the baby's cheeks appeared to be a little pinker than before, and surely that tiny rosebud mouth had bloomed ruby red?

Hardly daring to trust her eyes, she began to intently watch her daughter's chest to see if it was still inert.

Fumbling in her excitement, she began to blab. 'Oh my God, Doctor, I'm not sure, but I think she's breathing now!'

'Please, Kathleen, don't get yourself all worked up. You must be mistaken. There has been no heartbeat for almost an hour.' The doctor remained unconvinced.

'I know she wasn't breathing before, but now she is. I'm sure she is. It's a miracle, please, you have to see this. Oh, thank you, sweet Jesus, she's alive. Frank, take her and show the doctor.' In her excitement, she pushed the tiny bundle into his arms.

Perplexed and unsure, Frank numbly took the couple of steps to the doctor and passed the baby to him.

Still unconvinced, the doctor laid the tiny infant back under the bright lights. Not long ago, he and the nurse had both worked over this limp form in exactly the same place, trying to coax life where it wasn't. Now as he moved the last layer of the snug wrapping, the baby jerked her arms and legs in shock at being released from the security of the warm blanket, and she began to bawl loudly.

The nurse gasped and frowned at the doctor as he hurriedly began a post-birth examination. Checking her pulse, her reflexes, and flicking a light into a set of unique green eyes, he shook his head with disbelief.

'I can't believe it, but we have indeed witnessed a miracle here tonight. She was stillborn but now seems to be breathing unassisted. I really don't know how this could happen.' He stared at the newborn in wonder.

Kathleen kept looking from the doctor to the baby and then to Frank. All faces were a picture of pure rejoicing. Laughter rang out, and happiness replaced sadness and despair as the baby continued to cry loudly and confirm that she was indeed alive and hungry.

So, still in her suit of greasy white vernix, she was gently placed back on to Kathleen's chest to feed for the first time. Kathleen closed her eyes to thank God in heaven for this blessing.

Frank stood there grinning, with contradictory tears running down his face. 'My baby girl. Oh, thank you, thank you, God in heaven.'

Kathleen just wept with joy as she felt the mouth hungrily pulling against her nipple, looking for sustenance and comfort.

'We will have to monitor her closely over the next couple of days. I still have grave concerns because she was starved of oxygen for so long.' Staring fixedly at the blonde head and pulling at his short beard as he spoke, the doctor couldn't take his eyes off the vision before him or quite believe that the infant seemed to be fine.

As mother and baby were wheeled out of the labour ward and through the small observatory room, nobody noticed the flurry of soft white feathers with gold tips that rose from the floor when the bed passed over them, or when they fell to lay softly back on the polished floor.

This earthly sign of an otherworld transformation would await the cleaners in the morning.

Four

When Fallon took on human form, a shiver ran through the Silver City, and the angels all stopped as soon as they felt the disturbance. Every messenger looked at the other in disbelief, for they all knew at once that one of their own had chosen to become human. This act was unheard of, and the city was in turmoil. Some called for mercy, and others called for her to be penalised.

Puriel, the angel of law and order, was outraged that Fallon would take such liberties without sanction and went immediately to her unit leader, Gadriel.

'Brother, do you have any idea what this means? To take such risks is a rebuke of all that we stand for, our creed, not to mention our laws.' Puriel's inner light pulsed rapidly.

'Brother Puriel, please calm yourself. Fallon is one of our most successful field warriors, and I believe she would never take such steps lightly without considering the impact.'

Shaking his fist in Gadriel's face, Puriel shouted, 'You cannot protect her this time. She may be a favourite of yours, but the law is the law, and nobody is exempt from its wrath.' He stormed off before Gadriel could respond.

Puriel demanded an audience with the council: Remiel, Zinnia and Saraquel. 'Wise ones, thank you for this audience. It is of utmost importance that we seek your judgement. As you already know, one of our own angels, our sister Fallon, has broken our creed, which is to serve mankind. Instead, she has chosen to become one of them. With the fallen roaming Earth, the realm she'll now live in, it won't be a long, happy life. Should we allow Fallon to stay in this form, we are condemning the child and that family to years of heartache. The best course of action is to stop this mockery and end this life.' Puriel gesticulated wildly as he spoke.

Having followed Puriel to the council, Gadriel countered with a plea for mercy. 'Our council, I know this warrior and messenger. Her heart is blameless, and she would never do anything reckless without good reason. I ask that you trust her and that we do everything in our power to protect her in this vulnerable form. There is our creed to uphold. We protect humans; we don't take lives to honour a law or obey an order. This would only cause pain and suffering to an innocent family and compromise the principles of guardianship.' Gadriel stood steady as a rock with his feet planted wide apart.

Puriel stepped closer to clasp Gadriel's arm, desperate to make him understand. 'Gadriel, my friend, can't you see that this is a catastrophe? The child is not even human! It is an angel living within the confines of a mortal body. What if she has no control over her powers and someone gets hurt? What would that mean for us?'

Turning to clasp his other arm, Gadriel tried his best to argue his own point of view. 'My brother, I know that you speak the truth; however, this is not known to the parents of the infant. They believe she is theirs to love and to raise, and we must honour that life as much as any other.'

They stood facing each other before the council, Puriel with his black hair and matching wing tips, and Gadriel with his fiery red hair and wing tips. They were beautiful even as they quarrelled.

'Sometimes doing the right thing seems cruel, but there is too much at stake here, Gadriel.' Puriel softened his voice but stood firm in his opinion.

Zinnia spoke first.

'Both of you are right. There is a risk to leave one of our own so defenceless, and yet we preserve human life, not take it to keep the secrecy of our own kind.'

At her pause, Saraquel turned his harsh gaze upon the two supplicants and spoke his truth. 'There will be consequences for this action. Puriel, I understand your position that our laws are sacred and must be upheld by all messengers. This sister must face the rule of law upon her return, and as she is immortal, that time will come.'

Finally, Remiel spoke to complete the verdict. He stood and held up his hand for silence as he glanced across at his fellow councillors, before revealing their final decision. 'Brothers, we have decided to leave Fallon in her human form for the duration of this life, be it long or short. As Fallon was not authorised to take this path, there will be no interference and no angelic protection as she lives out a human life. The consequence of her choice is to suffer as a human, and as we know it, it will not be an easy time. The fallen that inhabit that realm will recognise her and follow her scent to destroy everyone she loves. It may be so that living this life is punishment enough.'

Puriel tried to intervene as Gadriel sighed with relief, even though his heart broke for Fallon.

Before taking his seat behind the high bench, Remiel raised his chin as he laid down his final word. 'Neither of you shall interfere, not in this realm or in the realm of man.' This signalled the end of the appeal, and both supplicants turned to descend from the bright light.

Gadriel had agreed to meet Josiel under the Blood Tree, and it was with a heavy heart he went to this rendezvous. He had done his best to represent Fallon and see her protected in human form, but he'd failed.

Rushing to him, Josiel took hold of his arms and looked deeply into his eyes. One glance was enough for her to turn away and cover her face with her hands.

'Tell me,' Josiel whispered behind her hands.

'They're not going to take the child's life.'

Josiel looked at him through the fingers splayed across her eyes, and he saw the grey glint of relief before he snuffed it out.

'But there is no protection. She must live in that realm with no guardianship from us.' His voice dropped to a whisper as he delivered the blow.

Josiel sucked in her breath in shock and began to pace back and forth. 'Lucifer and his kind will destroy her, destroy the family, all of them. She will be no match against them without her powers. Oh, my poor sister, she doesn't deserve this. That family doesn't deserve this.' Her voice broke as she stopped to wrap her wings around her form as protection.

'You must go to her.' Gadriel stroked her folded wings and stared into her wide eyes.

'How, Gadriel? You just told me we're not to interfere.'

'Saraquel has already banned me from the realm of men as he must suspect I would find a way, but you, Josiel, you are her sister. And the council always has you moving between the human and ethereal realms on their secret service. If anyone can move about without suspicion to keep an eye on Fallon, it's you.'

'Even if I watch over her, it wouldn't be full protection. I couldn't do anything too obvious or draw the council's attention.' Josiel moved away from him, and unable to stay still, she paced with her hands around the back of her neck as she considered the possibilities.

'Of course, it has to be random so it remains unnoticed, but even if you could teach her a little, influence the creatures around her as earthly guardians, at least enough to make her time on Earth tolerable. Fallon means a great deal to me as well, and my heart breaks to think of what is to come. Why did she do such a foolish thing?' He ran his hands through his gleaming, long red hair in despair.

'I know why she did it, Gadriel. She feels responsible for the suffering of humans, and feels we are not doing enough to protect them from the rebellious angels that we exiled to the earthly astral realm. Something must have gone very wrong with that soul delivery, and this is her way of fixing it.'

'Some fix.' Gadriel's eyebrows drew together in worry.

'All we can hope for is that she goes unnoticed for as many years as possible,' Josiel murmured with a far-off look.

'A vain wish, Josiel, and we both know it.' Gadriel turned away to look at soft, swirling twilight instead of the pain in his friend's eyes. He didn't see her grim nod but felt her sense of dread all the same.

Their thoughts collided. *What would it be like for Fallon to be human?*

Five

As Kathleen Harrison prepared for her daughter's birthday celebrations, she wondered where the years had gone. It hardly seemed possible that it was Gabrielle's, or Gabby, as everyone affectionately called her, seventh birthday already. Neither Frank nor herself had forgotten the trauma of her birth, and every year, the fourth of May was a day to celebrate and give thanks.

Family and friends squeezed into the clapboard Queenslander that sat on stilts, a shorter version of the traditional buildings so popular in Far North Queensland. The home was small, so the guests overflowed into the backyard to enjoy the feast and to gather around the little girl with the halo of blonde hair and wide green emerald eyes. Smiling shyly when she blew out the seven candles placed squarely in the chocolate frosting, the clapping and cheering announced the cutting of the cake.

All eagerly waiting for their piece of cake, little pink tongues then licked the icing off first until it was smeared over their sticky cheeks. The night didn't end until all children were carried home, exhausted from too much sugar and exertion.

Once all their guests had said good night and her own children were tucked into bed, Kathleen continued to tidy up until order was restored. She turned out the lights as she moved through the three bedrooms, one for her sons Thomas and Jacob to share, with Gabby in the smaller room and Kathleen and Frank in the main. The lounge chairs were leather that had seen better days, and nobody seemed to mind that the small television sat on a cabinet of recycled timber slats. Not a show piece but a family home where the kitchen table was a meeting place for friends and family.

Before going to bed, she peeked in to check on the children, first the two boys with their limbs flung across the beds in wild abandon, and then Gabby as she lay with her covers still tucked up under her chin. Her face was so peaceful and serene that it brought a smile to her mother's face. This little girl had been a blessing to their family from the moment she had come back to them that day in the hospital. The happy baby who laughed and smiled at everyone had grown into a child of sunshine, bringing their small family closer still. Old souls are what some people called them, the children with wisdom far beyond their years who seemed like they had been here before.

In Gabby's dimmed room, she saw the large, luminescent eyes of a curlew on the window sill. The birds had mysteriously appeared the very first night she was brought home from hospital, and at first Kathleen and Frank were frightened and chased them away, uncertain if they intended to harm their tiny daughter. Now they had become part of their daughter's uniqueness, for they were a constant companion, always watching over her. Kathleen nodded at the 'night watchman' who was on duty tonight before tiptoeing from her daughter's bedroom.

Beyond their small house and the white picket fence lay a world of adventure, one that sat on the edge of the Great Barrier Reef. San Remo Beach was a perfect playground for Gabby and her two older brothers. Jacob was already a young teenager and Thomas had turned eleven, and they were her heroes. She followed them everywhere, sometimes quite irritatingly.

Jacob was tall and thin like his father, Frank, whereas Thomas was a shorter, stockier build favoured by Kathleen's side of the family. Jacob was the leader, bossy and organising, while Thomas was softer and happy to take a support role in their adventures.

With the beach and bush always beckoning, the next-door neighbour Saila children, Lizzy, Nelly and Eddie, were willing accomplices. These six free spirits spent most of their time exploring and conquering enemies in their imaginary quests. The tree house became a fort, a last defence against hordes of attacking Indians, which were actually the youngest children clumsily wielding their handmade bows and making up in enthusiasm what was lost in skill.

Other times they were ocean voyagers, making a craft out of flotsam or driftwood and embarking on a journey around the world. Their homemade boat would usually unravel when it reached the breakers, forcing them all to float back to the shore upon various scavenged pieces of their craft.

With the bounty of the Coral Sea at their doorstep, sustenance was never a problem. The children learned to become skilled hunters and gatherers, harvesting a scrumptious feast with crabbing and fishing. It was all fun, but crabbing was their favourite pursuit.

Thomas, Jacob and Gabby itched to get out of house on the first day of their December school holidays, and they had made plans to meet the Saila children as soon as their chores were done.

'Come on, Gabby, we're going over to get the Sailas to go crabbing.' Thomas tapped his foot impatiently as he waited for her. Jacob had already run ahead, too impatient to wait for his little sister. Once she had finished drying the dishes, she ran out of the house with her older brother, her blonde hair flying out behind her like a river of silk.

'Tommy, the sand is hot. Can you carry me?' Gabby was hopping over the beach sand like a cat on a tin roof.

'Okay, little one, hold on tight.' He squatted down so that she could clamber on his back and wrap her arms around his neck.

'Don't choke me,' he gasped as he stumbled along bearing her weight.

'Come on, you guys,' Jacob yelled as he ran ahead with Lizzie, Nellie and Eddie trailing behind.

Once they reached the crab pots, the large green mud crabs furiously snapped their shiny pincers as they scrambled to escape capture, causing agony if they happened to catch any fingers or toes in their path. The younger children squealed and scrambled for higher ground every time one was released and crawled towards them. This was much more treacherous than fishing, but the likelihood of being bitten only made the catch more exciting.

During these outdoor forays, the children were never alone, for always the small cavalcade of curlews trailed behind Gabrielle wherever she went. One afternoon, she had reason to be grateful for these loyal little friends.

On this particular day when the Sailas had gone shopping in Cairns, Kathleen sent the boys to the beach to catch some prawns for dinner. Standing knee-deep in the water casting for prawns was a cool relief on such a hot day, and while they were busy, Gabby wandered along the water's edge looking for new shells. As usual there were three curlews following behind. Where the foamy waves rushed the shore, a little further out in the clear water, Gabby saw a shimmering red jewel sitting in the sand.

The jewel was so clear in the sparkling blue water and seemed teasingly close. Even though Gabby had promised she wouldn't go in the ocean without them close by, she carefully considered how deep the water was before deciding it was worth a scolding to retrieve the prize. She looked back again to make sure the boys couldn't see her, and then looked at the shimmering jewel. *It's so close, pretty and perfect. With the sea breeze, my shorts will dry out in no time,* she reasoned.

Without further hesitation, she waded through the breakers into the foamy water to seize her prize, but as her hand grasped the jewel, the sand suddenly collapsed from under her feet. With a squeal of alarm, she slipped into the deeper water just as a wave washed over her head.

Every beach kid could swim, and to save lives they were taught to swim almost as soon as they could walk. So initially Gabby wasn't too scared. She would get in trouble for being wet but she could easily swim back to the shore. However, the current was strong and kept dragging her away from the beach instead of towards it.

Over and over again she swam towards the beach, where she could see her curlews running up and down the shoreline, calling out to her with their wings extended. One even flew over her to encourage her to swim back to them.

It was the fourth time she tried that the panic began to settle in her stomach. Her throat was now sore from the salty water, and her arms and legs ached with exhaustion.

When she screamed for her brothers to come and save her, it was just a hoarse groan that escaped her lips. Flailing her arms and legs, she tried to swim against the current until she couldn't do it anymore and slipped beneath the choppy waters.

Drowning didn't seem so bad now. Gabby felt tired and content to drift into a deep sleep. The soft afternoon sunlight was shining through the surface, shimmering and dancing with the waves, its motion lulling her senses until the burning pain in her chest became secondary.

So easy surrendering to the embrace of the sea, she slipped into unconsciousness and let water fill her lungs. Oblivious to her fate, she didn't feel the two strong arms that grasped her shoulders, lifting her out of the water and carrying her back to the shore.

The respite was short lived when pain woke her from the frozen, dark void, burning her throat with bile and sea water. The same lifesaving arms held her close as she coughed and vomited water from her lungs. It was difficult to come back from the edge of oblivion to the harsh, callous light of day. When she could breathe normally again, Gabby opened her eyes to see an old man hovering over her. His worried expression sat within a criss-cross of lines that travelled over his face, his soft blue eyes lost in the busy commotion.

'You gave me quite a fright,' he said as he helped her into a sitting position.

Trying to speak, she was only able to croak out a response. 'Who are you?' Gabby asked, bewildered. 'Where did you come from?' Looking around, she still couldn't see her brothers.

'My name is Old Joe, and I live at the other end of San Remo Beach,' he answered, rubbing her back as she coughed.

'Thank you for saving me, Old Joe. I really thought I was going to drown out there.' Gabby's little body shuddered at the memory.

'You almost did, young missy. Lucky those curlews were kicking up a fuss and drew my attention that you were out there in the water.'

'Are you my guardian angel?' Gabby felt strangely safe with the stranger, almost as if she had known him her whole life.

Old Joe smiled, his face becoming even more wrinkly. 'I am certainly not an angel or a guardian, but I think those birds might be. Come on, let's get you home. Can you tell me where your house is?'

Feeling better now, Gabby decided first she wanted to show Old Joe the jewel that had almost got her killed. 'See what I found.' She held out her hand, and in her palm was the red jewel.

Joe took the piece of red metal and held it up to the light. It felt cool to the touch and shimmered with a life of its own. To his eye, it looked like a broken star.

'It's beautiful, young lady. Is that why you fell into the water?'

'My name is Gabby. Yes, when I reached for it, I fell into the deeper water and the current took me away from the beach.'

'Why are you here all alone on the beach?' Old Joe looked up towards the houses that lined the beach.

'My brothers are further up casting for prawns. I wasn't supposed to go in the water without them. But I just had to get this jewel. I felt like it was calling to me.' Gabby pointed and shivered as the wind fluttered through her wet clothes.

'Well, I think it's time we went and found them.' Joe scooped her up and walked in the direction Gabby had shown him.

Further up the shore, Jacob was the first to see a stranger carrying their sister along the beach, with the curlews running in front and behind him.

Running towards Joe, he shouted for Thomas to leave the net where it was on the sand. There were prawns flicking and leaping from the net, doing their best to scurry back to the water and freedom.

'Gabby, what happened? Why are you all wet! We told you to stay out of the water! And who are you?' Jacob shouted out his questions before coming to a panting halt in front of Joe.

'Hello there. You can call me Old Joe, young man. Your sister went into the water and very nearly drowned. Where are your parents?' Joe looked from Jacob to Thomas, who had just arrived on the scene.

'Gabby, are you okay?' Pulling her out of Joe's arms, Jacob checked her all over to see if she was injured. Her green eyes were edged with red rims from the tears and salty water.

Gabby nodded at her eldest brother with tears in her eyes. 'I nearly drowned, Jacob. I would have if this man didn't see me,' she stammered, her voice breaking.

Jacob kneeled down to hug her close. 'Why did you go into the water?' His voice was strained with worry.

'For this.' Gabby held out her hand to show Jacob the red metal piece. Thomas kneeled down to have a look as well. He shook his head as he hugged his little sister, so relieved she was all right. 'Then the current took me away from the shore, and no matter how hard I swam, I couldn't get back. Will you get into trouble with Mum now?' she asked timidly.

'Holy shit, Mum's gonna kill us!' Jacob stood up and combed his fingers through his hair. Their parents were particularly protective of Gabby. Maybe it was because she was a girl or the youngest child. Whatever it was, he knew that being the oldest, he would be held responsible.

'Jacob, that doesn't matter. All that really matters is that Gabby is okay. How can we ever thank you enough for saving her today?' Thomas now stood with his arms protectively around Gabby and held out his hand to Old Joe.

'No need for thanks. I'm just grateful I was there when I needed to be.' Joe solemnly shook the young boy's hand.

'Maybe you could come home with us and explain to our mother what happened?' Jacob suggested hopefully. Knowing his mum, she would not be quite so angry at him if the stranger was there as a buffer.

'I would be happy to, Jacob,' Old Joe said with a glimmer of a smile, fully knowing what the young teenager was doing to save his own skin.

Kathleen was hanging out the laundry when the troop arrived back at the house, Jacob carrying the cast net and bucket of prawns, Thomas was walking beside a wet, bedraggled Gabby with his arm around her shoulder, and a tall, very elderly man bringing up the rear. They were surrounded by the curlews, who seemed not too sure about this interloper.

Dropping the peg basket, Kathleen abandoned the washing and met them at the gate.

'What on earth happened, and how come you are saturated, young lady?' Kathleen demanded with her hands on her hips.

Joe could see the kids' mother was the matriarch of this brood. There was no question who was in charge as the boys sheepishly began to explain.

When the story was retold, Kathleen's expression went from horror to relief to consternation and finally to anger.

Lifting her chin, she turned towards her two sons and pointed inside. 'Both of you are grounded,' she said between gritted teeth.

'Mum, it's not our fault! Gabby promised to stay out of the water. It's her fault! She broke her promise to us.' Jacob tried to argue his position.

'How long?' was all Thomas said.

'Forever,' Kathleen snapped as the boys stormed angrily inside.

'Let me look at you,' Kathleen murmured as she rushed Gabby inside and lifted her to sit her on the kitchen table.

Gabby stared guiltily at the floor.

'Do you feel tired or have a headache?' Kathleen lifted her daughter's chin to look into her eyes.

'No, Mummy. Look what I found. See how it catches the light.' Gabby wanted to show off the prize that had brought about the catastrophe.

'Yes, my darling, it's beautiful, but it was very dangerous to go into the water for such a thing. You could have died if this kind man wasn't close by.' Kathleen's eyes glimmered with tears at the thought of losing of Gabby.

Turning to Joe, who still stood in the doorway, she said, 'Please come inside. How long do you think Gabby was unconscious for? She seems fine but maybe I should take her to the hospital to see a doctor?'

'I studied medicine a long time ago, and to my observations, she's seemed to come through unscathed, apart from getting a terrible fright. Luckily, I pulled her out just as she was going unconscious so I don't think we need to worry about any damage to the brain. However, I predict her chest and throat will be sore for a few days due to salty seawater. Maybe lots of honey drinks to ease her throat and some back physio to ensure the lungs are clear,' Joe advised.

'How can I ever thank you! You just saved my child's life.' Kathleen hugged Gabby close to her side as she stammered her gratitude.

'No need for thanks. I'm just grateful I was in the right place at the right time. But you probably should thank those curlews. It was their unusual behaviour that drew me to the shoreline. I don't think I've ever seen wild animals take an interest in human lives before. Have they always been like this?' Joe looked at the young girl curiously as he rubbed the bristles on his chin.

'Yes, they've been there since the day she came home from hospital. At first, we thought it strange, but now it's just part of the Gabby factor.' Kathleen squeezed her girl a little closer.

'Well, I think a hot bath is in order for you, missy, and then I'm going to make a nice pot of tea. Would you like to stay a little longer for some refreshments?' Kathleen felt compelled to show her thanks to the old man with something more than words.

Joe accepted her invitation with a nod and a smile.

Picking up Gabby, she turned to Joe. 'Please make yourself at home while I get this little mermaid in the bathtub.'

Joe looked around as he sat at the kitchen table waiting for Kathleen. The house had a good feel about it. Everything was clean and tidy, the furniture worn from many years of use, and he could feel there was love here.

Kathleen returned and made a pot of tea served with some crunchy homemade biscuits. She then invited him to sit under the Poinsettia tree in the garden. He could hear a little of the boys arguing about the injustice of their mother's decision as he followed her outside to sit on the wrought-iron garden seat.

'Do you have children, Joe?' she asked, thinking he looked old enough to be her grandfather.

'No, I never married or had a family. Not that I didn't want to, but there just didn't seem time.' He smiled over his cup.

As they drank their tea, they sat in the shade and talked for over two hours, like a reunion of old friends. At one stage, Kathleen left him briefly to see to Gabby after her bath, and she made her come out to say thank you.

Joe stood up to shake her hand, but instead she hugged him.

'Thank you for saving me, Old Joe.' Gabby hugged his bony ribs with gratitude.

Joe had never seen eyes like that on any child. It was difficult to concentrate on her words when her face was dominated by orbs of such colour and expression.

This interaction would become one of many, as each time he'd walk the beach, he would drop in to see the Harrison family. Before long, none of them could imagine an existence without Old Joe being a part of it.

That same night, Kathleen awoke and lay looking at the ceiling, unsure what had disturbed her sleep. The soft voice floated in again, and this time she threw off the covers and padded barefoot to Gabby's room. Gently pushing open the door, she saw her daughter sitting on the floor, having an earnest conversation with herself.

Stepping softly so that she didn't frighten the little girl, Kathleen stepped into the room. 'Who are you talking to Gabby?' she whispered.

'Mummy, I was just telling my friend what happened at the beach today and showing her my new red star, or half a star.'

'Who is your friend?' Kathleen looked around the room with curiosity.

'Her name is hard to say, so I call her Jo Jo,' Gabby replied matter-of-factly.

Sitting on the floor next to her daughter, Kathleen gathered her in her arms and held her close, inhaling the innocence.

'How long have you known your friend Jo Jo?' She smiled at the fantasy world that children were able to create.

'She visits at night and sometimes leaves me one of her feathers.'

Standing up, Gabby reached under the mattress and drew out a handful of large, glossy feathers. Kathleen tentatively picked up a large feather. It was white and silky with dark shading along the edges. It was beautiful, like none she had seen before. Looking into her daughter's eyes, she saw something that sent shivers along her spine and goosebumps prickling her skin. Remembering her birth and the way she had come back to life, it seemed that anything was possible – really.

Kathleen never did tell Frank about Gabby's invisible friend or the feathers, but the next time she encountered the nocturnal visit, it was even more disconcerting.

It was a month before Gabby turned eight years old when a noise in the middle of the night again woke Kathleen. Slipping out of bed she went check on the children, knowing that sleep wouldn't return until she knew they were all safe and sleeping peacefully. She turned on the hallway light so that she could see the children without waking them.

The boys hadn't moved. They were still asleep and lying on their backs, but when she opened Gabby's door, she froze with fear when she saw the empty bed. Rushing into the room, Kathleen almost fell over Gabby who was curled up on the carpet amongst a scatter of red leaves. Frowning in confusion, Kathleen kneeled beside her daughter, unsure how leaves had blown into the room.

Stuffing the leaves into a small bin, she reached down to scoop her daughter up but drew back in shock when she saw dried blood all over Gabby's hands. Quickly placing Gabby on the bed, she looked for a wound to explain the blood. Unable to find any injuries, she ran back into their room and shook Frank awake, wanting to scream but also not wishing to alarm the boys.

Gabby woke up and rubbed her eyes as her parents rushed back into the room and turned on the bedroom light.

'Honey, how did you get blood on your hands? Did you fall and hurt yourself?' Frank turned each hand over, looking for cuts.

'It looks and smells like blood.' Frank was as confused as Kathleen.

Still half asleep, Gabby looked at them blankly.

'Gabby, can you tell us what happened? How did this get on your hands?' He held her hands up for her to see.

'Daddy, it's from the leaves that Jo Jo brought me. The red leaves that I always loved when I lived with her.'

'What is she talking about?' Frank asked Kathleen.

'I found these all around her when I came into the room.' Kathleen retrieved a handful of the red leaves she had thrown in the bin.

Frank examined the leaves and crushed one in his hand. Immediately, blood seeped out and stained his fingers.

'This is weird, Frank, really weird,' Kathleen whispered.

'Let's not overreact,' he whispered back. In a more normal voice, he said, 'Gabby, your mummy is going to clean this up and get you back to bed, okay.'

'Okay.' Gabby smiled at him tiredly, but was now more awake.

Gabby prattled on to Kathleen as she rubbed her hands clean with a warm, wet washer. 'Jo Jo said I was always at the Blood Tree, and she wanted me to remember where I came from. But I told her that I can't remember anything about that tree. Do you know the Blood Tree or Jo Jo, Mummy?' Gabby asked with the innocence of youth.

'No, honey, I don't know Jo Jo or the tree, but I do know it's time to go back to sleep. Sweet dreams, precious girl.'

Kathleen sat with Gabby until she relaxed into sleep, all the while holding her little hand in hers, rubbing her thumb over the sun-kissed skin. Her mind was in turmoil. *First my baby dies at birth and then when there seems no hope, she comes back to life. What if it wasn't my daughter, but some spirit that came back? I can't believe Gabby would be evil though, she is just too pure. But who is this nocturnal visitor that talks of knowing Gabby in another time, telling her to remember?*

Kathleen shivered in dread and felt her stomach roil, like she needed to rush to the bathroom, not sure if she wanted to vomit or purge.

What are we going to do? Should we talk to our priest about this or should we keep quiet? I want to protect this little one even if she isn't the child I think she is. I need to talk to Frank. He'll know what we should do.

Turning off the light in Gabby's bedroom, she found Frank in the kitchen.

He had taken the red leaves and placed them on the kitchen table. Over a cup of tea, they examined them more closely.

'Are you sure it's blood? Maybe it's just red sap?' Kathleen looked at him, hoping he would agree.

'It looks like blood and smells like blood,' he replied, lifting one eyebrow.

'Frank, what's going on here? Remember how our daughter died and came back to life? What if some other spirit took over her stillborn body?' Kathleen scraped back the chair and went to stand at the window, her arms wrapped around herself to ward off the unknown.

'Don't be silly, Kathleen, there is always a reasonable explanation. In the light of day, this won't seem so strange. Let's go back to bed before the sun comes up.' Frank rubbed his hands over his face in exasperation, staring at Kathleen's unyielding back.

'I can't just put this aside and go back to bed, Frank. I need to know that it is our daughter sleeping in that bed.'

'Of course it's our daughter! We were both there the day she was born. Yes, I agree there were some anomalies, but honey, that's life. Not everything is black and white, and sometimes we have to accept and be thankful for the grey. Come on, let's go to bed and face this together in the morning.' He drew his wife's stiff body away from the window, and with his hands on her shoulders, guided her back to their bedroom, even pulling the sheet up. He kissed her on the forehead before climbing in beside her to gather her close.

Ever so slowly, her breathing relaxed, and she grew heavy in his arms. It was Frank who lay awake contemplating the events when the sun peeked over the sea. Unable to sleep, he got up and made his way through the house.

When entering the kitchen to put the kettle on, he found the red leaves had turned to ashes on the kitchen bench. Gently, he blew on the small pile of rusty red smoke to watch it float up and then gently resettle to coat the utensils stored beside the stove.

It was a supernatural experience that neither Frank or Kathleen ever mentioned again. Who would believe them anyway?

After Gabby passed her eighth birthday, the Jo Jo visits seemed to stop. Slowly over time, Kathleen and Frank let their guard down, as apart from the curlews staying close, Gabby seemed a normal, happy child, just like any other.

Six

Nine years later

To the universe, one hundred years is like a day, and a day is like one hundred years. How does one measure time within this dimension? Is it the life of one man or the sum of many?

On this warm summer's day, the sky looked down upon two innocents, both on the cusp of adulthood. They lay like pick-up sticks strewn across the grass as they rested on their backs, looking up at the same sky that looked down at them. From their perspective, the wide arc above them appeared to be a limitless bowl of light-blue pudding with fluffy white dumplings floating across its surface.

An almost seventeen-year-old Eddie Saila had his head lying across Gabrielle Harrison's legs as he squinted up at the clouds, their wet clothes drying in the morning sun. Their last term of school had finished, and now the rest of their lives lay ahead of them like a book's pages not yet opened. This time was the end of something familiar and the beginning of something unknown and exciting.

'If you tilt your head to the right, that big cloud over there looks like Poseidon with his trident, can you see it?' Eddie pointed out.

'No, it looks more like the shape of America,' Gabby told him, and Eddie snorted at her lack of imagination.

'You need to get your head out of text books and read some fiction for a change. It just might stretch and exercise that mind's eye a bit,' he scoffed playfully.

'That's okay, Eddie. I'll learn all the important stuff while you just fill your head with cotton wool and clouds,' she joked back, ignoring his attempt at sarcasm.

Eddie didn't rise to the bait. He had become distracted by the sight of her framed by the sunlight, which seemed to enhance her essence.

She's like a fallen star, he thought. Light shimmered on her skin and glinted in the sea-washed blonde highlights of her long hair.

Lately he had been having dreams, inappropriate dreams of Gabby. His face flushed red just thinking about what happened in these fantasies. Thankfully, she diverted him from these traitorous thoughts. 'Eddie, if you stay very still, these little lady bugs will walk on you,' she told him in a hushed voice.

He raised his head to see twenty or more of the little bugs making intricate patterns over her arms and legs.

It became obvious they only wanted to be with Gabby, for no matter how many times she carefully picked them up and placed them on his brown arms, they always spread their tiny wings and flew back to her.

'How come animals and humans love you so much,' he grumbled in a good-natured tone. Laughingly, she scoffed, 'Andy Bolton and his friends don't like me much.'

'Yeah, but those guys don't fit into either category.' Eddie raised his eyes heavenward to make his point, and she couldn't help giggling.

'You're probably right about that, but let's not have thoughts of Andy ruin this moment of tranquillity. Tell me more about what you plan to do after school. Have you decided about uni?'

'I've made up my mind that I'm not going to uni. I hate burying my head in books when I could be outdoors. I want to work with my hands and build houses for rich academics like you.'

'I may one day become an academic but I never want to be rich.' Her voice became serious.

'Of course you do! Wouldn't you love to win a big lotto? What girl doesn't want to buy nice things?'

'Me! I don't need things. Everything that makes me happy is right here: my family, my friends and the beautiful world that we live in.' Her eyes became greener and pensive as she considered the pleasures of their simple life at San Remo.

'Not even for your mum and dad, to get them a bigger house or a better car?'

'I must have got my contentment from them because I don't think material possessions are important to them either. Mum and Dad are happy now, so how would a bigger house or car change that.'

'You are a strange one, Gabby. Well, I won't say no if fortune decides to smile upon me.' Eddie poked her in the ribs.

'Remember the saying? That money doesn't buy happiness?' Gabby's bright green eyes challenged his chocolate brown ones.

'Only rich people say that, but you would never hear of them giving all that misery away. You wouldn't be happy if you were poor either.'

'Of course I don't want to live in poverty, but I believe too much money is not good for the soul.'

'That sounds a bit naïve; the world needs rich people.'

'Why?'

'Because they create jobs, and jobs provide incomes for people like your dad and mine.'

'True is that, Eddie, but not many rich people are prepared to share their wealth. They always look for more and then hoard it away rather than making the world a better place for everyone.' A faraway look crept into her lovely eyes.

'What makes you so idealistic, Gabby?'

'You only have to read a little to realise the disparities within the nations. How most of the wealth is held by such a small percentage of the world's population and the difference we could all make if only more people understood what this life was all about.'

'Nothing is as simple as that. There are too many differences like race, politics and religion. No matter how much you talk about people sharing their money, it's never going to happen. Human beings are inherently selfish, greedy little creatures.'

'That's the problem, Eddie. We only see a tiny piece of the jigsaw instead of the whole picture. As a scientist, I want to live my life to make this world a better place and hopefully convince others to change their perception of what life should be about.'

'You're a dreamer, Gabby. You're gonna need a lot of help to change this world. One person can't make that much difference.'

Gabby shook her head in defiance. 'We all have to try. That's why we have the gift of life, to give back to this place.'

'Who are you, Gabrielle Harrison?' Eddie laughed.

'What do you mean?'

'Not many people think like you. Most of us are plain selfish.'

Gabby shook her head. 'There are lots of people who want to make a difference to their world, Eddie.'

He sat up and looked at her earnestly. 'It's not just that. It's the curlews and the way they follow you around. That's not exactly normal.'

'They're my little friends and have been with me since I was born. It's unusual, yes, but not that unheard of.'

'All I know is that there's this light in you, one that isn't in other people.' Eddie gazed at her fondly.

Gabby shook her head in protest this time. 'We all see something different in people, Eddie. I think it's just that we are such good friends that you see the best in me.'

'All this is going to change soon, and I don't want it to,' he complained.

'What do you mean?'

'The future, it scares me a bit. I get the feeling we are standing on a precipice. One wrong step and we'll fall into the unknown.' He sighed heavily.

'Eddie, most kids our age would feel the same. We're moving from childhood into the precarious adult world, and it's a daunting prospect. Despite this uncertainty, we are the lucky ones who've had the best families to prepare us for this, so we just have to trust all the energy invested in us and go out there and shine.'

'You make it sound exciting, but still, do you want to know what I wish? I wish all of this would never change and that we could stay here together. My future is going to suck without you, Gabby.' His voice dropped to a whisper.

She pushed his shoulder playfully. 'Eddie, I will always be in your life. Of course, I don't know what lies ahead for us, the how or where, but I do know that our friendship is everlasting. It will never change. Besides, we are just two kids from a small town. What bad things could possibly happen here?'

'Yeah, when you put it like that, I feel pretty silly. It must be just change that I don't like. These sensations or premonitions are just superstition, right?' he smiled contritely.

'Of course they are, Eddie.'

Gazing into his soft chocolate brown eyes, she thought about his much-loved traits. He was the best friend ever and always been there for her. Her earliest memories included Eddie and his family, his parents Ruth and Billy, and his older sisters Lizzy and Nellie. They were one of the many Torres Strait Islander families who called San Remo Beach home. Eddie embodied the best of their culture. He was kind, hard-working, loved the sea and had a great sense of humour. He was a gentle giant, slow to anger or speak ill of anyone.

Closing her eyes to enjoy a moment of peace, she listened to the steady beat of her heart, and taking a deep breath, she held the air in her lungs for a few seconds. The joy of this simple exercise felt strangely satisfying. For some unknown reason, it was a novelty to be alive and here in this wondrous place. Maybe she was an old soul who appreciated another chance to live a good life?

Turning her head to the side, Gabby could see her curlews close by, their speckled plumage camouflaged in the dappled shade, always watching over her.

It would be hard to say goodbye when she had enough money to move south to Brisbane, where she hoped to attend university.

Across town, another young adult who had also just finished his final year at school was considering his future, longing to resettle in one of the big cities, maybe Melbourne or Sydney. A place big enough to disappear into as he felt stifled in this small town. Always someone was watching and judging, probably deciding he was short of decent.

Today he stood back to admire his handiwork, a hexagon with a serpent weaving through it, which was his tag. Andy Bolton sprayed his tag wherever he could on fences, shop windows or empty buildings, a mark of defiance on a society that snubbed him.

When he rubbed paint-stained fingers through his hair, the coloured strands stood up in spikes that only added to his bizarre appearance. Stepping closer to examine the twisting snake, he spotted some yellow eyes watching him, and his heartrate accelerated as he considered his next victim.

Slowly he backed away, then walked quickly across to his bag and carefully took out the bait. Opening the carton of long-life milk, he poured it into a plastic bowl.

'Here, Puss-Puss. Want some milk?' he said, coaxing the cat out of its hiding place.

The ginger tabby slipped out from under the bus, ribs protruding from his matted coat, an unloved, starving stray that had to scavenge to survive.

The milk smelled good, and soon the hungry cat was lapping it up with relish. As he enjoyed the treat, Andy ran his fingers through the scraggy coat, untangling the matted fur, and convulsively the cat arched his back to meet some longed-for attention.

'Poor little puss,' Andy murmured as he petted the cat.

In another life and another time, it may have been different. He would have been kind and compassionate, looking after a much-loved family pet. However, this was their reality and today their worlds crashed as predator and prey, and nothing was going to change their destiny.

As soon as the cat had filled its belly, Andy snatched him up and tipped him into the pillowcase he had ready. Alarmed by the turn of events, the cat cried out as he tumbled in upside down, snagging his claws through the fabric into Andy's back as he was bounced along. Going deep into the forest with his prize, Andy went far away from prying eyes and set up his tools. Tipping the cat out onto the dry grass, the Ginger did his best to escape, but Andy had done this many times before and wasn't about to lose his captive. Grabbing him by the scruff of the neck, the terrified cat fought for his life, claws and teeth scratching and biting Andy wherever he could reach.

With one hand, Andy held him steady as he looped the hang rope around the cat's neck and tied it to a tree. Now the harder the animal pulled, the tighter it choked him. As the distressed cat clawed at its neck to break the strangling hold, Andy moved quickly to splash some fuel over its back. The sting and stench of petrol made the animal panic and mewl woefully as he dug furrows in the dusty earth with unsheathed claws, digging trenches of despair.

Seeing the cat's fear and distress didn't move Andy in any way. He focused on spinning the flint of the lighter until the flame obediently leaped to attention. Andy hesitated to savour the moment before he touched the flame to the cat's bristled coat, then stepped away to watch rapturously when the hair singed black as the fuel ignited.

The Ginger screeched with pain as the fire burned into its flesh, but Andy stood intently to watch the cat burn alive, sucking in the smell of burnt flesh and watching the eyes pop and sizzle in their sockets until the cat finally stopped twitching and lay mercifully still. Without blinking, Andy squatted on the leafy ground and watched until the fire reduced the remains to bones and ash.

The only witnesses to his heinous act were the birds in the trees, and when the flames took alight, they screeched their outrage and flew away from the reign of evil.

With no conscience to prick him, Andy didn't feel any remorse. He had once tried to involve his friends John and Mick, but they were too weak. When the flesh had begun to sizzle, they both vomited and took off home. But not him. When he was hurting something, he felt more alive than at any other time.

It had begun as just a thought, a small urge that encroached upon his dreams, where he experienced the rush of killing. From his imaginings, it was only a small step to make it real. Initially he caught small creatures like frogs and mice and cut them up while they were still alive. It was exhilarating to see them squirm and squeal before death liberated them from his torture. Now his main prey was any vulnerable dog or cat he found on the streets. He felt like God when he killed. Death is God and he became one with it.

The obsession was getting stronger though. Now he had to hunt at least once a week to feed the craving eating away his soul.

Seven

Suddenly their seventeenth birthday was upon them. School had finished, and as Eddie and Gabby were born only a week apart, they were celebrating together with their families, friends and of course, Old Joe. Both sets of parents had planned a huge feast and bonfire on the beach for the party, and everyone gathered around the fire, drinking toasts and laughing. Jacob and Thomas were teasing the Saila girls about their boyfriends as they enjoyed a beer together. The air was redolent with the smell of sizzling meats cooked in Islander tradition, buried under the coals of the fire. The trestle tables were loaded with delicious fresh salads and fruit platters, and they all knew just how tempting the desserts would be when served later with tea and coffee.

Billy Saila got out his guitar and began to strum a tune, and like sirens, Lizzie and Nellie were drawn to the music to sit with their father and sing along. The songs were haunting and sweet, all about the sea, island life, families and love.

'Gabby, you look beautiful tonight.' Eddie leaned down to kiss her on the cheek and eye her outfit for the party. It was a simple white sarong, knotted under her breasts, falling almost to the ground. She had swept her long blonde hair up into a pile of curls with just some wispy tendrils curling around her face.

In response, she let her eyes roam over him. He was looking very handsome, now over six feet tall, he was dressed in a soft green button-up shirt and blue jeans, and the two colours went great with his smooth chocolate skin.

'You look pretty darn good yourself, Eddie.' Gabby nudged him in the shoulder and pointed across the crowd of young people from school. There was Laura, beautiful and athletic, being captain of the school basketball team.

'Look over there. The gorgeous Laura is checking you out,' she teased him.

'There's no point in teasing me, princess. You also have your share of admirers.' He nudged her back. It was meant to be gentle but the force made her stumble in the soft sand.

'So sorry, Gabby. I forget my own strength these days,' he stammered as he caught her before she fell.

'That's alright, you big bully.' She held on to him while laughing at his embarrassment.

Later in the night, Eddie and Gabby stood side by side to cut the cake bathed in the gentle glow cast by seventeen birthday candles. They hugged and kissed when their guests sang a boisterous happy birthday and bent to blow out the candles together, both laughing at the other's attempt to snuff out the flames.

There was plenty to feel good about as they finished Grade 12, Gabby receiving academic accolades and Eddie getting grades good enough. He wanted to work in a trade so was content to scrape through with a pass. Now the future stretched before them in planned formation of one good thing after another.

Gabby felt butterflies in her stomach, a mix of excitement and fear of the unknown, whenever she thought about the next phase of her life. First, she had to find a job in Cairns so that she could save for university. Once she had enough for the move and to carry her for another six months, she would be leaving the Far North and travelling to Brisbane to study science at the University of Queensland.

Tonight, as she looked around at her friends and family, she knew there would still be sadness to leave all of this. Distance would diminish some of these relationships, but in sharp relief there were a couple of boys Gabby would be glad to leave behind. Andy Bolton was one boy at school who had inexplicably taken an instant dislike to her from the first day and made it his personal quest to make her miserable.

John Pacey and Mick Willis were the two accomplices in all his nasty little tricks, and these two were much larger boys who provided the physical strength that Andy lacked. All three were intent on trouble, causing many headaches for their parents, teachers and fellow students at San Remo High.

The trio were notorious, and most students moved out of their way whenever they saw them approaching. Andy was always in the middle with his spiky brown hair and thin, cruel lips that twisted into a knife slash across his face, especially when he was enjoying one of his pranks.

They weren't considered dangerous though. Annoying was probably the best way to describe them. However, Gabby knew that Eddie thought differently and always said one day they would go too far and hurt somebody.

Gabby could clearly remember the first time she really clashed with Andy. It had been back in third grade when their class had travelled to a small town on the picturesque Tablelands, countryside that looked like a snapshot from England. It was all gentle rolling hills with hedges of dense rainforest that had once covered most of this land, long before farming dominated the landscape. Camping on the fringe of the forest right beside a beautiful waterfall, the excursion was a rainforest research field trip, an exciting introduction to the wonders of nature.

At night, the class went exploring by torchlight and discovered the forest was alive with wildlife. They saw possums gliding through the high branches and little bandicoots snuffling through the moist soil looking for roots, while strange noises filled the dark forest. Their torch lights sought out the mysteries like beams from an alien spaceship.

Within the forest, the air was humid, like a living green house with a sweet undertone of rotting compost from the thick carpet of leaf matter. A myriad of insects buzzed around their heads as they carefully followed the teachers. Suddenly, one teacher stopped the children and pointed up into the branches. There were gasps when they spotted dappled tree snakes sliding silently and sinuously along the branches as they hunted for roosting birds.

Nervously, they all moved through the darkness until moonlight pierced the dense landscape and lit up a secret, peaceful glade. This open area had a small trickling stream winding itself between pristine tree ferns until it disappeared once again into the thick rainforest.

They had stumbled upon an enchanted, sacred place, undisturbed in a long time, with magical glowing fireflies drifting through the air like fairies going about their business. Before long, one student squealed with delight when she discovered many tiny green tree frogs clinging to the underside of the graceful tree ferns. Each one so cute in their miniature form, they had the recognisable light yellow smiley grin and lime green smooth skin.

The class took their time inspecting the amphibians, being very careful to not stand on any or touch them with their fingers. The teacher explained that the acid on human skin could burn their sensitive green suits, and as the night waned, the teachers called out for them to start the trek back to camp. The tired children fell in behind, and as she moved away, Gabby glanced back to take one more look at this precious sanctuary.

The peace was shattered when she screamed in outrage. Gabby could hardly believe her eyes when she saw Andy, John and Mick running around snatching at the baby frogs and squishing them with their hands. If one managed to leap away, they killed it by stomping it into the ground.

Running back, propelled by fury, she launched herself at Andy, hitting him with such force that the two of them toppled over into the stream, Gabby raining blows over him as they fell.

'How can you be so cruel, destroying something so beautiful. You and your friends are monsters,' she screamed at him.

'They're just frogs, you stupid freak! What's the big deal? And get the hell off me,' he yelled back.

'Gabrielle Harrison, get off him now.' The teacher firmly grasped her arm and dragged her away. The other two teachers had grasped John and Mick by the shoulder and once the children were separated, the three boys were marched back to camp with a teacher close behind them.

Wet and crying with rage, it was the first time Gabby had felt such contempt for her own kind. Why did humans have this desire to destroy something beautiful and good? Why couldn't they just leave the earth in peace and let other species live their lives?

The three boys were banned from participating in any further camp activities, and they also had increased camp duties to make up for their misdemeanours against nature.

Andy hated Gabby even more after that incident, and in a school with only two hundred students from preschool to senior, it was impossible to avoid him and his cruelty.

He delighted in grabbing Gabby's long hair as she walked past, or pushing her roughly up against the concrete walls whenever the teachers were not around.

One lunch break when they were in Grade 9, Eddie decided it was time to take a stand. As Gabby passed him an apple, he saw two bruises on her arm. 'What's this?' Eddie demanded as he took hold of her arm and turned it around to better see the marks on her skin.

'Andy made a grab at me as we passed in the corridor.' Gabby shrugged off his concern.

'Did he now?' Eddie tossed the apple into his school bag. 'Come with me,' he hissed as he grabbed her hand and dragged her along.

They walked briskly to the part of the school where the trio usually hung out.

John and Mick were sitting close together and reading a magazine that they snatched behind their backs as soon as Eddie and Gabby got close. This made them suspect it may have been a Playboy or something that would be confiscated with consequences if discovered.

'Where's Andy?' Eddie demanded.

The boys pointed to the toilet, and without ceremony, Eddie marched Gabby ahead of him into the boy's cubicles. Finding Andy at the sink, Eddie picked him up under the shoulders, pushed him against the wall and hissed menacingly. 'I am so sick of your bullying tactics, Bolton, and I swear that if you ever hurt Gabby again, I will do the same to you, but much, much worse.'

'Chill out, man. I'm just joking around,' Andy stammered as he looked over at Gabby and then back into Eddie's very close face.

'Eddie, please put him down. It's nothing. Truly, it's nothing, and I don't want you to get into trouble because of a few marks on my skin.' Gabby grabbed his arm and tried to make him lower Andy back to the ground.

'No, it's not nothing. I've had enough of this, and you'd better listen to me and leave her alone,' he growled as he lowered Andy to the ground and unhurriedly took his hands away.

Gabby dragged on Eddie's shirt to pull him away.

Andy put his hands up in surrender. 'Okay, I hear you, okay!' Andy's small, cold eyes flicked across to Gabby.

'Remember, I'll be watching you.' Eddie looked back as they both left the boys bathroom.

'You shouldn't have done that. He's not worth it, Eddie.' Gabby worried about Eddie and his school record.

'You're worth it, Gabby. You know I'd do anything to protect you.' He pulled her close against his shoulder to reinforce his vow.

After this warning, the harassment became more verbal than physical. Andy constantly called out cruel taunts whenever their paths crossed, most of which Gabby resolutely ignored.

If only she had known just how angry Andy felt every time he looked at her. If only she knew he was forming such a dangerous plan. How he dreamed about hurting her. How he wanted to leave a mark on her, one that she would never forget.

If only she had known.

Dragging her attention back to the present, Gabby shook off his ghost. Tonight was their special moment, a party that Andy Bolton was not there to ruin.

As the others settled around the fire to enjoy the music, Eddie and Gabby took some time out to walk down to the beach. Holding hands, they wandered beyond the sounds of the party until Eddie plopped down in the sand, dragging her with him.

Sitting beside him, Gabby rested her head on his shoulder, fitting it into the hollow just below his collarbone. Contented, they sat in silence, enjoying the starlit night for a while and listening to the rhythmic rush of the waves racing up the sand. Their only witness was the moon tracking its path across the dark waters.

Eventually Eddie broke their mesmeric contemplation of the scene before them. 'Well, here we are, Gabby, grownups now and able to make our own decisions. We've come a long way, you and me.'

He looked down at her resting against him and stored this memory away into his treasury for a time when she was no longer his to hold.

She smiled to herself and looked up into his eyes. 'Yes, but we have even further to go. Our lives are just beginning, Eddie.'

Eddie's smile faltered slightly. 'I am going to miss you so much when you leave.'

Gabby sat quietly for a moment, thinking about the future. When she left to study in Brisbane, she knew he wouldn't follow. His life was here at San Remo.

To cheer him up and distract herself, she laughed and elbowed him lightly in the ribs. 'Don't be silly, that's not going to happen for a while yet.'

Eddie grinned, and standing up, he pulled her with him. 'Always so pragmatic, aren't you! Come on, they're gonna think the worst if we're gone too long.'

She laughed at his joke and made her own comment. 'Don't be disgusting, Eddie.'

As they walked back towards the sounds of laughter, Gabby hugged Eddie's side. His friendship was the foundation of her life. She'd had so many experiences with Eddie by her side, and it seemed they had spent almost every day together. There was no one she trusted or relied on more than him.

'I will miss you too, you know.' Her smile was haunting in the moonlight as she tipped her head to look up at him.

Eddie simply grinned, mesmerised with her being his for this moment in time.

'I know.'

Eight

Only two weeks after their birthday party, Gabby was at Old Joe's beach cottage, which had become her second home over the years. She loved the timber-planked house with its veranda looking straight out to the beach and rolling waves. This was where they had sat sipping iced water and discussing changes in the numbers of sea turtles. Was it because of the trawlers that combed the coastline? Joe explained that when the turtles got caught in trawler nets, they couldn't get to the surface to breathe and unfortunately drowned. He also shared his concerns about coastal development that compromised their nesting sites.

Gabby loved anything science, especially when applied to nature or its impact on animals. She planned to study environmental science and work in the field to protect ecosystems and endangered species, and she had found a kindred spirit in Joe. His education had started with a medical degree but his passion soon became environmental biology. A hunger to know more had taken him on expeditions all over Australia and many other places around the world. From the Antarctic to across the Americas and some places Gabby hadn't even heard of, she never tired of his stories as they were an inspiration that fed her own dreams.

Old Joe had offered to sponsor her to study at a university in Melbourne. He had a small house there that could be her base, but Gabby wanted to be independent and fund her own path. She had decided on Brisbane.

'I had better head off, Joe. I need to wash my hair before going to the movies with Eddie tonight.' She stretched like a golden lioness in the afternoon light.

Old Joe nodded and stood up on his creaking joints to put the glasses in the sink.

Gabby turned to wave as she left for the bush path that ran parallel to the beach, and Joe noted the curlews had moved out of the shade around his house to loyally follow her home.

The bush was drowsy, sleeping to the lullaby of cicadas that drifted down from the treetops. The warmth of the sun enhanced all the scents, and the grass exuded a hint of coriander while the eucalyptus trees performed as well as any oil burners. Turning her head slightly to the side where the grass rustled, Gabby saw her curlews moving alongside, watchful and keeping pace with her stride.

Lost in thought, she wasn't really aware of her surroundings until she almost bumped into Andy Bolton. Startled that he was standing across her path with his arms folded against his chest, she immediately stepped back.

Feeling more surprised than alarmed, she noticed John and Mick standing behind him, mimicking Andy with their arms crossed. Gabby stared at all three of them for a moment, then sighing in resignation, she stepped around Andy to continue on her way, thinking the best course of action was to ignore them. However, Andy had other ideas, and as she stepped around him, his hand snaked out and latched on to her upper arm, wrenching her body around to face him.

'Where do you think you're going, Little Miss Perfect?' he sneered in to her face. His breath smelled of cigarettes and rum.

Still not overly concerned, Gabby tried to shrug out of his grasp. 'I'm going home, so stop acting the fool, Andy, and let me pass.'

'I know you have been at that dirty old man's house all morning. What does he do to you? Maybe gives you some of this?' He leered as he grabbed at his crotch with his other hand and made lewd thrusting motions.

John and Mick laughed at his antics.

'Andy, you really are a sick moron sometimes. Maybe it's time you grew up,' Gabby said as she pulled away to break free of him.

'Are you angry, princess? Now that I would like to see.' Andy suddenly stuck his leg behind her foot and tripped her backwards onto the ground. Falling hard upon her backside, Gabby tried to bounce back on to her feet but Andy immediately fell on top of her in a spread- eagled fashion.

Realising this was no innocent prank, she began to fight in earnest. His strength was suddenly ridiculously strong, and she could hardly believe this was just skinny Andy Bolton. It felt like the weight of a giant was holding her down.

'This is crazy! What are you doing? Andy, please stop, you're hurting me.'

However, no matter what she did, she couldn't shake him off. Blood was rushing through her head, and in desperation she tried to shout for help, but fear had closed her throat so only a dry squeak came out.

Stretching her neck, she sank her teeth in to whatever flesh she could reach. Fear and survival instinct took hold, and Gabby became a tiger in his clutches.

Andy screamed in pain when her teeth latched onto his cheek, and he wrenched his head back in disbelief. Leaning in closer to spit viciously in her face, he snarled, 'You little bitch, I am gonna to teach you a lesson you won't ever forget.' His lips had thinned to a hard line on his now-bloody face.

Before he could move, Gabby smashed her forehead against his as hard as she could. Stars spun before her eyes from the impact, and maddened by the pain she was inflicting, he threw his own head back and screamed with rage.

'Come here you two good-for-nothing arseholes and hold her down,' he yelled at the other two boys.

Looking anxiously at each other, they ambled over, unsure whether this was a prank that was now going too far.

'I am going to hurt you, really bad,' he hissed into her ear as she twisted and turned to get away from John and Mick. They gripped one arm and leg each and held her rooted to the ground, but wisely kept out of reach of her teeth, knowing she would bite them too if they got close.

Andy sat back on his legs and fumbled with his zip, and like a matador he flourished his excitement for them all to see.

Gabby had seen her brothers at bath time a lot over the years but had never faced an engorged phallus before, and without the foreplay of love, it was especially repugnant. Andy's veined, purplish shaft seemed angry, intent on harm, and Gabby's breath rushed in and out in panic. To think being raped by Andy Bolton would be the first time she was with a man filled her with horror.

'Please don't do this, Andy,' she begged for any remnant of decency. *I don't want rape to be my first time. I don't want Andy Bolton to be my first man.*

Andy laughed at her plea for mercy.

Gabby knew she was in serious trouble and desperately started screaming for help. The curlews began crying out too, smelling her fear. They ran in close to Gabby, screeching over and over again.

This really spooked John and Mick.

'That's enough, Andy. These stupid birds are making too much noise. Let's get out of here before we get sprung.' John's face was flushed red with fear.

'Mate, John's right, this has gone too far. I'm not going to get charged for rape! She's not worth going to jail for. Come on, Andy, it's time to snap out of it,' Mick yelled at him.

Gabby was screaming as loud as the birds, and John and Mick shouted even louder for him to stop, so Andy did what he could to stop this spiralling out of control.

He crouched down and sat on her legs, bunched his fists together for more impact and punched her face over and over again until she couldn't call out for help anymore. Instead, she just lay there quietly whimpering as pain exploded through her broken face.

Consciousness was fading, and Gabby felt her spirit move away from her battered body. She could still see it all happening, but now it was like watching some other poor, beaten girl suffer.

'Far out, Andy. You've gone too far this time.' John and Mick backed away from the mess. It frightened them to see so much blood all over her nose, broken lips and from a gash on the forehead.

'Shut up and fuck off. Both of you get out of here!' Andy roared at them from on top of her body, his face flushed red from the exertion. There was snot running from his nose into his mouth, and his eyes were wild with frenetic energy. He had now abandoned all restraints of society and instead embraced the beast within that had been barely contained until now.

The curlews were darting all around them, hissing and striking out at the boys to scare them away from Gabby's prone body. John and Mick took one last look and ran away as fast as they could, both swearing that this time Andy had gone too far.

As she lay there, Gabby was slipping in and out of consciousness, no longer able to gather the strength or will to fight back or run away. Realising this was about to get a lot worse, she told her spirit to turn away. *Don't watch anymore. Go far from this place of shame.*

Dragging his pants up, Andy ventured a little off the track into the bush to find a broken branch and as soon as he moved away, the curlews rushed in to gather around her body in a protective circle. Andy rushed back at the curlews and began to beat them with the long stick, striking them again and again until they retreated back into the long grass, still hissing menacingly from their open beaks.

As soon as he turned back to Gabby, the brave little bodyguards raised their wings aggressively and dived back in to bite at his legs. Screeching with frustration, Andy swiped indiscriminately and struck them as hard as he could. The birds were flung shrieking backwards into the dirt, but they wouldn't give up. Time and time again they tried to scare him away from Gabby, but each and every time he beat them back.

Battered and sore, they retreated a little way off and kept calling out distress calls for Gabby, some rushing back along the path towards Joe's cottage.

Getting some breathing space, Andy came back, puffing, and he stood there to take a moment to enjoy the sense of anticipation. He looked at Gabby lying there unconscious and relished his moment of supremacy. With great excitement, he dragged his pants off and tore at her clothes, tearing them to shreds and exposing her naked flesh.

She was perfect, all golden skin and long limbs. The triangle nestling between her legs glinted like a pot of gold in the afternoon light. Like a conqueror, Andy threw her panties into the bush. Taking a deep breath, he dropped his body onto hers, shoving his hard erection roughly inside of her.

He shouted with pleasure as light flooded his body, encasing him in an ecstasy of sensations, shivering from the tips of his fingers right down to the end of his toes.

His ecstasy was her pain, and it was so shocking that it brought her body and soul back together again. She screamed as he ripped her apart, breaking and tearing the delicate flesh until blood ran down her legs. Andy grabbed her by the hair and spat into her face as he thrust his body into hers again and again. With humiliation and helplessness, she saw his eyes glaze over and lose focus until suddenly he shivered and groaned, releasing his poisonous infusion. One that spread hot inside of her like a burning iron, branding an insidious hatred deep within, consuming her like a raging fire of shame.

Laying there on top of her and panting for a couple of minutes, he whispered in her ear, 'Now you aren't so high and mighty, hey. You won't ever forget me after today.'

His face smirked with satisfaction as he put his clothes back in order. 'Thanks, bitch. That was one amazing fuck,' he said as he tore the red pendant off her throat, viciously snapping the leather cord.

Gabby couldn't open her eyes any more. They had completely swollen shut, but she turned her face to where she thought he stood and slurred through broken and swollen lips.

'What did I ever to do to you, Andy?'

In that moment, the mask slipped, and Gabby saw the force within. Andy's face twisted ghoulishly and a voice not his own rasped menacingly. 'Fallon, my old nemesis, now I am the powerful one, and in this human body you cannot stop me. Today's pain and humiliation is nothing compared with what is to come.' The threat turned into an insane cackle. Gabby just stared at him blankly. He had clearly lost his mind. He didn't even know who she was.

With that, Andy surrendered his whole self to the evil within, and drove his foot into her ribs, listening to her cry out with pain as he kicked again and again and again. Revelling in the beast, he did other things to hurt her, far greater than the actual rape, things that were too depraved to mention but would never be forgotten.

Gabby's spirit took her away, maybe forever this time.

Taking a moment to rejoice in the sight of her broken body before turning away, he waltzed down the dusty track as he shouted his exultation to the skies. 'Look out world, here I come. I am the angel of torture and death.'

Watching her suffer and bleed was far better than any cruelty he had exacted on a stupid animal. Already he wanted to inflict hurt again, and next time he wouldn't stop until he choked the life away.

This was the new beginning he had secretly longed for, and a flush of acceptance reinforced his talent to revel in pain. Not going home, not ever conforming again, he would hit the road and prey on innocents whenever opportunity presented the next victim.

Running off into the bush, he started making his way through the thick scrub heading west away from the beach, not caring where he would stop or spend the night.

Kathleen knew Ruth Saila was dropping over for an afternoon coffee, so she slipped the chicken and mushroom casserole into the oven before putting the kettle on to boil.

They had been friends since the early days of moving to the beach. Ruth and Billy lived in the same street in a house very similar to their own, and the three Saila children had grown up with Kathleen's brood. The Sailas were an Islander family who had moved from the Murray Islands in the Torres Strait when Lizzy was only a baby, settling soon after at San Remo with Billy getting a foreman's job at a nearby prawn farm.

'Let's sit outside under the trees, it's so hot today.' Kathleen took the tray to the small iron table and chairs set up under the shady mango tree.

'This is perfect.' Ruth gratefully accepted the mug of coffee as she settled her ample frame on to the small chair. The chatter of a willy wagtail in the branches above kept them company.

'Where's Gabby?' she asked.

'She should be home from Joe's any minute now. I think Eddie is taking her to the movies tonight.' Kathleen glanced at her watch to check the time.

'Oh, that's right, he did mention that this morning. I've got a head like a sieve lately. I just can't seem to remember anything,' Ruth complained as she sipped her drink.

They chatted with the familiarity of old friends, about family news and plans for the weekend, until the ringing of the phone changed their lives in one terrible moment.

Nine

Joe liked to swim each morning and afternoon. It was his daily exercise regime, and he had changed into bathers when Gabby left to go home. His mind relaxed as his body fell into the rhythm of the strokes, and he walked back to the cottage feeling refreshed and renewed. Then he saw one of the curlews acting crazy, running around in circles outside his house. He stared in consternation until it dawned that this may be a signal that Gabby was in trouble.

Throwing his satchel on the veranda, Joe took off along the track that she would normally take to go home. Three curlews now ran along beside him, and this only reinforced his fear that something was terribly wrong.

Gasping for breath, with panic and worry pushing him faster, he rushed along the dusty path until he spotted a group of birds surrounding someone lying on the ground.

Realising it was Gabby, Joe moaned from the depths of his soul when he saw all the blood. She looked like a bronzed porcelain doll lying there, shattered and broken on the ground.

Squatting down beside her, he cradled her misshapen, swollen face in his hands and crooned that somehow he would make everything right again. As he spoke, he scanned her body for injuries, noticing her breathing was short and sharp, so he suspected broken ribs. He could see the huge purple bruises already forming around her sides where she had been brutally kicked. Very gently he moved his hands over her limbs to feel for swellings and breaks.

One punch had ruptured a vessel in her eye, and a single bloody tear trickled down the cheek that was turning purple before his very eyes. This scarlet tear represented so much: the end of innocence and the beginning of his vengeance.

When he thought of her purity and goodness, this tear was the saddest thing Joe had ever seen in his long, long life.

His eyes moved to her lower body to discover a copious amount of blood coming from her groin and spreading over her legs, and his heart sank with the knowledge that these injuries were far more than just physical.

Taking his shirt off, he put it ever so carefully against the flow of blood, hoping to staunch the bleeding.

She stirred and moaned as soon as any pressure was placed against the wounds.

'Gabby, I have to run home to call the ambulance. I will be back as quickly as I can.'

'No, please don't leave me, Joe. They might come back.' She was whimpering with fear.

Torn between wanting to keep her safe and the urgency of medical treatment, he tried to reassure her. Not knowing how severe her injuries were, he didn't want to move her.

'It's all right, Gabby. I will only be a minute, I promise.'

'Hurry, Joe,' she mumbled through swollen lips.

He raced away as quickly as his bowed legs would carry him, and several curlews returned with him too, hissing their distress. The others remained and formed a circle around her.

How do I explain this to her family?

His mouth was so dry he couldn't even wet his lips, and he felt disorientated and dizzy with shock. His mind kept replaying the images of her until his blood began to boil with rage. How dare someone treat Gabby so cruelly. Unconsciously, he swallowed the bile at the back of his throat as his stomach lurched with nausea.

So many questions were rushing through his head. Who would hurt and rape her? Was there some escaped criminal hiding at the beach? Surely nobody they knew could commit such a crime? No one could possibly harbour such loathing for Gabby. She was a beautiful young woman who never had a bad word for anyone. In fact, she always defended the underdog, trying to understand people rather than judge them.

As soon as he instructed the ambulance where to come, he called the Harrison household. When Joe reached for the phone, he looked outside, and the first thing he saw was a group of curlews sitting on the grass keeping watch. A couple of hours or even minutes and a life can change so quickly. Literally in the blink of an eye, all of the previous expectations of what is in store can be gone, and only a bleak future traded in exchange.

With a cringing heart he dialled the number, and his breath quickly expelled as he heard Kathleen's familiar, cheerful voice answer.

Little did she know.

Kathleen laughed as Ruth described Billy teaching Eddie to drive, and how they argued about everything.

'That's why I left it to Frank to teach our kids. It's too frustrating for me by far. They won't listen,' she sighed in agreement.

'I think I hear the phone ringing, Kathleen.' Ruth poised with her coffee cup not quite at her lips and turned her head towards the sound.

'So it is. I won't be a moment,' she reassured her friend before going inside to pick up the phone.

'Hello, Kathleen Harrison speaking.' No answer.

'Hello,' she said again.

At first, Kathleen could only hear breath panting into the phone. As she was about to hang up in frustration, she heard Joe say her name.

'Kathleen.'

'Joe, is that you? Is everything alright? What's happened?' Kathleen immediately knew something was wrong. She couldn't miss that his voice sounded strangled and tight with emotion.

'Kathleen, Gabby has been hurt,' he whispered into the receiver.

'Joe, whatever do you mean?' Kathleen's breath sucked in with a wheeze, and she instinctively turned towards her best friend.

Ruth was watching Kathleen through the window and when she turned to look at her, she knew something was wrong. Kathleen's eyes were wild with fear and her face deathly pale, so without delay she rushed to her side and gently placed a hand on Kathleen's shoulder to support her.

'She's been brutally attacked, and the ambulance is coming to take her to the hospital,' Joe's disembodied voice was delivering the news like a judge's hammer.

The phone trembled and dropped out of Kathleen's hand as her knees buckled. Ruth caught her and supported her to a kitchen chair while she took over the call.

'I'm sorry, Joe, it's Ruth. Kathleen needs a moment. Can you tell me what happened?'

Who would hurt my beautiful daughter? Kathleen didn't want to believe what she had been told. Staring into space, she felt this was just a bad dream from which she surely must awaken from soon.

Ruth hung up the receiver and looked over at her friend with tears in her eyes.

'Come on, love. It's going to be all right, but we need to get to the hospital and be there when she arrives.' Ruth approached Kathleen with a heavy-footed walk.

Ruth then called Frank at work and told him to call the boys and meet them at the emergency department.

While Ruth fretted and cussed about speed limits and traffic lights, Kathleen didn't make a sound. Her world looked different, like she saw it in sepia, and everything moved in slow motion. Even sound was warped and distorted, unrecognisable.

As soon as he hung up the phone, Joe threw on some clothes and ran back to be there when the ambulance arrived. When he dropped down beside Gabby, at first she didn't respond no matter how many times he called her name over and over again.

Eventually his voice broke into her disorientated state, and the first sensation beyond pain was fear. She looked around wildly, thinking that Andy must still be lurking nearby. Even though her vision was filled with Joe's face, she still couldn't quell the sense of panic. Danger hovered over her like a silent assassin. The world she had known no longer existed. Light had become shadow and safety would never again be taken for granted.

'It's hurting.' With each breath, pain shot through her.

Gently holding her arms at her side, Joe murmured words of comfort. 'Hush, Gabby, the ambulance is on its way,' he kept whispering softly.

In spite of her injuries, she began to cry great, big sobs that tore through her ribs like a cyclone. She cried for all that was lost and her broken soul. Her heart had moved up and was choking her. Soon it would come out of her mouth, and she would spit it onto the dusty ground.

Old Joe leaned forward to hold her. It hurt him so much to see her suffer like this.

'Why did he hurt me, Joe?' she croaked, 'I never did anything to make him hate me like that. I wish he had killed me.' She turned her distorted face away from him and closed her eyes.

'Don't say that, Gabby. I don't ever want you to say that.' He sat there for a few minutes stroking the matted hair off her forehead. The blood was drying and crusting over the cuts.

She could feel his fingers lightly fluttering to find a place on her battered face that wasn't disfigured with swelling and wounds.

'Gabby, who did this? Who attacked you?'

'No,' she choked. 'I don't want to talk about it.'

'Gabby, no matter how much it hurts, you will have to tell us what happened.'

Still sobbing, but quietly now, exhausted and sore and barely able to make any noise, Gabby moved her broken lips so softly that he barely heard her say, 'Andy Bolton attacked me with the help of his two friends, John and Mick.'

Drawing back in shock and horror, a red mist moved across Joe's vision. *How dare they hurt her like this! Local boys, who were raised to know better. I know the parents of these children and there is no excuse for this. How dare they!*

Images of revenge against them flashed across Joe's mind.

Fighting hard to contain his anger and hatred, Joe tried to hide his reaction. He didn't want to frighten her with any more violence. His burning desire to avenge her suffering would have to wait.

She whimpered again when he mentioned that her mother would be at the hospital waiting for her.

'I don't want my family to know. Please don't tell them, Joe. I'm too ashamed.'

'Gabby, you have nothing to be ashamed about. Your family has only love for you, unconditional no matter what.' Joe consoled her as he looked into the swollen slits where those beautiful eyes used to be. Her face had crusted blood all over it.

'I'll be back in a minute, Gabby. I'm just going to flag down the ambulance and bring them through to the bush path.' He kneeled closer to the ground and gently kissed her forehead.

Gadriel was at the Blood Tree when Josiel arrived back in the Silver City. It had been heart wrenching to leave Gabby is such a state, but she dared not disobey her orders or raise suspicion of her movements.

'How is she?' Gadriel asked as she embraced him.

'Oh, Gadriel, it's bad, really bad.' Josiel looked at his kind face with her grey eyes swimming in a pool of tears. 'It is as we feared. You of all messengers know what the fallen are capable of, but now they are using humans as instruments of torture as well. Fallon and I are connected, so I feel what she feels, and the trauma her human self, Gabby, is suffering now is heartbreaking. Her pain is swelling in my chest and choking me. It's not just the mutilation to her body, it's the emotional and psychological damage that I'm struggling with.'

Gadriel held her away for a moment and said, 'You feel her even in this human form?'

Josiel nodded her assent. 'Yes, strangely I do. Humans have such a propensity for strong emotions. Their love is deep, their anger is hot and their hearts are so tender. I know Gabby's body will heal but this injury to her heart will be lifelong.'

Gadriel hung his head in shame. 'I should have sent another agent to discreetly watch over her. I'm so sorry, Josiel. I have failed you both.' He took her hands in his and tipped his forehead against hers; this was their way of conveying an apology.

'None of this is your fault, Gadriel. We knew there was no protection for her indiscretion. I'm just thankful I've been able to shield her a little and get to know this child. She was so precious and innocent growing up, and now as she approaches her adult life, it's going to be a precarious path to tread with danger on all sides.' Josiel moved away from Gadriel and leaped up on to the lower branches of Fallon's favourite tree.

Gadriel did the same and settled beside her.

'Do you think Puriel was right when he wanted to forfeit the life of the child at the beginning?'

'No, I still don't believe that. Her becoming human may have happened for a reason, and we don't know what purpose Fallon is fulfilling. What may seem a mistake may yet play out for the greater good.'

'You are known for your wisdom, Josiel, so I sincerely hope you are right. My question only came from a place of love: the desire to see Fallon safely home and to put a stop to her suffering.' Gadriel looked down at Josiel's bloody hands.

'Of course I know where your heart lies, Gadriel. In the same place as mine.' Josiel too looked down at her hands in dismay. In her disquiet, she'd plucked at some leaves without even thinking, and now the blood seeped across her palms. Guiltily looking up through the branches as if the tree would deliver a reprimand, she gently placed each leaf back onto the branch and waited for the tree to reclaim it and restore life.

'When can you return to her?' Gadriel took her red-stained hand in his.

'As soon my strength is restored, I'll go back.'

'If only I could move through the portal again, to seek and destroy any of our fallen brothers that even gets close to her.' He chafed at his own restrictions.

'Gadriel, these demons know how to move through the shadows and blend into society, and are working through humans.' Josiel looked down at their clasped hands in consternation.

'Lucifer always *was* clever, but it was his pride that became his downfall,' Gadriel agreed as he rubbed the bloody stain off the top her hand with his thumb.

Looking away into the velvet sky, its vibrant hue lit up Gadriel's fiery profile, casting a glow over his thick red hair. 'I still wish I was there to take care of Fallon in this vulnerable state.' He turned back to look at Josiel wistfully.

'We've been ordered to not intervene, and even my visits would be frowned upon if the wise ones on the council knew.'

'They probably already know, as they would do the same for their name day sister or brother.'

'You may be right, but for now we must hold on to hope and faith.' Josiel held tightly to the hand of her good friend.

'Hope is sometimes all we have, hope and faith,' he offered.

'Hope and faith is what the Blood Tree symbolises,' Josiel agreed.

Frank was waiting at the hospital emergency department doors when Ruth and Kathleen arrived.

After checking in at the triage desk, one of the nurses came from within the depths of the wards to usher Frank and Kathleen in to see Gabby, leaving Ruth twisting her hands in the waiting area.

'Oh my God, my poor baby,' Kathleen cried out in horror when she saw the bloody mess that was her daughter. Frank's face went pale with shock, and his knuckles whitened to the bone as he held onto the side of the bed for support.

Gabby was barely conscious and remained numb and mute to the outpouring of grief from her traumatised parents.

They were asked to wait outside when two doctors came to examine her. After the curtains were drawn again, they drew Frank and Kathleen into an empty bay to discuss her injuries.

'We think there may be some broken ribs but we'll do X-rays to be sure. She is young, so the wounds will heal with intravenous antibiotics,' one doctor reassured. 'However, apart from the evidence that there has been a sexual assault, there is also significant damage done to her vaginal region, deep gashes, and we think there is even some broken glass embedded in the flesh.' He stopped talking as Kathleen knees buckled.

'No, no, no,' she cried as Frank caught her.

Lifting her up, he held Kathleen against his chest and wrapped his arms around her and whispered in her ear. 'Gabby is strong like you, Kathleen, and now she needs that strength like never before.'

The first doctor looked very sad as he watched their distress and gently explained they would take her straight to surgery to repair the damage under a general anaesthetic.

Kathleen and Frank were desolate when the orderly came to take Gabby for the operation, and a sympathetic nurse led them into a small trauma room.

Soon the door flung open as Jacob rushed into the room, followed by Thomas. Both wrapped their arms around their weeping mother, trying to shelter her from this pain. Neither could even fathom the idea of someone hurting their sister, as nobody could be sweeter or as wholesome as she. After a family hug, Kathleen and Frank whispered to the boys what the doctors had told them.

Jacob, now a strong young man in his twenties, started pacing, thumping one fist into the other, while Thomas sat close to his mother, doing his best to comfort her.

A little later, the same nurse came back with Old Joe, followed by Ruth, Billy and their children, Lizzy, Nellie and Eddie.

'I think at a time like this you need friends around you,' the nurse murmured as she closed the door so that they had privacy.

Ruth immediately sat beside Kathleen and wrapped her arms around her. With their heads close together, Kathleen told her what was happening.

With Kathleen having her best friend's support, Frank drew Joe across the room to ask him some questions.

Joe told Frank what he knew.

'I can't believe they could do something like this. Are you sure Gabby said it was Andy Bolton?'

'Yes, sure enough to report to the police downstairs. They are going over to his house to arrest him.'

'Joe, please don't tell the family this, not tonight. Vengeance is best served cold, not with their blood boiling, and I just don't know what the boys would do with that knowledge the way they feel right now.'

Looking over at the three young men, Joe could understand Frank's wisdom. Eddie was squatting in the corner with his hands over his face, maybe to veil the tears that flowed down his cheeks. Jacob and Thomas were again sitting close to their mother and whispering how they would rip the perpetrators to pieces.

Staring into the worn sadness on Frank's face, Joe nodded his assent.

Billy was doing his best to comfort his daughters, feeling slightly guilty to have them safe and whole in his arms. He couldn't even imagine what Frank was feeling. It would destroy him if anyone hurt his girls, even if they were now young women.

Eddie couldn't believe this was happening. They should have been at the movies tonight, munching on popcorn and laughing at some stupid movie stunt. Instead, his best friend had almost been cut to pieces. If only he had been there to protect her. He should have sensed she was in trouble, but he had been in the shed at home, hammering wood, when he should have been with Gabby.

Time passed slowly, and sitting across from Kathleen and his sons, Frank stared at his feet, not seeing the black work boots or the polished surface of the grey floor. No, his inner eye was far away from this bleak place. It had cast back in time, going to a day when the cane was burning brightly...

'Look over there, Gabby. If we drive just a little way up here, we can hop out and safely watch the cane fire move across the paddock.'

Eager with anticipation, five-year-old Gabby scampered out of the station wagon and walked around to take her father's hand.

'Come up here, sweetheart.' Frank picked her up and placed her on his shoulders for a fine view.

They watched the flames leaping higher and higher, and the crackling of the burning underbrush filled the evening air. Heat pushed against their faces as the fire moved past them on its quest to consume everything in its path.

The heat and noise had been overwhelming when it climaxed. Once it had moved on, there was only blackened ash left in the aftermath, the cane grass turned to burnt sticks with a few green tufts left on top. The sky had darkened with pieces of cane ash that rained back to the earth, and when Gabby reached out and touched the black feather, it disintegrated on her fingers like a black stain.

Once the fiery glory had moved on, Frank reached up to take Gabby off his shoulders. 'Wasn't that something to see?' Frank asked as he merged the car back into the traffic.

'Daddy, why do they burn the cane?' Gabby tapped his shoulder to get his attention.

He quickly spared her a glance as he drove along the familiar road towards San Remo Beach.

'Well, honey, many years ago the cane cutters used to die from venomous snake bites and Weil's disease spread by rats, so they started burning the cane first to clear out these dangers before cutting. Now they only burn the low-lying paddocks that are susceptible to flooding.'

'What about the other animals that live in the cane, what happens to them when their homes get all burned up?'

'Oh, I'm sure they can sense danger and move out well before the flames reach them. If you stood at the very front of the fire, you would see all kinds of animals running out of the cane and safely away.'

'What about the baby animals? They wouldn't be big enough to outrun the fire, so what would happen to them, Daddy?'

He looked across at her and marvelled at the sight, those blonde curls falling around her shoulders, breathtaking eyes that were still too big for her sweet heart-shaped face. There was an adorable smudge of ash that she had rubbed across her pert, little nose.

Frank realised uncomfortably that she was one step ahead of him. How to explain to a child that these would perish? How to make her understand that the safety of people was more important than the baby bandicoots or other small animals living in the thick, grassy crop?

'I don't think they have babies at this time of the year, Gabby,' was the best he could come up with.

Frank saw the doubt lingering in her large, luminescent eyes but wisely she didn't press her point...

Always so clever and caring, now his little girl had been beaten up because of these unique qualities. Life was as fragile as a dream and without realising it, everyone lived on the edge of a knife; just a fraction to the left or right and everything that was familiar could become alien and unrecognisable. No one ever knew what waited just around the next corner, whether great joy or immense sadness.

Coming fully back to the harsh present while wishing he could stay in the past, Frank heard Jacob say to his mother, 'We will find out who did this and kill them.'

Kathleen shook her head as she held him in her arms and whispered, 'No, Jake. No more violence.'

Gabby was still in surgery when two police officers arrived to take her statement, so they spoke to Joe instead.

In another private room, he gave them his statement and then asked if they had been successful in apprehending Andy Bolton. The younger police officer said that Andy had failed to come home after the assault and that they had patrol cars out looking for him.

'Would you have any idea on his whereabouts?' the older, more experienced officer prompted Old Joe.

'No, no idea. He wasn't anywhere near Gabby when I found her. I assumed he would head for home and stay low. Surely he must know he would be charged for something as bad as this.' Joe held the gaze of the police officer.

'I'm sure he will be found and made to face the consequences of his actions.' The other officer dropped his gaze.

Once his statement was taken, Joe popped his head in to the room to bid the families goodbye and slipped out into the afternoon light, a plan formulating in his overactive mind.

Ten

Joe had a feeling that Andy had no intention of going home to face his parents or Gabby's family, so he gathered up what he needed and started tracking him through the bush.

It wasn't hard to find Andy's tracks. Like a bull elephant, he had crashed through the trees leaving his mark on the vegetation as well as foot prints on the sandy soil.

When he passed the scuffled ground where Gabby had lain, he could still see the red stain of her blood on the crushed grass where she had been left in that tragic state. His old heart twisted and hardened in his chest, and Joe swore to himself that justice would prevail this day. How dare a son of man treat Gabby like this. Surely Heaven had turned its face away from such brutality.

He maintained a steady pace like a hunting dog after its quarry. To stop from howling with anger and hate, he let his thoughts wander back to the time in his mid-forties when he lived with the Martu, one of the oldest Aboriginal tribes in Central Australia. He had gone there with a group of scientists to study desert insects and fell in love with the land and the people, deciding to take a sabbatical and stay on when the other researchers went back to Melbourne. Out there in the wilderness, time passed quickly, and he spent many years with '*the people*'.

The Martu were a nomadic tribe who moved from one waterhole to the next. With soaring daytime temperatures in summer, it became necessary to walk at night to avoid the punishing sun. Joe would march with them on feet as hardened and cracked as his Aboriginal brothers.

Joe took delight in learning their traditional ways, never regretting the decision not to return to the city. He discovered the benefits of natural medicines and listened in wonder to their Dreamtime stories, and in time he earned their respect to become a white brother. They astounded him with their generosity. Completely the opposite to the insatiable materialism of western culture, these people took delight in giving away as much as they could. It was prestigious to be a philanthropist in the red land.

Living as one of them for so long, the tribal council even gave Joe his own Aboriginal name, 'Mani', which means equal to us. Being an only child, he had never known the relationship of brothers or sisters, and these kind individuals filled that void in his life. It was easy to love such genuine people. Eventually, the elders were convinced of his sincerity to seek wisdom, and they met to consider Joe's request to sit on their council. A white man had never been trusted with their tribal secrets, and the wise ones wanted him tested away from the tribe.

The next day, Bindarra, a brother from the tribe, took him away from the camp to spend time in prayer and self-reflection. They walked all day on only a few mouthfuls of brackish water, and at night they curled into balls around the fire, cold and hungry.

With no provisions, they had to rely on the land to survive, and this took up most of the day. One morning during their foray, Bindarra grasped his hunting stick tighter and rushed towards a fallen log, seeing something Joe's untrained eyes did not. Suddenly reaching down into the dried grass, he shouted with glee and pulled out a large goanna by the tail, holding it well away from his body. As soon as they found some cleared ground, he dropped the large lizard and whacked it several times with his stick until it lay still at his feet. That night they feasted, enjoying the juicy, succulent meat as their teeth chewed it off the bones.

Once their bellies were swollen and full, Bindarra began to talk of the stars, gesturing with his hands to explain how they were placed in the galaxy. Joe watched the proud profile as Bindarra gazed into the fire, seeing a world that was as real as the dirt they sat upon. Everything had its own meaning out here. The world they lived in was balanced and purposeful, and far away from the distractions and greed of modern life.

Bindarra was not an educated man in the formal sense but he had spent his long life exhaustively observing the patterns and seasons of this land. Like a lover, he could intimately navigate every curve and hollow, and he agreed with Joe that the wind was singing of change.

'Our people have a strong connection to the land, and we have seen a shift in the seasons. The ancient ways are changing.'

'Those changes are happening all over the world,' Joe agreed.

'Mani, why are you so curious about our customs? Why not go back to your own kind?'

'For many years, my life was busy but empty until I came to the desert and found your people. Your beliefs are simple yet they sing to my soul and bring a peace that I have not found in the cities with my people. Only here have I found an acceptance that has nothing to do with what I have or what I can do, and I know this is the home of my heart.'

One morning when Joe woke up, Bindarra announced it was now time to go back to the tribe, so without ceremony they covered the fire with dirt and turned for home.

Upon their return, the council called a meeting with Bindarra in a cave with traditional drawings decorating the walls.

'Mani may have a different skin to ours but his heart is the same colour and beats with the same rhythm of our land. I would trust him with my own life and welcome his wisdom on our council,' Bindarra made his report.

'Thank you, Bindarra. We trust your wisdom and judgement. We now ask you to bring Mani to this council.'

Joe was ushered to sit with the elders. He held his silence and let them speak when they were ready. There was very little noise in the isolated, sacred cave. It was so quiet he could hear the scratching of a small lizard as it scurried across the sandy surface of the ground.

'Mani, Bindarra speaks well of you, and after much thought, we have decided to offer you a place on our council. There is only one more condition that you must agree to: You must take the journey from child to man and be circumcised and initiated alongside the other young men of our tribe.'

The process took many weeks, even months to complete. Joe was taken away into the bush by a group of elders, and during this time he had to learn to tell the Dreamtime stories and memorise the steps of the ceremonial dances that took a boy into his manhood. Learning the music and dances took quite some time. They chanted in rhythm to the Didgeridoo while others beat hollow logs covered in animal skins.

The dancing was exhilarating. As they moved around the fire with feet stomping and the red dust of their land filling the air, a brotherhood bond grew into a living thing, strong and powerful, and one that bound them together.

Joe found that nothing he had ever done could compare with tribal dancing and music. It was mesmerising as his heart picked up the beat to keep pace with the rhythm. Adrenaline rushed through his blood until he entered a trance-like state and moved without inhibition around the fire. It was so liberating to let go and become one with his new brothers, bonded together by blood and dirt.

The love and trust between them were so complete that he had no qualms to strip naked and stand proudly to get painted with red ochre. Intricate lines and symbols covered his face and body, and at other times all he wore was a belt made from human hair. This was tied around his waist and was what he slept, ate and learned in until he was considered an Aborigine man. Once Joe was deemed ready, the final step of initiation was performed: circumcision.

As a white Caucasian male, his parents had decided not to circumcise him as an infant. This was quite an unusual decision for that time as most babies had the procedure done soon after birth to prevent infection. Joe's parents had done their own research, talked to doctors and decided that it was unnecessary to inflict such suffering upon a newborn, so they left him intact. Until now.

Any fully grown male would appreciate Joe's apprehension at this final stage of initiation. Apprehension he decided was well deserved, especially when the procedure was done with a sharp stone in the presence of his new brothers. All the young men were very stalwart in their suffering, so Joe did his best to follow their example.

Ten days later, the tenderness and swelling had subsided, and he considered it was worth the suffering. Now that initiation was done, he was welcomed as a full brother and could enter the inner sanctum of tribal secrets.

These secrets were protected to ensure that they did not fall into the wrong hands. This was powerful witchcraft, one that was potentially dangerous without the understanding of their sacred purpose.

He was warned that if one betrayed these secrets, the medicine man's magic bone would be pointed at the perpetrator, resulting in coma and death. During his time, Joe never saw this judgement passed on an elder; they were all far too frightened to reveal the tribal laws. However, he had no doubt in the effectiveness of such punishment. This was a power that could not be explained by science. It was an otherworldly magic that could produce strange, unexplained phenomenon, like Spirit Ants.

The Spirit Ants looked like a meat ant that was found around Australia, but far larger. The size of man's thumb with large incisors, these particular ants were bred by the tribes, and once fully grown, the oldest members of the council performed a sanctification ceremony over them. This age-old spell empowered them with the sense of judgement they needed to fulfil their duty: They judged the spirit of a man, right down to the very soul. They were only used as a last resort if all other tribal investigations remained inconclusive. If there was any goodness in the heart, the ants would offer another chance.

The first time Joe saw the ants pass judgement, their verdict concluded that the soul was redeemable. There was great rejoicing from the tribe to see the accused given a second chance.

It was humbling to witness the ceremony of the Spirit Ants because the tribe knew that the ants could not be influenced or misled. They alone could determine if any goodness remained, and the tribe trusted the ants to carry out their punishment, even to death if that was the verdict.

In another case, a tribal man was accused of raping and murdering a young girl. They could have relied on white man's law but the elders preferred to call upon on their own traditional methods. The perpetrator vehemently denied the accusation, so after much investigation, the conclusion was still uncertain. The elders called a declaration ceremony and restrained the young man with the some very specific vines then released the ants. As soon as they moved towards him, he screamed and strained against the vines that held him fast.

The tribe watched in complete silence as the ants moved around the terrified man, whose large brown eyes looked fit to pop out of his dark, sweaty face. When the ants began to touch his skin, he wriggled in the red dirt trying desperately to discourage them. Maybe it was the scent of fear that determined their decision; however, once the ants began to feed, everyone moved quietly away to let them to do their work and give privacy to the person seeking redemption from his ancestors.

There wasn't much left when the Spirit Ants had finished. All the flesh was completely consumed, and only the white bones were left glinting in the harsh sunlight.

The same ants, the same appetite. It was just that one human still had a residue of goodness and the other had succumbed to evil. The ants' accuracy was proven time and time again whenever their special skills were called upon. The truth would become apparent once all the layers of lies and mistrust were lifted away, and only the Spirit Ants could reveal the true quality of a man.

Joe had to swallow the bitter bile that rose in his throat when he came upon Andy sleeping peacefully, propped up against a tree. The setting sun softened the scene before him, making it picturesque. The flat, grassy land with a shale cliff rising up behind hardly looked like a hide-out for a criminal. Not wanting to wake him, not yet anyway, quiet as a mouse Joe crept up and carefully prepared the vines around Andy's ankles and wrists.

Placing them in loose circles, he had them ready to restrain him in a moment.

Watching his quarry blissfully lost in slumber, it hardly seemed possible this young man could act so cruelly. His cheeks were flushed from the afternoon sun and there was just a hint of stubble on his chin, small signs of the awakening man.

No matter how beguiling, this state of innocence didn't trick Joe or make him falter from his decision. He only had to close his eyes to see Gabby's bloody, battered face and the light of innocence snuffed out of her clear sea-green eyes to stay true to his path.

Clenched in Andy's curled hand was the pendant Gabby always wore around her throat. In the afternoon sun, it shone blood red, and the same stain was smeared across his knuckles and spattered over his face. Joe's resolve hardened even further.

When all was ready, Joe leaned back and pulled on all four ties at once to tightly bind Andy to the trees around him. Waking up with a jolt, Andy looked wildly around to find Joe sitting a couple of metres away from him, regarding him as a spider to a fly. Andy did his best to break the bonds holding him captive, but the harder he pulled against the vines the tighter they gripped his limbs.

Choosing to bluff his way out of the reprisal, he put on a brave face and spat on the ground in contempt.

'What the hell are you doing here, old man? What do you think you can do to me? You're just a weak, decrepit, disgusting paedophile!'

Joe just sat there quietly on his haunches during this tirade of abuse and obscenities until Andy lay there panting, with blood pooling around his wrists and ankles.

'You're a frigging lunatic. What do you think to prove from this? You trying to make me say 'sorry'? Well, I won't, because that stuck-up bitch had it coming to her anyway.' His face fused purple with fear and frustration, the blood vessels standing out prominently across his forehead.

Throughout all of this, Joe remained detached from the boy's suffering. It was almost like Andy were one of the insects he was impaling on a board.

With no more energy to fight or curse, Andy slumped against the bindings. Sweat was pouring off his face, and it slicked his hair wet upon his skull.

'What do you want from me?'

Walking over to his pack, Joe took out a large wooden box. Lifting the lid, he examined the contents before approaching Andy and sitting just out of his reach.

Looking deep into the young man's eyes, he took a moment to explain.

'Andy, these are Spirit Ants from a sacred site in Central Australia. They seek the truth and test the spirit of a man to see if there is anything decent to redeem. These vines will hold you restrained until the morning, and if there is any hope of re-demption left in your soul, the ants will leave you unharmed. However, if they discover that evil has spread throughout your heart, they will enter your body and devour the darkness. You are here with your judge and jury, so your fate is now in your own hands.'

Taking the lid off the box, Joe placed it at the base of Andy's feet and a great hoard of huge black ants scampered out onto the ground.

These were biggest ants that Andy had ever seen, black as night and each one was at least the size of his thumb with large incisors for devouring meat. His eyes filled his thin, pinched face when the first couple tentatively made their way up his feet and onto his legs while he desperately squirmed around to dis-lodge them.

'You can't leave me here tied up in the bush with some bloody man-eating ants! Crazy old prick, this is murder. Don't you understand they will put you in jail and throw away the key once they find out what you've done to me!' His voice cracked with more than a hint of hysteria.

Old Joe packed up his bag and stood up holding the box in his arms, unmoved by the scene before him.

'Andy, you should be saving your breath to ask for forgiveness for what you have done today.'

'Hell will freeze over before I do that, you old religious fanatic. Today was the best day of my life,' Andy panted through clenched teeth.

Joe's fists curled in anger. Desperately wishing he could unburden his own pain on this vile creature, it was his humanity that held Joe from stooping to the same low level. With resignation, he walked up to this despised creature and forcibly uncurled Andy's bloody fingers from around Gabby's pendant.

'Goodbye, Andy.'

'You can't fuck off and leave me here! Come back, you lunatic. I will make sure the police lock you away for the rest of your miserable life!'

Joe didn't look back, and with each step the shouting got louder and louder.

Andy couldn't believe this was actually happening. A part of him wanted to scream and another part of him wanted to laugh hysterically.

Tied up to a tree with man-eating ants that apparently could determine if he was redeemable? The whole concept was ridiculous, or would be if he could get himself out of this.

He tried pulling with all of his strength to get free from the restraints, but all the vines did was cut into his flesh. He thrashed his legs over the ground to either crush the ants or at least scare them off. Any normal insect would scarper away, but these seemed determined to climb upon him.

What if the old man was right? What if these weird creatures were going to eat him alive?

A cold sweat broke out across his skin, which prickled with trepidation as his heart began to race. He didn't want to die a death of a thousand painful bites.

'Piss off, bloody ants,' Andy yelled, causing the birds in the trees above to squawk in protest.

Initially his actions seemed to work as the ants hesitated, but then they ran in like bloodhounds to smell his skin, checking first before deciding if they would proceed or leave him alone. They kept touching his skin and backing away, then rubbing their antennae against each other to share their first impressions. They seemed wary of Andy, undecided, touch and retreat. Each ant danced the same little ritual, touch and retreat, over and over again.

Andy sighed with relief, reassuring himself that the old man always tried to scare people with his ridiculous superstitions. Everyone at the beach said he was a fruit loop. He had been predicting for years that the world was going to end.

His relief was premature for just as Andy started to relax, the ants made their decision. Grouping together one last time, they rubbed against each other, and after this final council they charged up his body, each going for a different location, sure now in their advance.

Then they began eating, and it was a death of one thousand stinging bites for Andy Bolton.

As Joe walked away, he knew exactly what the final result would look like. He had seen it before in the territory. There would only be bones left when the ants had completed their sentence.

The same birds that had watched Andy commit torturous crimes against his innocent strays now watched as he suffered the same fate. This time they didn't fly away but stayed as witnesses to the justice of nature.

Eleven

The rock rippled as the demon entered the tunnel, his dark shadow hovering in the air until it took on the image of the form he once knew. He had once been a symbol of awe, a messenger of light, but that was before the decay had set in. Now Jinn's stooped shoulders no longer held his wings high. Instead, they dragged slightly behind, and the claws that had grown out of the winged tips scraped on the low ceiling as he shuffled through the warren of tunnels towards the red glow that lit the way.

He had been there when Fallon confronted the butcher in the shack all those years ago. The body he'd possessed had been feasting on the blood and flesh like a ravenous hound from hell until she had interfered. Unable to withstand her power, Jinn had been returned to the dirt and shadows, but all was not completely lost as he still held a piece of her red star, a prize for the future. He remembered the shape well as it was a replica of a leaf from the Blood Tree at their former home, the Silver City, the cradle of angels. He'd tucked the piece of pendant away for safekeeping before he submitted his report to Sut, his superior. That another agent had lost to that zealous warrior Fallon, she was a former friend he now longed to crush.

Years after the attack against Scarlett in the shack, he had once again encountered Fallon; however, this time he was the hunter and she was his to toy with. It had begun when her scent had blown in on a breeze. Inhaling deeply, he'd followed it without hesitation. To his astonishment, he had found his nemesis in the body of a small child – a human child, weak and within his grasp.

Sut had cruelly pinched Jinn's face in his excitement with this new discovery and began to drool with anticipation. They spent a long time discussing how to remove Fallon from her forbidden life. Jinn suggested they use the broken star to lure her out to sea, but on the day, their plan was thwarted by the arrival of a good Samaritan. After this botched attempt, they reconvened and agreed it would be more satisfying to allow the angel to live a little longer as a human, especially while she was within their reach.

Tonight, he would report that Andy Bolton had played his part admirably, giving himself over to Jinn's debauchery, and Jinn had enjoyed every moment of that brutal rape. However, Joe Campbell had managed to remove Andy from their control with his damned Spirit Ants, once again ruining their entertainment.

He knew Sut would be pleased about Fallon's suffering, and Jinn looked forward to many more diabolical plans. There were still many humans out there who were open to their evil influence and would act for them when the time came.

As he shuffled into the cavernous room, Jinn heard Sut whispering in the gloomy room. There was no furniture except a chair sculpted out of rock. It couldn't be called a throne but it did speak of leadership.

Sut looked up as Jinn stood in the doorway. 'Sut, I see you are busy. I can come back later.' He tried to move backwards out of the suddenly too-warm space.

'Not at all. We were just talking about you. Come forward and submit your report.' Sut advanced towards Jinn, his dusty wings fluttering with excitement. 'This is very good timing, Jinn. I was just telling Lucifer, and he is thrilled a messenger has fallen within our grasp.'

Out of the shadows, a form materialised and turned its burning gaze upon Jinn. 'Yes, my brother, come forward and speak your truth.' Lucifer's velvet voice sent shivers skittering across Jinn's bony shoulders.

Jinn stumbled under Lucifer's compelling gaze. Here was the Morning Star, the one who had challenged the light to become the creator of all life. One would think such a devil would be odious to look upon, but even in the shadows, his golden eyes glowed bright. It was strange how living away from the light had destroyed their glory. Exile had turned the once-beautiful and light-filled rebels into a hideous mask of decay, but their leader was somehow regaining his former splendour. He was as bright and beautiful as before, his golden locks shone and his wings had a shimmer of gold along the edges.

'My Lord.' Jinn dropped to his knees and lowered his gaze, swallowing nervously.

'Pray tell us what happened today,' Lucifer prompted Jinn to continue.

'Lord Lucifer and my leader, Sut. I have some news to share. The messenger who is living as a human by deceit has suffered greatly today.' Jinn chanced to look up as his voice faded away.

It was Sut who broke the silence first. 'Did she suffer as much as we hoped for?' he asked, with a little dribble leaking out of his mouth.

'Even more than we anticipated.' Jinn smiled at the memory as he bent his knee in submission.

'Tell us exactly what happened.' Sut brought Jinn upright and turned him to face Lucifer.

Jinn proceeded to describe how Andy initiated the attack, Gabby's suffering, and ended his account with how Andy Bolton met his demise by Joe's own form of retribution.

Neither Lucifer nor Sut made a sound, until a laugh that started as a suppressed snicker began to swirl around the cavern. It became a storm of sound and malevolent movement that threw Sut against the rocky wall and pulled at the loose skin on Jinn's darkened face, causing it to flap in the force of Lucifer's delight.

Finally, he slapped Jinn on the back and he declared, 'So, Fallon, the most active operator, a warrior messenger who has sought and destroyed so many of our agents over the ages, has suffered a significant setback. It seems she has friends, but they can be easily disposed of.' He waved his hands to demonstrate how easily they could be removed.

Then grabbing Jinn by both shoulders, Lucifer spoke quickly and intensely as he stared into Jinn's bulging eyes.

'My brother, Jinn, this is good, it's so good. This is just the beginning of us hurting those who injured us so long ago. Do you remember how beautiful the Silver City is?' To which Jinn nodded a fraction.

'Do you remember bathing in the light? Do you remember being filled with power and strength?' Lucifer painted a picture with his beguiling words.

Jinn nodded at Lucifer's face, which was almost pressed up against his own, a picture of beauty and the beast, and briefly Jinn did remember the past. He closed his eyes, his thin purplish lips parting wistfully as his hand crept up to hover over his rotting heart. For the tiniest moment he could almost touch the melodious music of creation, but it danced away from him illusively until the burning, claustrophobic reality brought him back to the present.

Pulling away from the hypocrisy of his face against Lucifer's, Jinn stood back and stared at Lucifer's flowing hair while scratching the few tufts left on his almost-bald head.

'Do you remember the banquets?' Lucifer taunted him with all that they had lost. 'How would you like to go home?' he asked softly.

They both hissed together. 'Yes.'

'But how, my Lord. You know we were banned for all time, and that is why we live here in the dirt and fire, our exile for the rebellion.' Sut stepped carefully to the side of Lucifer, uncertain if he would burst out laughing again or slap his face in frustration.

'My brothers, I have found a new source of power, one that has almost transformed me back to my former glory.' He turned in the glow of the fire, showing off his magnificence. 'There is only this atrocity that remains.' He held out his hands, which were still covered in coarse hair and long claws.

'However, times are about to change. You are here because you chose to follow me, to take orders from me, and now it is only a matter of time before you can return to your former selves.

'I have a plan. A way has become clear to take back what is legally mine. I shall be The Light, The First Dawn, and you, my brothers, will rule over all the realms, bathed once again in power and glory. Until then, we must use the seven sins that tempt mankind. We know they cannot resist pride, wrath, lust, greed, envy, gluttony and slothfulness. We just have to use these human weaknesses and possess mankind as instruments of vice.

'Sut and Jinn, I charge you both to make Fallon and anyone she loves miserable in every way. Glorify in their suffering while we anticipate the most tragic end to this pretender.' Lucifer's deep-timbred voice echoed through the cavern, causing the others to lift their heads and throw their shoulders back in determination.

'Morning Star, we faithfully followed you to this realm and will be at your side when we re-enter our beloved Silver City.' Sut bent his knee along with Jinn, and they prostrated themselves before the golden creature.

Kathleen slowly drew out the cold casserole dish. She hadn't even noticed Ruth turn the oven off when they rushed out the door hours earlier.

As she scraped out the ruined food and tipped it into the trash, her head dropped and harsh sobs disturbed the quiet night.

The family had left Gabby at the hospital sleeping off her anaesthetic. Frank and Kathleen had sat by her bed for the longest time, with the boys leaning against the wall, both staring in desolation at their sister and parents.

Eventually the nurse suggested they go home and get some rest. 'We'll keep a close eye on her overnight, and I promise I'll call you if she wakes and needs you here.'

Reluctantly they all kissed Gabby's now-pale forehead and squeezed her hand, hoping she could sense their love in that miniscule contact.

So immersed in her grief, she didn't hear Frank come up behind and reach his arms around her crumpled frame. Gently he turned her around and took the dish out of her numb hands and carefully placed it on the kitchen bench.

Kathleen, who was normally so resilient, someone always in control, now stood immobile, unable to move away or halt the pain that refused to be contained one moment longer. Frank could see that his beloved was about to collapse and knew it was his turn to be her rock.

With his arm around her shoulders, he guided her out to a bench seat in the garden and held her in his arms as she wept for all that her daughter had lost. Frank couldn't cry anymore, he just held Kathleen tightly against him and placed loving kisses on the top of her hair.

Eventually the sobs turned to hiccups and then when all the emotion was spent, she slumped exhausted into his embrace. They loved their children so much and would gladly take away any pain. All they ever wanted was to keep them safe and happy. Now events had shifted Gabby out of their protection, and their love had to help her rebuild something of worth from the ashes.

No words were spoken between them. Words were unnecessary to share what had happened today. Sitting so still in the starlit night, they noticed the curlews had moved closer.

Nature itself was there for them as well. This little sign gave them hope that with all this support, Gabby would come back to them, back to all she loved.

As her injuries were mostly flesh wounds, bruising and lacerations, apart from her ribs, Gabby only stayed in hospital for forty-eight hours. The doctors sent her home with topical antibiotic ointment and a prescription for oral antibiotics if there was any sign of infection. Thankfully by some miracle, the broken ribs had not punctured her lungs.

Gabby couldn't sit on the car seat as it was too painful to place any weight on her damaged nether region. Instead, she lay on the back seat and stared at the flashes of tree tops and slits of blue sky that flashed in the window. Her head ached, her body ached, her soul ached, and at this very moment she wished she had never been born.

Once they arrived home, Frank assisted Gabby out of the car, and placing his arm around her shoulder, he led her into the house.

'Would you like a cup of tea, love,' he asked.

'No, I just want to go to bed if that's alright with you.' She looked up at her dad.

'Of course, whatever you want is fine by me,' he reassured her.

Kathleen settled her into the fresh, clean sheets and helped her swallow some Panadol tablets to ease the pain.

'The doctor wants to see you in a few days to see how it's all healing.' Kathleen couldn't say the words that her daughter's vagina had been butchered.

'The hospital also wants to set up counselling sessions.' Kathleen cringed when Gabby turned towards the wall and said nothing in response.

Gabby just closed her eyes and pretended to fall asleep. She purposely slowed her breathing to make her mother go away.

All she wanted was to be alone.

As the afternoon light softened into twilight, the Sailas arrived, and Eddie went straight to Gabby's room.

Kathleen watched from the door as he lay on the bed and held her in his arms.

'Gabby, I am so sorry that I wasn't there for you,' he whispered into her hair as he cradled her body against his chest.

Kathleen heard Eddie whispering plans for their future, encouraging her to see beyond this, but no matter how hard he tried to reach her, Gabby remained mute and numb in his arms.

Eddie had his own demons chasing him. If only he had been with her that day, none of this would have happened.

Like a turtle in a shell, Gabby had withdrawn from the world to a safe place. She didn't make a sound and had barely spoken a word since coming out of surgery. Her statement to the police had been just a nod or a shake of her head.

Eddie held her until he saw her breathing soften and slow.

Once he was sure she was asleep, he went to join the others who were now congregated around the kitchen table. Everyone had tear-stained faces.

Ruth took Eddie in her arms and let him drop his head down on her shoulder.

'I just wish I could fix this, Mum,' he whispered hoarsely.

'I know, son, we all do. To us, family is everything, and somehow we will get through even this,' she tried to comfort her man-child.

The two fathers watched on, helpless to stop their families hurting.

Eventually it got late, and their visitors had to take their leave, but instead of going home, Eddie asked Kathleen if he could crash on their couch for the night. She squeezed his arm and nodded at him gratefully.

When Eddie left the room, Gabby woke but lay there pretending to sleep, taking some comfort in the solitude. Lying in her bed, she looked at the curlew sitting on her window sill. The night watchman was in place for the night. There were no more tears to shed. Her heart was wooden, and the splinters tore a hole in her chest every time she took a deep breath.

'I don't think I can ever go back to my old self,' she whispered to her silent guard as its large yellow eyes intently watched over her.

'Thank you for fighting for me that day. We just weren't strong enough to stop him.' His strength still baffled her as Andy was such a weed of a boy.

Every time her eyes closed, she relived each horrific moment and couldn't stop thinking that there should have been a way to avoid the depravation and violence. Even now, the pain was hot and hungry, like an insatiable fire burning out of control, until she had to either move or scream.

Rising out of the bed, she went to the dressing table and stood there looking at her face. The bruising and swelling obliterated her features, and her sore ribs prevented any deep breathing. Even though the pain would be excruciating, she longed to fill her lungs to capacity and let some of the tension out in a long, slow sigh.

The physical pain aside, it was the sensation of being violated that was the most abhorrent. She felt guilty and dirty, and no matter how much she washed and scrubbed the stain, it just wouldn't come out. She knew her rationale was skewed, but somehow even now, it felt that everything that had happened was her fault. Why hadn't she been strong enough to fight him off? He was just a scrawny kid. What had empowered him that day to hold her down and hurt her like that?

So many questions that she couldn't answer or come up with a reasonable explanation for. Unable to let it go, her analytical brain went over every word that had been spoken, each threat, and then the rape itself.

If only she could go back to earlier that Sunday afternoon when the world felt safe and her head had been full of dreams. Dreams of a future that seemed brighter than the sun at that moment and yet now, such a short time later, the sun was covered in a grey blanket of fog. Life had become a burden, and already halfway dead, she had woken up wishing she never had to face another morning.

Gazing through swollen, bruised eyes, she looked around her room. The walls were covered in posters promoting green choices, solar energy and recycling, and her desk had a globe of the world sitting on it. Sunny yellow curtains were tied back with daisy flowers, so bright, so happy, and so naïve.

Gabby stood there taking stock of her childhood keepsakes, special craft projects from school and awards for scientific achievements. Everything looked so, normal, so yesterday. She felt altered, like a stranger here, where she no longer fit or belonged. This was a child's room and whether she liked it or not, she was now a woman, one who could not consider fondly the passage from innocence to carnal knowledge.

Gently placing her hands down to her private area, she could feel the damaged, torn flesh, like a crushed and broken flower. Swollen beyond recognition and so tender, fear would now dominate all intimacies from this point on. All anticipation of pleasure and girlish fantasies had been stolen. Instead, all she felt was overwhelming dread and heart-pounding anxiety when she thought of anyone even wanting to touch her.

'You have ruined me. These injuries will heal but my mind can never forget the pain and terror of that day. Because of you, Andy Bolton, I will never marry or have children. You were right when you said I would never forget you. Well, I will never forgive you either. I will hate you forever,' she spoke to the stranger in the mirror.

Gabby went back to her bed and closed her eyes, seeking the oblivion of sleep, but it eluded her. To distract from her feverish thoughts, she drew her knees up and rocked back and forth. The movement felt comforting. It must be a connection with her mother's love, backwards and forwards over and over again, focusing on nothing else until sleep finally came and took her away to a better time and place.

Unseen, another watched over Gabby as she thrashed about in her dreams. 'Fallon, it's Josiel, your name day sister. Please remember who you are and come back stronger, regain your powers and defeat the demons you so despise. No one understands why you are here at this moment in time, and I refuse to believe it is a mistake. Surely you living in this form has happened for a reason, one we just don't understand yet. I love you, dearest. Feel my presence and let it comfort you.'

Gently placing her hand upon Gabby's feverish forehead, she whispered comforting words in a heavenly tongue, until her sister's breathing slowed and a peaceful sleep descended.

The reprieve was temporary, as later that night horrible images ambushed Gabby's dreams. It was a hot summer's day with the cicadas drowning out all other sounds. Just when she thought her eardrums were going to burst, the air suddenly became strangely silent. In this eerie twilight, Andy Bolton appeared holding a broken bottle in his hand. No matter how much she told her legs to run away, they were sluggish and heavy. Desperate to escape, they refused to move, standing immobile with her pounding heart as he came closer with that wicked smirk on his despicable face.

Finally, her legs decided to make a run for it but it was too late. Andy slashed the sharp glass and opened up her face from forehead to chin, slicing right through her eye. Gabby's sight blurred, and she felt the pain of her skin peeling back as her mouth opened wide to scream and scream.

The still night was torn asunder as Frank and Kathleen dived out of bed and raced to Gabby's room.

Jacob, Eddie and Thomas got there at the same time, and they all reached out as she sat there in bed with her eyes wide open but not seeing anyone. Not matter how they tried to break the spell, she fought them off ferociously.

In the struggle, Gabby's fist struck Thomas in the face. He fell back in surprise and put his hands over his nose as the blood began to seep through his fingers.

Eventually Frank managed to get in close enough to hold her and whisper, 'Gabby, wake up. I'm here now, and no one can hurt you anymore. Wake up, honey, it's going to be okay.'

It was his love that broke through her bonds of terror.

Their hearts constricted that little bit more when they looked at her swollen, disfigured face and helplessly listened to sobs of such an aching sadness. After the onslaught of tears subsided, Gabby huddled deep into the covers and turned her face away from the pity in their eyes.

Kathleen passed Thomas a t-shirt to staunch the blood from his nose and then hovered over her crying daughter.

'My poor girl, I'm going to stay with you tonight.' Kathleen lay down beside Gabby and held her tight, murmuring words of comfort and love.

The men retreated to the kitchen where Frank got ice from the freezer and wrapped it in a soft cloth for Thomas's nose.

After pressing it into his hands, he then found some comfort in the routine of putting on the kettle to make tea.

Jacob started pounding his fist on the kitchen cupboards. He had to vent his rage on something physical, and nobody commented or bothered to stop this bizarre behaviour.

Once his nose stopped dripping, Thomas dropped his head down on the table in despair and mumbled that he wanted to 'kill those sons of bitches' for what they had done.

Eddie just sat there staring into space as his hot drink went stone cold.

Frank rubbed his hands over his face, feeling the rasp of whiskers. *How did we get here? Everything feels upside down.* He kept trying to remember that time heals all wounds and softens the edge of pain, but just now, this truth provided little comfort.

The police charged both John Pacey and Mick Willis with assault and the deprivation of liberty, but with consideration that they were first-time offenders, the judge put them on good behaviour probation for two years. Andy's bones were eventually found in the bushland by an Aboriginal tracker. It seemed he had suffered a fatal attack from wild animals and speculation was rife over the possible predator.

Andy's parents were devastated by his actions and their own loss. For no matter how wicked a child can become, it is still yours to love, and they mourned him as much as any parent would.

The whole beach community was shocked by news of the assault and many dropped off small notes, flowers and hot meals to the Harrison home.

The small town of San Remo would never be quite the same again.

Twelve

For the next three months, the Harrison family kept trying to reach the silent, introverted young woman that had replaced their daughter and sister. Her ribs didn't hurt so much, and her bruises were all gone, but still she seemed lost in a world of introspection.

Jacob and Thomas chafed with the notion of revenge against the two boys, who they felt were just as guilty as Andy Bolton. It was a volatile state of affairs just waiting for a spark to ignite the pent-up testosterone, and it wasn't long before that night was upon them.

One evening after work, the two brothers pulled up alongside Eddie as he was walking home from the prawn farm. He hadn't been able to seek an apprenticeship. Since the attack on Gabby, he just couldn't find the motivation, so he spent his days working with Billy, his father. Instead of learning a trade, he was feeding prawns, harvesting prawns and shovelling prawns onto the sorting tables. It was hard, physical work but it kept him from thinking too much.

'Hey, Eddie, want a lift home?' Jake pulled his car over to the side of the road.

Eddie looked in the window and saw Thomas sitting in the passenger seat, and nodded his consent as he slid into the back. The boys spoke little as they took the turns towards the Saila's house, and it was Jake who broke the silence with profanities when his headlights caught John and Mick walking along the sidewalk.

Jacob screeched the car to a stop and sat there with white knuckles gripping the steering wheel.

'Leave it, Jake. Taking your anger out on them won't solve anything. Think about your parents and Gabby now. Haven't they suffered enough?' Eddie reached over and grabbed Jacob's shoulder to hold him back.

Jacob shook him off and swung open the car door.

'It's about time these two grubs got a taste of their own medicine. Are you coming, Thomas?' Jacob's brown eyes met the matching pair staring back at him.

'Thomas, don't. Even if you agree with Jake, don't do it.' Eddie did his best to keep both of their tempers in check.

'I think we owe it to Gabby to at least shake them up a little and scare the crap out of them.' Jacob had already gotten out of the car and now spoke through the open window.

Thomas turned around to look at Eddie.

'You don't understand, Eddie. It wasn't your sister they hurt.' His eyes begged for absolution.

'No, it was my best friend,' Eddie muttered as he eyed the boys, one standing stiffly outside in the cool night air and other on the brink of joining him.

'Don't fret, we're not going to hurt them real bad.' Jacob's grin had a tinge of malice.

'Harming them will only make it worse. Walk away, guys. Let it go.'

'No, why should they get off Scot free? Especially when I think about how they stood by and let that monster hurt Gabby. Come on, Tom.'

Thomas got out of the car, and they both walked quickly across the street to intercept John and Mick.

Jacob grabbed John from behind and twisted his arm up so hard that he cried out in pain. Thomas went for Mick and gripped him around the throat while Eddie hung back just wishing they would listen to him.

'Don't hurt me. Please don't hurt me,' John snivelled.

'Hurt you? Dirty rotten scum. Do you know what your buddy did to our sister? He took a broken bottle and cut her up. How much do you reckon that would hurt? Only God knows how much I want to do the same to you and your spineless mate.'

Whimpering from the pain, John was waiting to hear his bone snap, and Mick was wheezing short puffs of air from under Thomas's stronghold on his windpipe.

'We didn't mean her no harm. We thought Andy was only going to scare her a bit. We never thought he would go that far, and anyway he's dead ain't he, so can't we just leave it alone?'

John was doing his best to calm Jacob's fury.

However, the appeal for mercy left Jacob cold. Rather than placate his anger, it only made his heart race faster. With a trace of his distant ancestors, he lifted his face to the moon and yelled his rage at the world. This roar alone was not enough to release the tension, so with murderous intent he spun John around, grabbed him by the shoulder and head butted him hard in the face. Instantly the skin above John's eye split open, and a deep red flow began to gush down over his face. It was such a still night that Jacob could smell the blood. The metallic aroma jerked him back to his senses, and he stepped away from the grisly sight.

'You know what, you are not even worth the trouble of a beating. You're both snivelling cowards and you have to live with what you've done.'

Jacob's back was tight as he walked away to the side of his old car, and with relief, Eddie saw Thomas release Mick and go over and put his hand on Jake's shoulder.

Eddie had already turned away when he heard John savagely mutter, 'Bloody stupid bitch, she probably deserved it anyway.' He pulled his t-shirt up to mop the blood oozing down over his nose.

A burst of light flashed behind Eddie's eyes, and he snapped. After all the years at school, he just couldn't stand their attitude one moment longer. Without saying a word, he walked up to John and grabbed him under the armpits to raise him up to eye level.

John began to blabber, saying how he didn't mean it. Eddie just glared at him with contempt and threw him backwards towards the sidewalk. John landed heavily, and instead of his backside taking the impact, his head snapped back and cracked against the concrete guttering with a sickening sound. Everyone turned to watch in horror as it rolled to an unnatural angle and his body lay deathly still.

Mick ran to him in panic and yelled, 'John, buddy, wake up.'

There was no response from the prone form lying there in accusation.

'Bloody hell, he's not breathing! You bastards have killed him!'

The three boys couldn't believe their eyes when they realised Mick was right. John wasn't breathing. Thomas ran to the nearest house and shouted for them to call an ambulance, while Jacob and Eddie tried resuscitation on John.

There was blood all over John's face but Jacob was too busy to mop it up before he placed his mouth over his lips to breathe for him. The blood smeared over his face, and he later told Eddie would never forget the hideous taste of shame.

Mick was in shock. He sat beside them and rocked backwards and forwards as they worked on John's still form. He was moaning 'no, no, no' over and over again. Blood and fear filled the air. It was acrid in their nostrils and left a bitter taste in their mouths.

No matter how hard they tried, John was still unresponsive when the ambulance arrived. The medical officers immediately tried to resuscitate him but could not get a heartbeat. They shook their heads at the female police officer when she squatted down beside John's inert form. Looking at his pale face, he seemed to be sleeping if not for the blue tinge to his lips. All of the boys were silenced in shock, unable to believe the outcome of their intent to intimidate. It only began to seem real when climbing into the police car for the short ride to the station.

Eddie sat with his head in his arms. He couldn't believe what had just happened. His body rocked back and forth as his sobs filled the cabin, drowning the silence of death. *I'm a murderer. I've just taken another person's life. Yes, it was a mistake, but John is dead all the same, and there is no way to rewind what just happened. Oh God, just kill me now as that's what I deserve. How will my family see me now? How can they still love me when I can't stand myself? I wish it was me dead and not John. Either way, my life might as well be over.*

He looked across at Jacob and Thomas with their hair all dishevelled. Jacob still had dried blood all over his face and Thomas's lips had disappeared into his white face.

John was taken to the hospital, and his parents were told he was DOA, dead on arrival. He had sustained a mortal blow to the back of his skull, one of those unfortunate moments when a person can die from a simple fall. This tragedy rocked the whole beach community once again. Thomas and Jacob were charged with assault, and Eddie was kept confined in the police watch house with a likely murder charge.

When the police knocked on the Harrison's door, it was the beginning of a new nightmare, one with its own set, plot and characters to play out the tragic tale. Only this wasn't some elaborate drama, it was their lives that were unravelling. Overwhelmed by circumstance, Gabby sagged on the couch and buried her head in her arms as she moaned, 'No, no, no.' Frank and Kathleen immediately went to the police station to see the boys and unwillingly left her alone to consider a bleak future.

After another sleepless night, Gabby was at the police station early the next morning, begging to be allowed to visit Eddie. After waiting what felt like an eternity, the officer returned and agreed to take her to his cell. When she tried to console Eddie, her tongue felt thick and sluggish from the anti-depression medication, and the words just wouldn't come out. They sat opposite each other on stools. Eddie's face now looked more like her own, gaunt and hollow with dark circles under his eyes, the stress apparent on both. The silence stretched out until he began to cry, and Gabby moved her stool closer so that she could hold him in her arms, trying to absorb some of his despair.

'What fools we were, making all those elaborate plans for the future, and thinking we were so clever, so dammed invincible. Now I'm going to spend half my life in jail.'

She put her hand over his mouth. 'Don't say that, Eddie, you don't know that yet.'

'Yes, I do. A manslaughter charge is the best I can hope for, and that will be ten years if I'm lucky. So I'll be a lucky man in my mid-thirties by the time I get out. Gabby, please believe me when I say I really never meant to hurt him. Your brothers just wanted to scare them a bit, and when John made some half-arsed comment, I lifted him up and shoved him away in anger.

I only heard his head crack as I was walking away. I feel so rotten about John, even if he was a complete prick. I never thought I would take another person's life. Can God forgive me?'

'Eddie, there is nothing to forgive. Nobody blames you. John's death was a freak accident.'

'Yeah, well, tell that to his parents. I'm sure it will be a great comfort to them.' Eddie looked back at her with tears trembling on his long lashes.

There was no answer to that, for it was true. It didn't matter how your child died, he was still dead, and nothing, not remorse or regrets, could ever bring him back again. They sat there in silence as there were no more words to say. He saw the bruises on Gabby's beautiful pale face had finally disappeared, only to be superseded by dark shadows of pain.

Eddie was released on bail, and his case would be called sometime after Christmas. Jacob and Thomas were charged with assault and given a twelve-month jail sentence. However, with their clean record, the sentence was suspended to a good-behaviour bond and a significant fine to pay.

Thirteen

Christmas came and went with very subdued celebrations, and it was the first time that Old Joe didn't join them. Kathleen did her best to involve Gabby in the preparations, but it was a waste of time. She had become a shadow of her former self, a zombie, one who lived without spirit or hope. Kathleen still made her meet with a rape psychologist once a week at the hospital, but she remained closed and non-responsive.

Gabby's favourite place was her bed, where she would lay down and listen to the words of the song 'Wonderful', often wishing she had died like Andy, then there would be no more questions without answers. What had made him hate her so much? Why did she still feel guilty?

Her mother had been there every night to help her through the nightmares, reliving the horror over and over. Time didn't seem to be healing the mind as much as it had the body.

The world continued without her participation, and events swirled around her like planets circled the sun. Conversations continued around the dinner table, and Gabby was relieved to hear that Old Joe had insisted on covering the cost of Eddie's defence, an offer Ruth and Billie had gratefully accepted.

George Hudson QC came to Cairns and spent numerous hours with Eddie to build the background for his case. He wanted to know all the facts around the incident, to examine the street where it happened and to walk through the scenario with Jacob and Thomas to gain a picture of what had transpired between the five men that fateful night. Everyone felt a little more hopeful with George around. He was a big man with a gruff, gravelly voice and no-nonsense manner. They sensed he was accustomed to winning, and his confidence was contagious.

The first meeting was hard for Eddie. It was imperative that George knew he wasn't a murderer. For some reason this was of vital importance to him. If his counsel didn't believe him innocent, then how could they convince a jury?

His family had vacated the house so that Eddie and his QC could talk in private, and Eddie looked across the shabby wooden kitchen table at his liberator.

'Eddie, how are you holding up, son? George looked into his eyes, searching for answers.

'I'm not too bad, considering what's hanging over me right now, sir.'

'No need to call me sir. George is fine,' the QC suggested.

'Okay, George. Before we go any further, I want you to know that I didn't mean to hurt John Pacey. It was an accident.' Eddie leaned forward in his seat and looked into George's eyes to convey his sincerity.

'Eddie, it doesn't matter if I believe that or not. My job is to convince the jury that you are innocent.'

'It matters to me. I need you to see that I never meant to hurt him.'

'Well, Eddie, what I do know after meeting your parents and sisters is that you are from a decent family. When I look at you, I don't see a murderer. I see a kid who did one hell of a stupid thing, which has landed you into a whole world of trouble, and that's where I come into the picture.'

'Thank you, George.'

'Now listen, Eddie, with that said, it is true that what I believe counts for jack shit. It is the jury that needs to think of you as a stupid kid, not a murderer. So we have to work together to get you out of this mess. And to do my job I need to know everything. Even the smallest, insignificant detail can be a mighty tool in the courtroom.'

Their conversations were lengthy and exhausting. Eddie took George all the way back through his childhood. He described how Andy Bolton had a vendetta against Gabby from an early age and how John and Mick were just as guilty in all the tormenting and bullying at school. He got tearful when they talked about the assault against Gabby and how much they hurt her, both physically and mentally. He also felt remorse for shoving John and that he never in a thousand years imagined it would result in his death.

'Eddie, I have to warn you that the legal system has pulled out their big guns to fight this case. Ethan Miles is a new attorney flown in from Brisbane to lead the prosecution. He's young and looking to make an impression, so we can expect some fairly decent opposition from him. It may help if we portray you as disadvantaged because of your race.'

'Disadvantaged? But I'm not disadvantaged. This can't be about colour. To me, that is completely irrelevant. We have to argue that this was an accident, one that I never intended to happen,' Eddie protested angrily.

'Son, anything that can help us win your case is certainly relevant.' George frowned from under his bushy eyebrows to make his point.

'No, sir, this is not negotiable. You have to respect my decision, George. I don't want anyone to think I have been in any way disadvantaged for being born a Torres Strait Islander. I'm proud of whom I am and how my parents have raised me, and I'm not gonna bring any shame to them or my culture no matter how it plays out for me. You will have to fight to win my case without that angle.'

George had no other option than to agree.

That afternoon, Frank took a few beers over to share with Billy Saila. They sat side by side on the sand, which was still warm from the afternoon sun. The beach was deserted and peaceful before them, with the setting sun illuminating the mountains behind. Frank took a long sip of the refreshing drink then broached the topic that was never far from their minds.

'How is Eddie's case coming along?'

'Well, it all depends if George can convince the jury that it was an accident and not premeditated. He'll use the evidence from Jacob and Thomas to verify that Eddie was actually encouraging them not to take their frustration out on the other two. I guess we just have to hope and pray that this lawyer is as good as everyone says.'

There was nothing Frank could add to bolster their hopes, so he just nodded and sat quietly, sharing this moment of tranquillity with his good friend. He knew how much his family cared about the other.

Those intervening months flew past quickly, and the monsoon season was intense and prolonged. This suited Gabby. She lay like a mannequin, barely moving for hours in her bed, staring unblinkingly out at the sleeting rain and waiting for the day of

Eddie's hearing. She barely remembered that young girl with stars in her eyes, the same person who planned to get a job, to save for university, to learn about how to save the planet. That girl had died the day she was attacked, and now another girl inhabited the same body, a sad, lonely girl who didn't look forward, only back into the past.

Longed for and dreaded in equal measures, the day finally arrived to see them all at the Cairns Courthouse. It was an austere building, built for practical purposes with no waste on beautification. Gabby wore her long blonde hair scraped back into a tight ponytail, and a classic grey dress, which hung off her frail frame.

Every eye followed her across the room as fervently as the whispers, '*There's the girl that got raped.*' Inwardly cringing and hunching her shoulders as a shield from their stares, she quickly slid into her seat with the rest of the family, the ever-present tears not far away, just trembling behind her lashes.

Sneaking a glance through half-closed eyes, she saw Ruth and Billy with their daughters across the room. Just then, Ruth happened to look up. Gabby could no longer hold back the tears at the sight of such sadness, that rich dusky skin looked clammy and pale with fear. How does a mother cope when the son she loves has been accused of murder?

Their gazes met, and even though the colours clashed, the expression was identical: raw pain and bewilderment. With tears awash, both heads turned to look at the one they cherished. There was Eddie sitting on a dais at the side of the courtroom with his lawyer whispering in his ear.

Knowing that Old Joe was here should have been a comfort, but her sense of shame kept her gaze averted. It was that same self-reproach working against her, the monster inside who never let her rest or heal, a voice in her head that softly said that everything and everyone is different now, making it impossible to pick up the threads of her old life. Maybe she never would. Her skin didn't fit anymore, it no longer felt right. The old Gabby was gone and now this new version was all she knew.

Love and loyalty glued her to the seat when all of her senses cried to return to her shell. Like a crab, she longed to retreat back into the bedroom that had become a sanctuary, safe behind the door that shut out the rest of the world.

There were mixed feelings amongst the crowd that had gathered. Everyone felt sorry for the Paceys, but not all thought Eddie should go to jail to pay for his mistake. At the back of the courtroom, there was a small group of onlookers who supported John's family, and they wanted justice.

Ethan Miles, the Pacey family's lawyer, looked like a slick southerner. He wore an expensive suit and shiny black shoes that creaked as he strode over the tiled floor. Young, smooth and determined, he pursued Eddie's guilt like a bloodhound following the scent of a fox, smelling the verdict he sought to bring to light.

It was impossible not to be affected by the tension from all of these opposing forces. Gabby felt like an impending disaster was again about to sweep in to devastate her fragile grip on sanity.

The first day in court was to set out the rules of engagement, how the jury had to maintain objectivity and the court's expectation for them to deliver a clear verdict

Over the next few sessions, all the facts of the case were examined, including time and cause of death. The medical reports from the attending medical staff at the hospital were presented to the jury, and every aspect of the incident was combed through with minute attention to detail. After these initial procedures were completed, the battle lines were drawn, each contender setting out the challenges ahead.

The prosecution drew a picture of an aggressive black man who had no respect for the law and as first witness called Michael Willis. Once he was sworn in, the lawyer got straight to the point. 'Michael, I ask you to describe to the jury how Andrew Bolton was threatened and bullied by Edward Saila.'

'Well, you see, in our ninth grade he was alone in the school bathroom when Eddie grabbed him and threatened to kill him if he ever touched Gabrielle Harrison again.'

'Was Andrew Bolton scared when Edward Saila treated him aggressively?'

'Hell, yes, will ya just look at him. He was a giant even then. After that threat, Andy kept his distance from both of them.'

'Do you think Andrew Bolton believed that Edward Saila was capable of hurting or killing him?'

George Hudson shouted 'Conjecture, your honour,' but the judge waved the prosecution on.

Ethan Miles nodded at Mick to continue.

'Yes, sir, I do,' Mick replied.

The prosecutor turned to the jury and spoke with a hushed voice.

'From this account, there is a history of violence. Edward Saila had a habit of pushing people around, only this time he went a little too far, and because of this unbridled temper, John Pacey is dead.'

He took his seat and nodded to the prosecution table.

George Hudson approached Mick and stood in front of him, his eyes boring into the young man's until Mick dropped his gaze.

'Michael, you mentioned that Andrew Bolton told you of an assault. You know second-hand information is never a reliable witness, especially if a life depends on it. To validate your statement, we need Andrew Bolton here, but he is deceased. Can you tell us what happened the day that Andrew Bolton passed away?'

Ethan Miles countered with, 'Irrelevant, your Honour,' but the judge also gave George permission to continue.

'Well, you see, Andy got carried away when he started teasing Gabby Harrison, and she hit him, so he hit her harder until it turned into a big fight.'

'Michael Willis, do I need to remind you that you are under oath, and if you do not tell the truth, you may find yourself behind bars. Now tell us what really happened that day.' George's deep, gruff voice pinned him down in his own lies.

'Okay, but I heard it was bad luck to say bad things about the dead.'

George frowned at him. Mick swallowed loudly and continued. 'The day that Andy died, he beat and raped Gabrielle Harrison. We thought he was just going to scare her a bit, like he always did, but when those birds started going crazy and he was punching her face over and over again, John and I pleaded with him to stop, but he told us to 'fuck off' so we did. We ran home as fast as we could and just somehow hoped everything would be alright.'

'You didn't alert the police that you had witnessed a crime?'

'No.'

'Why, pray tell us.'

'Because we were worried that we would get in to trouble too. We did hold her at first but not for long when he really started bashing her.' Mick stole a glance at Gabby as he restated the events of that day. He saw her face, white as a ghost, and felt a tiny slip of remorse for what she had suffered.

'Michael Willis, just so that the jury can see the 'history of violence' that you have participated in, we should mention your extensive records. Here is the list of misdemeanours from your primary and secondary schools.'

He proceeded to hold up several sheets all taped together into one long, sad tale.

'All of this represents a sorry story of school bullying that could have destroyed a young woman's future, both academic and social. Instead, Gabrielle Harrison rose to be an honour student with grades good enough to enter any university in this country, a young woman who has many friends who think highly of her. She has two loving brothers, two dedicated parents and a best friend who has been there for her every step of the way.' His voice got louder and louder as he stated these facts.

Turning to the jury, he said, 'Eddie Saila saw his best friend get pushed and shoved and verbally abused her whole school life. If he was of a violent nature, he would have given each of these boys a serious beating back then; however, Eddie's record stands clean and a good example of his upright character and the self-control that he upheld throughout all these years.' As he finished, his voice dropped to a lower cadence so that the jury had to lean forward in their seats.

When Eddie took the stand, Ethan Miles circled like a shark, looking for the best side to attack. He knew he was unnerving Eddie, and this was exactly his intent.

'Edward Saila, are you romantically attached to Gabrielle Harrison?'

'No, sir, our parents are close, and we have been friends since we were babies.'

'So you can put your hand on your heart and honestly say that you do not love Gabrielle Harrison, and Edward let me remind you are under oath to tell the whole truth and nothing but the truth.'

Eddie's face flushed red and he hesitated.

'Well, the jury is waiting Mr Saila,' Ethan taunted as he made a show of pulling back the cuff to look at his watch.

Eddie raised his head high and looked straight at Gabby as he said in husky voice, 'Of course I love her; she is beautiful, smart, compassionate and kind. Everyone in the world loves Gabby, even the animals that follow her everywhere. I ask you, Mr Miles, who could not fall in love with a girl like that?'

'So we must shift our viewpoint from a concerned best friend to a jilted lover who was bent on revenge that day for Andrew Bolton assaulting his girlfriend.'

'No, sir, we are not lovers. Gabrielle probably isn't even aware that I harbour these feelings in my heart. I have never voiced them until today, so you *cannot* cast me as a boyfriend or lover.'

'Young man, that will be for the jury to decide.' He left his questioning with this hanging in the air.

George approached the witness stand to lay an arm along the bench, like a friend who was coming over to have a chat.

'Eddie, we have heard the facts until we are blue in the face, but tell me friend to friend: Why did you push John Pacey that night? Did you want to see him dead for his crimes?'

'No,' Eddie gasped. 'I tried to convince Jacob and Thomas not to retaliate, but when John said Gabby deserved that beating, it broke my heart. After I shoved him backwards, I was walking back to the car. I promise that the worst I expected to happen was for John to land on his backside. Never in a thousand years did I imagine my dislike for John would cause his death. I want to say sorry to his family, to everyone, and surely if I could turn back time to that night, everything would be different.'

'Ladies and gentlemen of the jury, you have heard it from the accused himself: He is remorseful for his actions that night. This is a tragic accident, not a murder case, and it would be an injustice to ruin another young life to make amends for a simple mistake.'

The court proceedings and evidence went on for over a week until the final case for each lawyer was presented to the jury. Gabby sat on the edge of her seat for each closing statement.

The prosecutor did his best to persuade the jury to see the three men as revenge-driven persecutors. Striding up and down in front of the jury, he strenuously declared his case against the accused. 'Tell me, ladies and gentlemen of this jury, why else would three strong men stop their car and accost two unsuspecting juveniles who were just walking along the street minding their own business? I can tell you that it is the type of men who turn to violence first then plead for mercy only when they are caught. Now is the time to bring this particular miscreant to justice and uphold the law before it becomes unsafe for any of us to leave the shelter and protection of our homes.

'You must understand that the purpose in waylaying John Pacey and Mick Willis was the intent to harm. These two boys had not raped or beaten Gabrielle Harrison. They were led astray by Andrew Bolton, and now John Pacey has paid the ultimate price for this association: his life. For justice to prevail, Edward Saila should pay by forfeiting his freedom. He has an outstanding debt to society that should be recovered in this courtroom today.'

He did his utmost to beseech the jury to punish Eddie as an example to other aggressive young men, those who thought they could step outside the law and deliver their own version of justice.

John's parents were sitting stiffly side by side with their hands gripped tightly, unable to show any emotion lest the flood gates opened.

In Eddie's defence, George Hudson gave a full explanation of his lifelong friendship with Gabby and her family. He drew out the virtues of the close and loving relationship that they shared, describing Eddie and her brothers' pain when she was sickeningly assaulted by Andrew Bolton.

'That boy raped Gabrielle Harrison.' He pointed at Gabby while she shrank back in her seat. 'As if that wasn't bad enough, he then beat her and kicked her in the ribs over and over again until he shattered several of them. He broke a bottle and slashed her genitals, leaving broken glass embedded in the mutilation. The damage was so extensive, it took hours in surgery to repair. This has had an unthinkable effect on her life, removed her as an active member of society and ruined her plans to attend university. This attack and her ongoing depression have reduced this vibrant young woman to live within the four walls of her bedroom as a recluse who has lost faith in life and humanity.

'John Pacey and Mick Willis held her down while Andrew Bolton punched her face over and over again. Sure, they didn't actually rape her, but they were historically guilty by association.

'Of course, this didn't give Edward Saila or her brothers the right to accost the two boys that unfortunate night.' He dropped his shoulders in understanding.

'Their motive was to demonstrate anger and disgust; certainly, none of them were murderers or had intent of that course of action.' As he voiced this statement, his voice and body language strengthened to convey his belief.

Dropping his voice to a gentler timbre, he laid the final truth over all of this information as gently and lovingly as tucking a child into bed at night. 'None of these boys intended to seriously hurt John Pacey or Mick Willis. Yes, they were protective and angry, but not then and not today is Edward Saila a murderer. Everyone here today feels a great sadness for John Pacey's parents and family, and as Edward Saila said himself that if he could turn back time or change the course of this tragedy, he would. But to see Edward Saila as a murderer, this too is wrong. He was a protective young man who wanted the two bullies who hurt his best friend to know how much pain they had inflicted. Not murder, my friends, but a reproach gone horribly wrong.'

George took a moment to look around the room, a poignant pause, and then he walked across to stand in front of the jury and looked them squarely in the eyes to say this.

'Edward Saila is saying to you today, "*I am not a murderer. Don't see me as a murderer and don't punish me as one. See* me instead as a young man whose actions that day accidentally caused the death of another. It was never intended and will be forever regretted. Two wrongs don't make a right; don't take another young life in exchange for one that is already lost to us.'"

Scanning the courtroom, Eddie's gaze settled gently on his much-loved family, the small spark of hope in his mother's face as she listened earnestly to their lawyer doing his best to save her son, his sisters sitting on either side holding tightly on to her hands.

With Gabby's head hanging forward under a curtain of blonde hair, he was unable to see her eyes. Only a hint of the dark shadows now framed those magnificent windows to her soul. Eddie wished he could see his own reflection. What would his eyes say? He imagined they were expressing regret, remorse and despair, for this was how his heart felt.

The jury rested for the remainder of the day and the next until they called for the court to be reconvened on the third morning.

Eddie may as well have been carved from stone when he stood to accept the verdict of the jury. One small bald man with a note clutched tightly in his fist literally held his life in his hand, and a shiver of dread ran over his skin when the judge asked if they had reached a verdict.

'Yes, your honour, we have.'

'Speak up then.'

'For the charge of murder, we find Edward Saila not guilty,' he proclaimed loudly.

This was followed by a great wave of sighs and claps around the courtroom. He hesitated slightly for the reaction to cease and then continued.

'For the charge of manslaughter, we find the accused guilty.' The rush of sighs suddenly hushed to a morbid silence.

The judge thanked him, and the juror took his seat with the rest of the jury.

Eddie's shoulders slumped in despair. Secretly they all hoped and prayed that he would not be charged but let off with probation. A manslaughter charge was infinitely better than murder, but now that it was here, it suddenly hit him that this was it. He really was going to jail. This wasn't just a bad dream after all, here he was wide awake and still living it.

Gabby hardly heard the judge give out the sentence. There were words spoken but they didn't make sense. She thought she heard him say 'no prior convictions and a lighter sentence.' However, the next words out of the judge's mouth could not be mistaken or ever be forgotten.

'Edward Saila, I sentence you to fifteen years of imprisonment, with a non-parole period of nine years, effective immediately.' He slammed down his gavel.

Gabby looked down at her clenched hands with despair. She really was going to lose her best friend to a place that was a hell all of its own.

Ruth and the girls began to keen, a chilling cry that ran across the skin like ants, anguish ripped from the soul, which was heartbreaking to hear.

'No, not my baby, not my boy,' Ruth cried. Everyone felt the hair rise on their necks at such a gut-wrenching sound, a mother losing her son. It was such a great price to pay, a pain so raw that most eyes in the courtroom pricked with tears to see her suffer like this.

Maureen Pacey was the only one who could really empathise, for she too had lost a son, not for nine years, but forever.

Lizzie and Nellie wrapped their arms around their mother in support, their cries adding to the lament. Billy looked carved in stone. Kathleen rushed over to join them, and Frank stood with his arm around Billy's shoulders to comfort his old friend.

Eddie saw their suffering and felt so bad to see them hurting. They had always been the best parents anyone could wish for and now he repaid them with sorrow and tears.

Old Joe was immobilised by shock and despair. Who would have thought that life could be so cruel? He had always watched over these kids, but now his two adopted grandchildren were moving beyond his reach, one lost to society and the other to depression.

The judge asked the court officials to take custody of Eddie and hold him in the watch house overnight, ready for transporting to the security prison in the morning.

Ruth had to be supported by Billy as the police handcuffed Eddie and walked him out the side entrance to a waiting car.

Time slowed as Eddie cast his eyes once more over his loved ones before he exited the room. He saw his mother on the verge of collapse, and saw the concern in his father's eyes as he tried to convey a goodbye with his own.

The last faces he saw were John Pacey's parents.

They stared back at him with a glint of satisfaction. For them, his incarceration in prison was some small compensation for taking John's life.

Eddie did his best to convey his remorse. There was no happy ending in this sad tale.

A kind-hearted police woman sat with the family and explained to a distraught Ruth and Billy that Eddie would be taken to the Copeland High Security Prison on the Atherton Tablelands.

Time stood still when his eyes fell on Gabby in those last few seconds. Earth met the sea as their gazes locked. They were both pale versions of their former glory. Eddie had discreetly watched her during the proceedings. He was worried about his best friend, especially when all the details of her attack were dragged out for everyone to hear and see.

Sitting there emotionless, he knew her blank face was just a mask. Graphic descriptions of what she had suffered would have taken her straight back to the blood and dirt. Eddie knew she had such a tight grip on herself, but he wondered how long before she snapped and broke completely. There must be a limit on how long you could maintain staying numb or detached.

As she returned his stare, her mind flashed back to their time growing up at San Remo Beach. In her mind's eye, she could clearly see images of them running along the beach with kites, building sandcastles, swimming in the warm waters of the sea, holding hands under the stars at night.

Her last thought was their birthday party on the beach such a short time ago. They were very different back then, so innocent and naïve! So sure the world was good. *How we have changed Eddie, or did the world change us?*

Silence reigned at the Harrison dinner table that night. Food was pushed around plates listlessly, and after cleaning up, every one retired for an early night.

There was no way that Gabby could sleep. She lay there on top of the covers and looked at the night watchman on her window sill, her dear friends that had always been there in good times and bad. She kept praying for Eddie, especially when her mind thought about the terrible stories that she had heard about prison.

'Please, God, look after him, keep him safe and don't let evil take over our lives.' She kept repeating these words like a rosary, trying to find hope.

She couldn't forget the expression in his beautiful brown eyes, so frightened and wounded, like a cornered animal with no way to escape.

She buried her face in the pillow and hoped it could muffle her sobbing.

He must be so scared tonight.

Kathleen lay in bed staring at the ceiling, and her thoughts and prayers were with her best friend.

Ruth was normally such a strong woman. She had always been a shoulder for Kathleen to lean on. She thought back to an incident many years earlier when she had turned to Ruth to take control. It had been a hot November day when Kathleen had heard a cry coming from the beach, yet when she ran to see who was in trouble, she found a group of Islander men butchering a live Dugong. The poor creature was wailing as they sliced along its back. Horrified by the senseless cruelty, she ran to Ruth's to ask her to stop them.

The look of determination that had settled upon her friend's proud features reassured Kathleen that she had the men in hand. Within an hour, Ruth was back and explained that at first the men wouldn't listen to a woman, but she had pulled rank as Billy's wife and wouldn't leave until she saw the animal humanely slaughtered.

'Thank you, Ruth. But why did they do that?'

'It's a cultural practice, one that I personally don't agree with. After I finished with them, I don't think they'll try that again in a hurry.'

'You're amazing, Ruth.'

'Bossy, you mean.'

'No, amazing.'

'Well, those young men are sure to make their feelings known to Billy.'

'I'm sure Billy will stand by you, Ruth.'

'He better,' she smiled cheekily.

Today, this strong woman looked broken in body and heart. When they took her son away, she seemed to shrink before their eyes.

Fourteen

Eddie was kept in the watch house at the police station. He lay on the hard cot and stared at the concrete ceiling most of the night, listening to the drunken ravings of his neighbours. Most of these itinerants would be released the next morning once they sobered up, but for him it was the first of many nights behind bars.

He left the tiny cereal box unopened that was supposed to be breakfast and waited for someone to take him away. Ensconced in the back of the police van, he stared vacantly at the floor. His mind was numb, and he couldn't even feel upset. He welcomed this detachment and wished it could last for the next nine years. Refusing to think about the horrors awaiting him, this new version of himself didn't want to acknowledge the nightmare that was about to begin.

The only fear that seeped through his shield was the suffocating panic of confinement. After the freedom of roaming the beach, he felt like a wild beast, caged up. Through the slit of glass at the top, he could see the landscape changing as they travelled along, the dark green of the rainforest to the open forest trees with the blue sky framing their branches. And as the trees thinned, he knew they must have almost arrived.

In no time at all, the car crunched to a stop on the gravel, and he could hear the police officer talking to staff at the prison entrance. The vehicle slowly progressed along the interior of the barbed-wire fence going through several security checks as it moved ever closer to the imposing buildings. Gate after gate slammed shut behind them, sealing him off from the world.

Eventually the back door was flung open to the morning sunshine. Eddie looked up at the mocking blue sky and took in a huge gulp of fresh air.

'Come on, young fella. They have to go through the process of checking you in.' The police officer was a decent sort of a guy and lightly guided Eddie into the building.

Checking me in! Eddie thought hysterically to himself. *As if this was a five-star hotel.*

The smell of bleach was his first impression, harsh chlorine to sterilise the infection of pain. Escorted through heavy metal doors to a reception area, the prison warden checked his date of birth and then asked Eddie to remove any jewellery and surrender personal belongings.

Eddie took off the watch that his parents had given him for his seventeenth birthday, and strangely enough this brought tears to his eyes. It was hard to surrender this small link to his family, and suddenly he wanted to shout at these people that this was all a mistake. He wasn't a murderer, he was just a stupid kid who had let his anger get the better of him, only once, and with tragic consequences.

Blinking rapidly to disguise the moisture, he handed the treasure over to the surly guard.

The prison officer took out an official-looking stamp and slammed it down on the paperwork from the police. Once finished, he tossed the stamp onto the counter where it tumbled over and over, spinning until it rested up against the wall.

For some reason, Eddie couldn't take his eyes off its crazy movement.

He felt the same way, spinning out of control with no safeguard to protect him now. Would there be a wall to stop him plummeting into the pits of hell? Some sanity to hold back the madness? In here there was no soft place to fall, no one to swoop in and rescue him. No parent or friend to attend to his wounds or comfort his fears. The enormity of his predicament was starting to seep in.

'We are going to take you to the medical examiners room, and a doctor will do a physical. After that, you will be kitted up.'

Eddie nodded past the lump in his throat and followed the warden along a corridor and into a brightly lit room.

The doctor seemed very ordinary, wearing the typical white doctor's jacket. He was a man in his mid-fifties with short grey hair and a matching clipped beard.

He introduced himself as Doctor Stanton.

'Come in, Edward, and let's have a look at you.' He tried to reassure the scared young man who walked slowly in and sat on the very edge of the examination table, poised to take flight.

The warden stood by the door as the doctor instructed Eddie to remove all of his clothing. Eddie glanced across at the big, burly warden, feeling embarrassed to undress in front of two strangers. But there was obviously no choice, so he took everything off and folded his garments neatly on the table beside him.

The doctor listened to his heart and breathing, took his blood pressure and checked his pulse. Then to Eddie's mortification, he bent down and examined his testicles, rolling the testes in the sac to see that they were both descended and firm.

Eddie quickly flicked his eyes to the warden but he seemed to be staring off into space. He must have witnessed this scene more times than he cared for.

Then the doctor explained that he would have to do an anal examination to make sure there were no caches of drugs being brought into the prison.

'Please try to relax. If you tense up, it only makes the sensation more uncomfortable.'

Doctor Stanton then asked Eddie to turn around and bend slightly forward over the consulting bed. Eddie did as he was told and could hear the doctor putting on his plastic gloves. It reminded him of all those corny jokes during senior year science classes. The students would put on their gloves and jokingly say 'bend over for your examination'.

However, today it was no joke, it was his reality. He jerked as the doctor's fingers slid into his anal cavity. It burned like crazy, and he wanted to step away out of his reach to break the unwelcome intrusion. The doctor took his time wriggling his finger this way and that until he was fully satisfied that there were no secret packets hidden inside.

Eddie couldn't have it finished soon enough, and when it was over, it felt like he had soiled himself from the leftover lubrication jelly.

The doctor gave him some antiseptic scrub and showed him a shower cubicle to wash down. It was an open space with no door so both men talked quietly and watched as Eddie scrubbed himself clean.

'I wouldn't want to be this kid tonight.' The warden nodded at Eddie as he spoke quietly to the doctor.

'Can't the prison manager put a stop to that barbaric initiation?'

'Nope, he won't. In some weird way, he thinks it keeps the newcomers scared and less difficult to handle. Once the older prisoners are finished with them, they don't have any self-worth left to get cocky about.'

'It's a cruel introduction to prison life, especially for kids like this one. You can see that he isn't some street punk. He seems like a decent sort and is quite possibly still a virgin.'

'Well, he won't be no virgin after tonight, I can promise you that.'

After the shower, the doctor took his pile of clothes and gave them to the warden, and in exchange gave Eddie prison jocks, grey overalls, white socks and sneakers.

Eddie hurriedly donned his new clothes and looked at both the men for the next instruction.

'Ok, you're mine for now.' The warden raised his brow sardonically at the doctor as he led Eddie away to his incarceration.

They walked through several locked corridors until they came to one long corridor of cells, not stopping until they reached Eddie's new place of abode. It was just a couple of metres wide and long. Just enough room for a bed and a small toilet bowl in the corner. There was no privacy; everything here was bare and exposed, just like his fear.

Not long after Eddie arrived, all the prisoners shuffled in to the dining hall, and he took his place in the line while discreetly looking over the crowd. There were mostly men of average appearance here, quite a lot of indigenous who seemed completely disassociated with their surroundings. The line also held a group of men who seemed to know each other. They nudged and shouldered one another in the queue until one who stood taller and broader than the rest turned his gaze upon them. Immediately, they froze, like children caught doing wrong. Eddie watched and knew he was the one in charge, and as if he had called out to him, the brute turned those cold eyes on him. They seemed to promise suffering.

Eddie took his plate from the pile and started along the food line. There were a couple of young prisoners helping to serve the food. As Eddie held his plate to get some mashed potato, a young, lightly coloured man discreetly pushed a note into his hand. It wasn't until he was back on the hard wooden bench seat that he unfolded it in his lap and glanced down. In a childish slant was written: *They gonna fucken come for you tonight.*

Eddie's face drained of colour as he looked at the other inmates. He was suddenly all too aware of the knowing looks passing from one prisoner to another. He felt a current of excitement running through the place and suddenly understood that it was because of him.

The buzz seemed to be humming 'new blood, new blood'. Eddie looked at the food on his plate and felt like throwing up. The trouble was there was nowhere to hide in here and no chance to get away from these perverted monsters.

Oh, God in heaven, help me. Old Joe says everything happens for a reason but what purpose could all this have? Eddie felt completely forsaken at that moment. There was no one to turn to and no one in here cared what was about happen to him. The guards didn't seem inclined to step in and protect him from prison violence, so now he had to look after himself.

Time to man up. He tried to mentally prepare himself for what was ahead.

As they all shuffled back to their cells after dinner, Eddie noticed that the guards didn't bother to lock any of the doors.

'Excuse me,' Eddie called after a guard. The guard sauntered back to Eddie and raised his eyebrows in question.

'If you aren't going to lock the other prisoners in their cells, will you at least lock me in mine?'

The other prisoners who had heard him shrieked in laughter at this request. They all knew the guard had instructions from the prison manager not to lock the doors for the first night when a new prisoner arrived.

The guard just smirked knowingly and shook his head then strolled back along the walkway between cells.

Eddie retreated to the back of his cell and pushed himself into the very corner. He would go down fighting, at least, if they were going to hurt him. Well, he would make sure some of them got a dose of their own medicine.

The lights dimmed just after nine, and Eddie could hear an exchange from one of the other cells. There was a group in there making plans. When he heard them creeping along the walkway, Eddie bunched his muscles in readiness for the fight. He was big, in the prime of life, and heavily muscled after lifting crates at the prawn farm where his father worked.

Three large, tattooed men from the knucklehead group jostled into his cell, almost filling it with their bulk. Flushed with excitement, they were looking forward to a fight and some long-awaited excitement.

Two of them reached for Eddie in his corner, and he came out fighting. Kicking high he connected with a jaw and heard the bone crack. The guy screamed in pain as his teeth bit right through his tongue. Blood poured out of his mouth, and he staggered back from the shock of being hit so pretentiously.

The third man hungrily took his place, and this time Eddie brought his head forward as hard as he could and butted him right between the eyes. A nasty gash split the man's brow, and blood spurted out to blind him. Eddie felt his own skull throbbing from the impact but he didn't have time to stop. The first brawny brute was trying to twist Eddie's arm up behind his back to subdue him enough for his mates to give him a pounding.

Instead, Eddie did a move he'd learnt in Judo where he twisted his own body into the attack to lessen the pressure, and as soon as his body got close, he turned to bring his knee up and crunch it into the man's crotch. This one dropped to the ground and cried out in agony as he clutched his bruised testicles.

Of the three, one had a broken jaw and split tongue, the other had blood pouring over his face and the last one was on the ground holding his groin while he squealed like a pig.

Not a bad first round but there were plenty more to take their place. As the first three stumbled out, another three men, just as excited, took their place. Eddie did his best to keep up his defensive moves, but as one backed away with an injury, another took his place until he became so exhausted they just dragged him out of his corner and into the walkway.

The prisoners ranking lower in the prison hierarchy were not permitted to actually participate. Nonetheless, they began howling with excitement when they saw Eddie get dragged out of his cell. Two burly thugs held him tight while their collaborators hit him over and over again until he could barely stand. His legs trembled like jelly and his kidneys were burning from the punches pummelled into his back.

The volume of the audience really escalated when the men dragged Eddie's underwear off and threw them up in the air like a trophy, and one of the non-participators dashed out of his cell and grabbed them with glee. They gazed hungrily when the light gleamed on Eddie's mocha-coloured buttocks.

'Move out of the way, you bastards. He's mine first.' Bruce the brute shoved his way to the front.

They held him tight as the leader of this pack of dogs lined himself up behind Eddie. Shouting with triumph, he grabbed those firm young buttock cheeks and plunged himself deep inside.

Eddie lunged forward and screamed in agony as the thug started moving in and out. But no matter how he tried to draw away, the other men held on to him so tight he couldn't break away.

Enthusiastic shouts and howls of encouragement drowned out Eddie's groaning.

Only one cell was quiet as the inmate sobbed quietly in the corner. He relived his own humiliation every time they did this to a newcomer, and it never got any easier. He felt so sorry for that young black man. From the first glance, he could tell that he wasn't a thug or accustomed to animals like these.

They took turns, until Eddie's consciousness started to blur, and he couldn't make any noise or cry at all. Shock was setting in, the welcomed separation taking him away from the trauma until it wasn't him anymore, just some other poor kid in this horrendous predicament.

Behind his closed eyes, he was transported back to San Remo Beach, a child again, innocent and free, swimming out into the ocean and floating without a care in the world, and always with Gabby. He saw the halo of blonde hair floating around the fine bones of her face and those unforgettable green eyes. These images rescued him from what was unbearable and protected his inner core from desolation.

'Come away from this evil, Eddie.' Her mesmerising eyes beckoned him with an escape.

Once they had vented their fury and sadism, the inmates literally threw Eddie's broken and mutilated body back into his cell, and eventually quiet settled on their floor.

Eddie remained unconscious, safely in his world of dreams where sanity still reigned supreme.

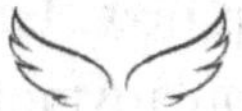

Upon discovering Eddie's battered and unconscious body the next morning, the prison guards placed him on a stretcher and took him to the infirmary. The same doctor who had seen him at check-in barely recognised the good-looking young man. His face was swollen and battered, his nose was broken and several of his teeth were knocked loose. As he examined the damage, he thought to himself that the teeth would tighten up again, bones would mend, bruises would fade but the internal damage would be another lifelong scar.

He could see there was blood seeping from Eddie's anal passage and knew the poor kid had been raped repeatedly. This was the real injury done to a man. His heart and mind would never fully heal from the depravation of liberty and dignity. He silently treated his injuries while his own heart burned with anger.

The doctor contained his emotion until after lunch when he couldn't stand it anymore. He decided that it was time to confront the prison manager.

Crashing the door back against the wall, he stormed into the manager's office. He was sitting at his desk studying a ledger book and looked up with an angry frown on his face at the rude intrusion. The doctor was standing in front of him, his face taut with anger, jaw clenched tight and hands fisted at his sides.

'Doctor Stanton, you seem a little upset over something.'

'You bet I'm upset. I have a young man in my surgery who was a decent human being until last night, until you ruined his life. Your policy to allow the inmates to have some fun has done more damage than all the other dumb things you have done. Do you ever think of the consequences of these activities, which I don't need to mention are illegal and entirely unprofessional? This has to stop now. I will not keep quiet about the way you manage this prison anymore.'

Running out of steam, he stood there huffing and puffing and watched the manager slowly close the book and fold his hands carefully on top of it. He was a big man in his fifties with too much weight on his girth and heavy jowls that sat on the stained collar of his shirt. Here sat a clever manipulator of others and one who knew how to target their weaknesses for his own gain.

'Doctor, please calm down. This young man is in prison, not some church youth camp. All of the men here are in jail because they did something very wrong, and society no longer wants them. I think we need to remember not to get emotionally involved with the prisoners and their little misdemeanours.'

'Misdemeanours! You can't be serious. These are crimes and it doesn't make any difference if they are in prison or still out in society. This is criminal activity that you are condoning.'

'Doctor, do I need to take this one step further and remind you of our agreement? I have not asked you to stretch yourself unnecessarily to pay me back. I have been patiently waiting for my money, but if you want to push me into a corner, then I will no longer support your urge to gamble and instead call in the debt immediately, and in full too.'

The doctor suddenly lost all of his fight. He literally shrank in stature in front of the manager, and he could see that this bastard still had him exactly where he wanted him. Blackmail had always been an efficient way to control weak people.

'Well, debt or no debt, Edward Saila's kidneys are so badly bruised that he will have to stay hospitalised in my infirmary for at least a week. You are just lucky that they didn't kill him, it was this close.'

He showed a tiny gap between his two fingers to show the prison manager that he could have been explaining away a death in custody to the authorities.

'Okay, okay. I will tell the guards to tone it down in the future. Are you happy now?'

The surgery was kept busy all morning as the medical team attended the perpetrators with a broken wrist and jaw, a gash in the mouth and a nasty cut above the eyebrows that needed stitching. Everyone had seen it before, and they struggled to maintain their professional detachment. Their hearts were with Eddie, and they didn't bother to make it any easier on the perpetrators. The doctor hoped to drag out Eddie's treatment for as long as he could. Any excuse to keep him away from the cells.

As Eddie lay there in a small, sterile room, he marvelled at his bruises, which were a rainbow of colours, ranging from purple to an orange, pinkish hue. Even his bones ached, and every muscle felt warped from its original position. His lower region was constantly on fire with a deep burning pain. It was this sensation that he found the most distressing, being violated in his own skin. The stain of it had burnt into his soul.

A small voice whispered that he should have fought harder, and even though he knew he had held them off for as long as he physically could, his heart still felt betrayed. It would be so easy to lose his way from here, and now he had an even stronger connection to Gabby and the depth of her suffering.

During his recovery time in the infirmary, Eddie was tormented by nightmares. He kept reliving that twist-of-fate night and was tortured by the sound of John's head hitting the curb. The impact in his dream was magnified, and it was now as loud as a crack of thunder with the high drama of the judge's gavel crashing down, emphasising the cataclysmic moment that stole John's life and ruined his.

His personality shifted, and hate now consumed him. There was a rage inside him that wanted to kill every one of those bastards who had attacked him. Violence bred violence; the vicious circle had begun. Eddie lay in his bed for hours hatching plans on how to kill Bruce and the others. Some days he knifed them in the stomach, and other days they died from having their skulls bashed in by a large stone. Every day in his mind, the men he hated died in a different way. Especially Bruce.

Whenever the doctor asked him how he felt about the rape, he refused to talk about it, too ashamed to acknowledge what they had done to him. It wasn't so much the physical affliction, it was the changes in his personality. He didn't realise emotions could be so strong, but the need for revenge consumed his every waking thought. He wasn't the same person anymore. Joe and Gabby would no longer recognise him if they could read his mind and all the evil plans he devised.

Eddie had always considered himself to be a good person, from a decent family. That was a time before Bruce (BB), which was how he saw himself now. The person before and after were completely altered, and now a darkness resided in his soul, one that his former self never knew existed.

The pastor at the Baptist Church once preached, 'If you think of an evil deed, you may as well have done it. If you lust after your neighbour's wife, you have already committed adultery.'

So now I am a murderer through and through, for I have killed several men day after day, over and over again. I have chosen wrong over right, and all that I was is no longer. It's all gone. Tell me, how do I explain all this to the doctor? Really no point, is there.

Eddie's parents were told he had come down with a very virulent strain of flu, and they would have to wait until he was well again before visiting him. The prison manager didn't want anyone to see Eddie's present state. There would be all kinds of enquiries if anyone on the outside saw him now, but secretly he was impressed that this kid had put up one hell of a fight. Too many of the inmates were pussies wrapped up in tattooed skin.

Over time, the doctor got to know Eddie quite well and asked him to call him Gregory, not the formal title of Doctor Stanton. Eddie told him stories about growing up at the beach with his family, and he talked a lot about Old Joe and Gabby. The doctor envied the strong family bonds as not everyone had such a good start to life. This was the first part of the healing process, without realising the lifesaving role he was playing, the doctor slowly drew this young man back from the brink of suicide.

Eddie still wouldn't talk about the night of his attack no matter how much Gregory encouraged him to open up. He kept that pain and hurt locked up deep in his heart, and even before the kindness in the doctor's eyes, the shame was too deep. These scars would be a cross he would carry forever; some things just cannot be shared.

When he was escorted back to the cells, Gregory missed the gentle giant's company and considered how he could bring him back with some other excuse.

One morning soon after, the prison manager called Eddie in to his office. When the young man came in and stood up straight in front of his desk, he looked him up and down then cleared his throat.

'Edward, it's unfortunate that you suffered an attack on the first night. Now, you don't want to distress your folks with the gory details, so I would suggest we keep this to ourselves. Your parents have been told that you have been sick with the flu and if you know what's good for you, I suggest you go along with the story.' He raised his eyebrows in question.

They both knew the cells were not locked some nights and that nothing was done to stop the atrocities that went on. In spite of this, Eddie just nodded at the manager and made a note to add his name to his kill wish-list.

That evening, Eddie was lining up for food when Bruce decided to toy with him again. Pushing his way through the other prisoners, he stood close to Eddie and whispered wetly in his face.

'Hey, boy, I gonna have me another piece of your black arse one of these nights. They say you killed by accident, but you need to know that when I kill, it ain't no accident. I kill people for real.'

Eddie kept his face vacant of all emotion. He would not even let his knuckles tighten on the food tray. Only his mind was busy with the many ways he planned to dispose this vehicle of filth. His stare only faltered when in his peripheral vision he saw the guy who had tried to warn him on the first night. He stood frozen to the spot, his eyes wide as his tray began to shake. It was this clattering crockery that broke the stalemate between the bully and his prey.

'Remember, you're mine, and I gonna get ya again.'

Only when his bulk moved away did Eddie take a breath to fill his shrunken lungs and went to sit beside the nervous young man.

'Suddenly lost my appetite,' Eddie muttered as he pushed the tray away.

'Even if it chokes you, fucken eat it. They're looking for any sign of weakness, and you did a good job so far to show them they don't rattle you. Better than I could have done, that's for sure.'

Eddie looked at him intently until he relented and drew back the tray. 'The food in here chokes me even when I'm hungry, but somehow I'll make it go down.'

They sat in silence for a while, Eddie drinking glass after glass of water to wash the tasteless food down his throat.

'Tell me, how did you end up in this rat hole?' Eddie asked as he reached for the jug to refill his glass.

'Got caught with a big bastard stash of heroin. Was supposed to meet a buyer but the cops must have got tipped and they were fucken there instead.' The stranger smiled at Eddie to take the sting out of his profanities. 'How did a decent guy like you get here?' he asked as he scraped up the last of the gravy and popped the stale bread into his mouth.

'Let my temper get the better of me.' Eddie bunched his shoulders in self-contempt.

'What happened?'

'Got angry one night and when I shoved a snivelling coward, he cracked his head and never woke up. I never meant to hurt him, but now that's all history and my future is here.'

'Some fucken future.'

'I know. Most of the time I wish it was me who had died that night.'

The young man looked wanly at Eddie. 'I'm Barry, by the way.'

'Hi Barry, I'm Eddie,'

They didn't shake hands like most people at an introduction. This was prison not polite society, so they just nodded at each other with a hint of a smile.

Fifteen

The world didn't stop spinning, and life outside the prison walls went on without Eddie. Babies were born, people continued their daily grind at work and slowly a different rhythm returned for the Sailas, even when life had lost its purpose.

'Ruth, how did your visit with Eddie go yesterday?' Kathleen had called to find out about the first visitation.

'Kathleen, it was horrible, even though I longed to see him. There aren't any words to describe how it feels to see your child locked away like some wild animal. The process to get in there was tiresome and nerve-wracking. After taking off all our jewellery, they walked us through a metal detector, then we were put into an X-ray booth to make sure there were no concealed weapons, as if I would do such a thing, but I guess it must happen. Once cleared, we were taken to the visitor's room to see Eddie. There were guards hovering all around us the whole time, so there was no privacy.'

'How was he?' Kathleen asked.

'Not good. He looks exhausted and scared.'

'What do you mean, scared?'

'I don't know. He won't talk about it, but he can't hide his fear, and I can see that something terrible has happened to him.' Ruth's voice quavered as she started to sob over the phone.

'Ruth, I am so sorry. Everything feels broken, and I don't know how to put our lives back together,' Kathleen's voice faded as emotion closed her throat with sadness.

There was silence while Ruth struggled with her composure. It took a little while to release the tightness that had a vice-like grip around her heart.

'His eyes are so sad, and we could see him hanging off every word, just devouring every little detail, trying to make the moment last. The hardest part was leaving him there. I felt like I was abandoning him when we had to leave, and it broke my heart to walk away.' Ruth was openly crying now.

The next weekend, Kathleen and Frank took Gabby to visit Eddie and were subjected to the same security protocol.

As soon as they were ushered into the visitor's room, they were shocked when they saw Eddie.

Gabby could see the difference in him immediately. There were shadows in his eyes now, and his gaze was no longer direct and open but one that slid away from her probing look. She wondered what had happened here to cause these changes from a strong, confidant young man to a whipped dog.

What a ruin our lives have become. It seems my pain now has a rival, she thought miserably.

Eddie did his best to keep his gaze averted. He knew she would see the truth and didn't want her to bear his pain as well as her own.

Visiting time went far too quickly. Eddie was desperate for any news from the beach, so Kathleen and Frank tried to drag up every local piece of gossip to satisfy his thirst for home life.

'Mrs James had her operation and will be able to walk without her stick once the pain eases.'

'That's so good. Is Thomas still mowing her lawn?'

'Yes, he promised he would look out for her, Eddie.'

'It's a relief to know that he will keep her yard tidy until the replacement hip is fully functioning again.'

Kathleen smiled and held on to his large hands.

Gabby hardly spoke a word, just sat there staring at Eddie until the guards told the visitors that their time was up.

When they hugged goodbye, tears welled up in Gabby's eyes and trembled on the lower lids until in surrender they spilled over her face.

'Don't cry, Gabby. Everything is going to work out for us. If not now, then one day, I promise you.' Eddie did his best to comfort her.

She just nodded mutely at his reassurance.

Kathleen and Frank both tearfully promised to come back soon.

The hardest part of the visits for Eddie was when it was time for them to go home without him. It hurt even more than the first day he had been brought here.

As they all walked away, Gabby looked back for one more glance. She attempted to smile but it came out all wrong. Eddie stared back at the gaunt shadow before him, and this time he was her mirror image.

When the angels were first exiled, it hadn't seemed so bad to Jinn. They'd had each other as brethren and could still roam freely in the earth's astral realm. It took a while for the light to begin to fade within and for their strength to fail, then slowly over the ages, their features blurred and changed into the grotesque masks they now wore.

Now they had infiltrated the earth itself, and either wandered unseen among the living, stalking their prey and plotting for vengeance, or they removed their shroud of concealment to dwell deep beneath the Earth in dark, dusty caves.

At this moment in time, he stood in the doorway and looked around the chamber, only to find it empty. He knew not where Sut was. Advancing further, he stared at the chair carved in stone, a symbol of authority. It gleamed with a life of its own in the flickering light from the fire. This was where Sut had sat and talked to Lucifer not so long ago, the same hour their leader had ordered them to cause havoc in Gabrielle Harrison's life.

Looking left and right, Jinn moved to sit on the stone chair, and slipped to the back so that his legs dangled over the edge with his wings tucked up behind. Sighing, he tilted his head back to rest against the high back. It was strangely comfortable, considering it was made from the caves they had been forced to retreat to. From a city of glory to these dusty caves that smelled of smoke and dirt, how they had fallen, not just in dimension but also in their quality of life. And it was an eternal life, so their exile had no end.

Considering the consequences of the decision to follow Lucifer, did he have regrets, or would he do it again? Yes, was his answer. Especially now, he was relishing the torture of this angel–human and planned to drag it out until she begged him to end her human life. Jinn's long claws tapped the arm of the chair, his mind feverish with ideas on ways to make her suffer.

This fallen angel, Jinn, loved blood. The spilling of it brought such gratification. Any desire to look after the welfare of mankind had vanished long ago. Enjoying this moment, Jinn closed his eyes as he pictured his triumph over Fallon, until his reflections were abruptly interrupted with a loud harrumph.

'What do you think you are doing sitting in my chair,' Sut demanded from the doorway.

'Sorry, my Lord Sut. I only sat there a moment to rest.'

'Well, have you made progress in tormenting the trespasser?' Sut queried as he wiped the blood from around his mouth and settled himself into the chair he had come to enjoy. Long ago when they'd made these caves their base on earth, he'd ordered the unit he commanded to fashion the chair out of the stone that surrounded the cavern. It had the most glorious fiery colour running in streaks, like veins throughout a body, and some said only opals gleamed with a fire like this.

'Indeed, I have,' Jinn answered as he sat on the floor at Sut's feet.

'The human Fallon's best friend has committed murder and been sent to prison, which was utterly out of character. Conveniently he suffered a terrible attack, one that almost killed him,' Jinn declared, fluttering his closed wings with glee.

Sut looked down at him with consideration. 'You orchestrated this?' he asked with a hint of suspicion as his thumb rubbed the coarse skin that sat taut across the bridge of his misshapen nose.

'Yes, it wasn't that hard to prey on the prisoners' weaknesses. Lucifer was right. Humans are so prone to sin, it's like they were born to do it. First the friend Eddie, who was bent on retribution, then Bruce and the other inmates in the prison.' Jinn couldn't contain his eagerness and leaped up to pace about the dusty room.

'Who is Bruce?' Sut commanded.

'Well, Bruce, he's so easy to influence. His heart was already filled with filth, and all I had to do was ensure his world collided with Eddie's and the outcome was assured.' Jinn stopped his pacing and turned to Sut.

'Sut, there is one concern.' Jinn's tattered wings fluttered in trepidation as he turned to stare into the flames that made shadows dance across the chiselled walls.

The silence dragged on as Jinn waited for Sut to ask him to go ahead.

'Go on, Jinn.' Sut stood up and waved his clawed hands to encourage him to continue.

'The messenger living as a human is now on the brink of suicide. Have we pushed her too far too fast, when there is still plenty of torment and peril ahead?' Jinn hunched his shoulders in question as his eyes stayed glued on his leader.

'I believe you worry too much, Jinn. The human Fallon may seem weak and defenceless but she is hardly about to give up so soon. Watch and wait, and your nemesis will rise from these ashes like a phoenix, and all you have to do is be ready to strike again.' Sut smiled devilishly.

'I'll trust in your wisdom and devious streak,' Jinn's smile mirrored Sut's.

'Now tell me more about the wicked plans in store for her and those piss-weak friends.' Sut clapped his hands together with glee.

After a lively exchange, Sut reached forward to grasp Jinn by his bony shoulders. 'Jinn, there is something you must do for me,' Sut asked of his fallen brother.

'What is that you ask?' Jinn bowed before his liege.

'Promise me you will deliver a chalice of her blood when it's done. It would be the sweetest bouquet of all.' Sut began to drool in anticipation.

The blood of an angel, surely this was a first. He had never tasted one of his own kind who had juice in her veins. The fallen had taken to drinking blood to bolster their flagging strength, and many of their kind welcomed the opportunity to partake of sacrificial human blood at cult ceremonies. But to drink the blood of an angel, that had him licking his lips with fervour, and a look of pure malice settled on his grotesque features.

Sixteen

Time passed in the routine of prison life. Eddie kept one eye open at all times, even at night. The luxury of deep, innocent sleep was no longer his to have, and he was always ready to react at a moment's notice. He never lowered his guard no matter what he was doing. Bruce and his thugs still hated him for putting up such a good fight, and they did everything they could to make each day harder than it had to be.

They slipped contaminants in his food making him vomit and run to the toilet, and they smuggled illicit drugs into his cell to get him in to trouble with the guards. He spent many days in solitary for no good reason, bearing his unwarranted punishment stoically. It was just as well he had Barry looking out for him. So many potential disasters were averted by his sharp eyes and his own network of contacts amongst the other prisoners.

Barry Vilphene's mother had emigrated from the Philippines and became pregnant not long after she arrived in Darwin. Every time Barry had asked who his father was, his mother just said he was a fisherman from the Islands.

Left alone while his mother constantly tried to get enough work as a cleaner to provide for them, he had little supervision or parental guidance, and it was too easy to get led astray by the brotherhood of a gang. Natural progression was a drug addiction, and eventually selling to pay for his habit. He'd only been in Cairns a couple of months before he was caught red-handed.

In spite of his tough, brash exterior and constant swearing, Eddie came to love Barry like a brother, and this unlikely friendship was a buoy to cling to in their stormy sea.

Doctor Gregory was aware of the vendetta against Eddie and did his best to keep him away from the thugs as much as possible. He asked the prison manager if he could get some assistance to archive the records that the government required on each inmate. The manager approved the request and wasn't surprised when the doctor asked if Eddie could be his assistant for a while.

Extending the work for as long as he could, Gregory did his best to distract Eddie with questions and always drew out a story to delay the end of the shift.

When the lights were dimmed, Eddie sat in his cell and fondly remembered life before prison, especially the smell of the salty breeze blowing off the ocean at San Remo Beach. He would have given anything just to go home and see all the loved and familiar places, the smell of his mother's cooking, the sound of laughter as his sisters helped her in the kitchen, his father watching the news with a cold beer in his hand.

So many ordinary day-to-day moments that he had always taken for granted. Now each of these memories were precious keepsakes to be treated reverently and kept safe for recollection. He lay there and let these images flood his mind, evoking senses from a life that was no longer his.

During the day, he tried not to think about what they were all doing beyond the prison fences. Instead, he kept his mind on this moment, this day, making no plans for a future, dreaming no dreams of a new life, just here and now, doing his best to get through this madness.

There was a storm brewing in San Remo. Old Joe was struggling to accept that Gabby was prepared to throw away her future and stay trapped in her pain.

The day dawned when he awoke with a determination to confront her and, if necessary, force her to return to the present and lay the past to rest. It was time to start looking forward instead.

Kathleen opened the door to his knock and her face lit with pleasure to see him again. 'Joe, please come in. It's been far too long since we've seen you. Would you like a cup of tea?'

'No thanks, Kathleen. I've come to see Gabby if that is alright?'

'Oh, she'll refuse to see you, I just know it. It's not just you, she won't see anyone anymore, Joe. I can barely get her to come out of that room, even to eat. Nobody or nothing seems to break the hold of depression, even the counsellors have given up on her. We don't know what to do anymore.' The tears welled in her eyes, and there was such sadness in her voice.

'Kathleen, I still want to talk to her. Would you mind?'

'You are welcome to try, Joe, but I don't like your chances.'

'Well, let me see what I can do.'

Kathleen led him down the hallway to knock on Gabby's door.

'Gabby, you have a visitor. It's Joe.'

A hollow voice called out to say she wasn't feeling well and didn't want to see anyone.

Kathleen looked at Joe and raised her eyebrows in despair.

Joe mouthed for her to move aside. With some reservation she stepped away from the door, torn between protection and hope.

He pushed open the door and closed it behind him.

'Why are you here?' a pale shape spoke from the gloom. With all the curtains pulled tight and windows closed, it was a stifling and oppressive space.

Joe didn't answer but went to the windows, pulled back the curtains and opened the panes to let in some fresh air.

'Gabrielle Harrison, it's time to get out of bed and start living your life again.'

'Get out. I said I don't want to see anyone,' she whispered as she huddled in the dishevelled sheets.

'No, I'm not going anywhere until you stop feeling sorry for yourself and re-join the living.'

'Get out, Joe,' her voiced dropped to a husky, threatening tone.

'No, I will not.'

'Mum, can you please come and get Joe out of my room?'

In response, Joe went across and locked the door. Kathleen rattled the door and asked him not to upset her daughter.

'It's just you and me now, Gabby, and I will not leave this room until you promise to make some effort to get well again.'

'There is no way to get well again, and I don't care if I never leave this house.'

'Well, that's a depressing thought. What about your plans for university, your aspirations to make the world a better place?'

'Andy Bolton stole all those hopes and dreams, Joe. I am no longer that person.' She pulled the covers over her head so that she didn't have to look at him anymore.

Joe went to sit on the side of the bed and gently tugged the sheets away from her face.

'Gabby, there is so much love for you here. You need to let it in to heal the pain and help you forget the trauma of that day.'

'How can I forget, Joe, when my body has been mutilated. Every time I have a shower, the scars take me straight back to that day.'

'You have to let go, Gabby, before his poison destroys you.'

'I can't let go. This is me now. Go away and leave me be. Our friendship is over.'

'I won't let you go, Gabby.' In desperation, he grabbed her bony frame and held it close. 'Let the pain go. Come on, I know you are strong enough to do this.'

Gabby cringed at the touch of another man, even an old one like Joe.

'Get your hands off me before I hurt you,' she threatened.

'I'm not going anywhere, Gabby.' Joe held fast to her, trying to lend her his strength.

'Mum, help me. Get him out of here, get him off of me,' Gabby choked.

'Joe, that's enough. Don't you see how much she has suffered already? Please let her go, please leave us alone.' Kathleen shouted through the locked door. She knew he was trying to help, but she couldn't bear to hear her daughter in turmoil.

'I'm not losing you, Gabby, not again. I won't let go until you come back to me, come back to life,' Joe whispered.

'Don't you see, I'm already dead,' she spat.

'Not to me, Gabby. Not to your family and not to those birds who still watch over you day and night. Don't give in to the demons. Fight for your future. Fight to survive,' Joe continued to whisper, despite her raging emotions.

Knowing he wasn't about to give up, Gabby felt trapped all over again. All the suppressed emotion and pain erupted into a lava flow of anger.

Rage that had been bottled up for so long burst forth like a fire from her belly. It moved up her throat like sulphuric acid and streamed out of her mouth, expelling the demon within. She pushed Joe away from her with such force that he flew across the room and smashed through the door and into Kathleen, who stood just outside.

'Oh my God, Gabby! What have you done!' her mother cried. 'Joe, are you alright?' Dropping to her knees, she checked his prone form crumpled before her.

Gabby flew out of bed to grab Joe and hold him against her.

Sobbing, she said, 'Joe, I'm so sorry. I never meant to hurt you.'

'Gabby, what have you done?' Kathleen repeated fearfully.

Their tearful silence seemed endless until both women took a breath when Old Joe grunted and groggily opened his eyes.

'Gabby, was that you?' Joe groaned as he struggled to sit up.

'Joe, I am so sorry. Please forgive me. I don't know what came over me.'

Holding on to her shoulders, he looked deep into her eyes, searching for the girl he once knew.

With her apology, the tears began to fall. Gasping and choking on her grief until collapsing, she laid her head in his lap like a little girl again. He stroked the oily golden strands back from her face and made small, comforting sounds as Kathleen sat on the other side, hugging her daughter's back, all three crying in relief.

After a long time, Gabby raised her head, and a small smile tickled her lips.

'Are you ready to come back to us, Gabby?' Joe asked.

She just nodded, too overcome for words at that moment.

'Well, I think we should get up and clear out this mess before Frank gets home,' Kathleen suggested.

Once the door was taken off the hinges and removed to the backyard, Kathleen made them all some lunch. It was a thrill to see Gabby freshly showered with her hair washed and out of her pyjamas.

As she sat with them nibbling on a sandwich, Joe started sowing seeds for the future.

'Kathleen, how would you feel about me taking Gabby to Melbourne to study? It might be good for her to have a change of scenery for a while?'

Gabby just stared at Joe as if he had lost his mind and shook her head wordlessly.

Kathleen looked at both of them and as much as it would break her heart to see her daughter leave, she thought that his suggestion might be the best for Gabby. Far away from the shame of her rape to give her time for the memories to fade.

'I think that's a great idea, Joe.' She smiled at Gabby encouragingly.

'I have a lovely brick cottage in Carlton that has sat empty for far too long, and it's close to the university. Gabby, we could move there in time for the mid-year enrolments if you are interested in a fresh start?'

'What about Eddie?' The effect on him was her first concern.

'Well, Eddie is going to be in the same place for a while, and I think he would be relieved to know you were on the path to recovery again, even if it meant you would not be visiting as much. To make it easier for both of you, I will make sure you fly home every couple of months so that you can see him and your family, or even more frequently if you like.'

'What will Dad say?' Gabby looked at her mother for support.

'Your father only wants what's best for you, Gabby, so if you want to go, he'll be fine with it.'

'Okay, well, there's no hurry, so we can discuss this further with the whole family, but please think about my idea and let me know.' Joe let it go for now.

'Thanks, Joe, for everything.' Gabby hugged him when it was time to leave.

'I'm happy that today we are on the same page again, Gabby, and I will come back tomorrow to find out what you have decided to do. One more thing,' he murmured as he took out her broken red star. He'd kept it safe since taking it back from that abhorrent Andy Bolton. 'I believe this is yours.' He smiled as he passed it back to its rightful owner.

She clutched it to her chest. 'Unbelievable. I thought this was lost forever. How can I thank you, for everything?'

'Focusing on getting well is all the thanks I need, Gabby.'

'See you tomorrow then, Joe.' She smiled for the first time in a long time and closed the door.

Joining her mother in the kitchen, Gabby stood at her side as they quietly prepared dinner. There was no need for words, for it had all been said, and now an easy silence sat between them.

Frank and her brothers were surprised to see that Gabby had left her solitary confinement, and this evening the family meal felt a little like the old days, with a happy banter passing amongst them.

The shattered door was repaired and replaced with little comment from Frank. He felt it was a small price to pay to get his daughter back, and how she did it was not dwelled on too much either.

Old Joe was relieved to hear that Gabby had agreed to move to Melbourne, and they began to make plans. Boxes of clothing and chosen household pieces were freighted to Melbourne, waiting to be delivered once they arrived in Carlton.

After some phone calls, it was arranged that the Tropical University would happily come and collect the tanks of many species of insects Joe had been studying over the years. Except one. This prized specimen was delivered personally to an old friend who knew of its significance and pledged to return the Spirit Ants to their rightful place in the desert to once again live amongst the tribe who respected and understood them.

Seventeen

Two weeks before their departure to Melbourne, Gabby went to see Eddie at the prison. Eddie's face lit up when he saw her waiting for him.

'Hi, Gabby. You don't know how good it is to see you.'

'You too, Eddie.'

Once he sat opposite, he took her hands in his and looked intently into her face. 'What's happening in the real world?' he probed.

'Eddie, I've come to tell you something and please don't get angry.' Gabby's eyes pleaded with his.

'What's wrong, Gabby?' he anxiously held on to her hands.

'No, nothing is wrong. It's just that...' her voice trailed away.

Suddenly, the words gushed out in a rush. 'Well, you know I haven't been myself since that day?'

Nodding to let her know there was no need to explain what day that was, he encouraged her to go on.

'Old Joe wants to take me away to Melbourne to make a fresh start and attend uni down there later this year.'

Gabby looked down at her lap so that she wouldn't have to face the hurt she knew would be in his eyes.

Eddie's heart squeezed painfully at her news. He knew this would be good for her but selfishly he didn't want these visits to stop. Even though Gabby was a shadow of her former glory, her countenance was pale and she was far too thin, there was this quality in her that he couldn't find the words to describe. There was something within her that shone, an essence he had never experienced with any other human. This light was the slither of sunshine that snuck through his dungeon window, something he wanted to sit and soak up and save the memory of its warmth when darkness fell again.

Gabby kept quiet while he took his time to absorb her news. Eventually, she stole a quick look at his face to gauge his reaction.

Soft chocolate brown eyes met sea green ones, and he smiled just a little bit.

'I think it's a good idea, Gabby. It will help you forge ahead without the constant reminders of what happened.'

'But what about you?' She held his hand tightly.

'Gabby, it's alright. Remember everything happens for a reason, we just can't see it yet. Do you recall that verse in the bible that says we see through a glass darkly but one day we shall see face to face?'

She nodded.

'One day it will be clear to us why we had to go through all of this.'

'Eddie, I came here today expecting to comfort you, not you me.'

'Somehow all this bad stuff will work out for the greater good. I don't know how but I feel that there is still a plan waiting for us.'

'I don't know what I believe anymore, Eddie. Nothing is like what I thought it would be.'

'Just have faith, Gabby. It's easy to be true to yourself when times are good. It's only when life gets tough that you really reach down deep inside to find that inner core of strength. To be honest, at the moment, this belief is the only thing keeping me from going mad. If I don't hold on to this then I would feel completely forsaken and give up on life.'

'My heart speaks the same truth. I had almost given up too, but now I have regained a small spark of interest to discover what is still in store for me.' There was a ghost of a smile on her lips.

'Gabby, I only have to look at you now to know that everything is going to be alright. We have all been so worried, but today I see some of the old Gabby resurfacing from the ashes, like a phoenix. This time, she will be even stronger and more magnificent than before.'

'I hope so, Eddie. It all feels very fragile just now. I'm like a glass house, one stone away from shattering.'

'Take one day at a time, and then in a few years I'll be released and can visit you in Melbourne. It will be so much fun when you show me all around the big smoke. Plus, by then you'll be a famous environmentalist.'

He even managed to inflect a little of his old teasing nature into those words.

It was gut-wrenching to give her his blessing but no matter how much it hurt him, Eddie didn't want his best friend to suffer any more than she already had.

'I love you, Eddie. You will always be my best friend.' Gabby smiled back at him.

Eddie did his best to memorise every detail of her during that last visit because he knew she wouldn't be back for a while. He was like an alcoholic, nursing his last drink and trying to drag out the moment. Like the way her hair trapped the colour of sunshine, those magnificent eyes, still mesmerising in spite of her gaunt face and dark shadows. Her smile that lit up a room, white straight teeth peeking out from full pink lips. He would never see such a fair sight again and wished that these few seconds would last forever. He tucked away every little mannerism away to revisit later, including the way she chewed her lower lip when she was worried about something. Surely he loved her more now at this moment than any other time he could remember.

All he wanted to do was wrap her in his arms, and resentment burned in his chest at another liberty lost within the prison walls. Hugging her with his eyes, he knew that holding on to Gabby was like clutching at a moonbeam. For a brief moment, she had lit up his world, but deep down he had always known she was far beyond his reach.

Before leaving, Gabby held on to his hands so tightly that their knuckles shone white, like the moonlight they used to watch track cross the sea.

Gabby looked at him one last time.

'Always remember what you mean to me. I am going to miss you so much, Eddie.'

'I know,' he smiled back at her ruefully.

The night before they were due to fly out, Gabby crawled into Kathleen and Frank's bed, and they lay there with their arms wrapped around each other.

'Mum, do you think I'm doing the right thing, leaving everything I know behind and going to a place where I have no friends?'

'Yes, I think this is absolutely the right thing. You're going to make wonderful friends who have the same passions, and I know you are going to be very happy.'

'I'll miss my family though.'

'Of course you will, as we will you, but we all love each other enough to be close even when we are apart, and Joe is going to make sure you are home as much as possible.'

'Mum, there are no words to say how much you mean to me.'

'If you could find them, Gabby, I would use them too.' Kathleen held her tighter in her arms as she silently said her goodbyes.

Later that night, Frank and Kathleen stared at the ceiling, looking for their own answers.

'Honey, I hope we're doing the right thing. Melbourne is such a big city, and Gabby has only really ever known this small town.'

'I know, Kath, but even in this small town we couldn't keep her safe. Something bad did happen to her, so I don't think size has much to do with it.'

Kathleen sighed as she turned and snuggled deep into his arms.

'It won't be the same without her.'

'No, it won't be the same, but I would rather miss her knowing she's happy than see her growing mouldy in that room.' Frank rested his face on her soft hair, and as he gazed into the darkness, he could hear the mournful cries of the curlews as they moved around the house.

It seemed they knew their beloved was moving beyond their reach as well.

The following morning it was time to say goodbye. Before the sun came up, Gabby was outside sitting with the curlews. 'I will never forget you my little friends. We have been together since I was born. Every memory, good and bad, has you in it, and I won't forget how you suffered with me that day.'

Sensing her mood, they circled her, sitting as close as they could with their feathers fluffed protectively, like they did when caring for their own young.

At the airport, Gabby's face was puffy and her eyes were red from crying as she looked around at the people who loved her. To one side, Joe stood with her father, both wearing a sombre expression.

Joe spoke first. 'I will watch over her closely, Frank, and if this doesn't work, well, we can always come home,' he assured him.

Frank shook his hand and nodded at Joe. He was not good at expressing his feelings and could only hope Joe knew how much it meant to him. The effort Joe was making to bring Gabby back from the precipice, to relocate from his beloved beach and go back to the city he had escaped from long ago.

Jacob grabbed Joe's wiry old frame and hugged him.

'You had better take care of her, old man, or you will have all the Harrison kids living with you,' Jacob joked to break the sombre moment.

'That's alright with me, Jacob, both of you boys are always welcome,' Joe replied seriously.

'Are you kidding, you would be sorry, Joe. You haven't seen how much he can eat,' Thomas joked with them as well.

'Yes, I have, Thomas. Your mother is always in the kitchen.' Joe smiled at them.

'Seriously though, come down as often as you can. It will be good for Gabby if you do,' Joe assured them.

'Thanks, Joe, we will,' they both answered at once.

'Gabbs, you be careful in the big smoke. Don't go out at night alone and don't trust people that you don't know.' Jacob tried to pre-empt any more trouble.

'Okay, big brother. I'll be careful, I promise.' Gabby hugged him back affectionately.

Thomas hugged her tightly and whispered, 'Take care, little angel.'

Gabby cried a bit more, loving him so much at this very moment.

Then she turned to their good friend and hugged Ruth.

'This is your place of dreaming, your home, Gabby, and if you are not happy, promise me you will come back.'

'Thank you, Ruth. Nothing can ever replace what I have here. When you see Eddie, please tell him I'll call him and come back often to visit. No matter how much everyone tells me differently, it feels like I'm abandoning him and moving on while his life is shut away in that place. Please tell him that I love him.' Gabby sobbed against her shoulder.

'He knows, baby, he knows that you do. You have his blessing to be happy so don't be hard on yourself.' Ruth held her tightly to her chest. She loved Gabby like her own daughters and knew that Eddie would feel her absence sorely; however, in spite of their own loss and pain, they had to let her go.

Pulling away at the final boarding call, they hurried up the ramp to board their flight. Gabby buckled up and wiped her damp face with the handful of tissues that Old Joe passed across to her. As they flew south across the country, a strange thought came to Gabby. '*Andy Bolton, why?*' In a strange way, he was responsible for her sitting here on this plane today.

I don't hate him anymore, nor can I honestly say that I have forgiven him either. When I think about the rape now, it feels numb. I have locked away all those bad memories and feelings and put them into a box buried deep within my soul. I know the events of that day have left lifelong scars; something died inside me and now I have to get used to living with this loss.

Old Joe sat there pensively as well, but he was deeply grateful that Gabby had broken free from her own prison. One other thought teased at his consciousness, one that he hadn't let himself fully consider: How did a 45-kilo girl get the strength to toss him across the room and through a door?

He'd always suspected there was something more to Gabby. There was this aura that glowed around her, but he could never have known her strength until that day. Another thought that wouldn't go away was how scrawny Andy Bolton was strong enough to hold her down. Surely there were forces at work here that were of a supernatural nature?

Time passed, and before they knew it, the flight landed and they stepped out into the cool Melbourne air.

Joe gave the taxi driver his address in Carlton, and driving through the city, Gabby took in the sights of her new home. It was so much bigger than she had imagined. Eventually, the car pulled over in front of a charming brick cottage that was set back a little way off the street. The garden was very overgrown. A climbing rose bush covered most of the veranda and a quaint timber sign hung crookedly off the gate welcoming them to 'Carlton Cottage'.

'This is the house I was telling you about,' Joe said as they both stepped out of the taxi.

'It looks lovely, Joe, even in the moonlight.' As Joe paid the driver, she dragged their suitcases from the boot of the car.

'How long have you owned this place?' Gabby asked as the taxi's lights lit up the front when he backed out of the driveway.

'I lived here many years ago, but got tired of the cold winters, so I followed the sunshine and moved up north. I could have sold it but it has too many special memories, so it's sat here vacant for a long time now.' Joe pushed the key into the lock, opened the creaking front door and reached just inside to flick the light switch.

The house smelled musty and stale from being locked up but Gabby had time to note the lovely timber floors, furniture covered with sheets, cobwebs in the corners and dust that had settled on every uncovered surface.

'We'll have to do some cleaning up in the morning to make it feel like home,' Joe murmured as he walked around taking sheets off the furniture, coughing and sneezing from the clouds of dust.

'Tomorrow I'll get the hot water system working, but tonight it's going to be a quick, cold shower for us then bed. Luckily I brought some fresh sheets with us to make up our beds.' Joe found the sheets in his suitcase and gave a set to Gabby as she chose which room she would prefer.

She chose the front bedroom that opened up onto the veranda, with the smell of roses drifting in through the open window. Sinking into the soft, deep mattress, for the first time in many months she drifted off to sleep with a smile on her face.

The next day, they were up bright and early and worked all day cleaning up the house, buying groceries and meeting their new neighbours. Over dinner that night they planned how they were going to attack the garden and put it to back to rights, and the next week was spent busy at the house, getting their little cottage running smoothly. Once the house and garden looked tidy and organised, Old Joe began showing her around his old haunts in Melbourne.

Gabby soaked up the city atmosphere, which was so different from the casual lifestyle at the beach. Here most people in the streets were dressed in dark colours: blacks, dark greys and lots of business suits. Long boots, short boots and dark leggings should have made an overall depressing scene, but it didn't. It was right for this place, and she wouldn't have changed it even if she could. Embracing the new style, she soon felt at home as she navigated around the large and dynamic metropolis. She grew to love the buzz of city life and the throngs of people that moved along the streets or sat at the many sidewalk cafes sipping aromatic coffee.

Gradually her bloom of youth returned to draw many admiring glances.

Visiting all the tourist sights, they also enjoyed meals in some of the best restaurants in the heart of Melbourne. This was the beginning of Gabby's love affair with Italian cuisine. Her parents were reassured when they heard some of her former spirit returning as she described all the sights and flavours of Melbourne.

Kathleen told her that Jacob and Thomas were already planning a visit, and Gabby could hardly wait to show them attractions like Lygon Street, where restaurants and eateries lined each side of the road.

Joe was filled with nostalgia as he explored his old city. He had been a young man studying medicine, burning the midnight oil with his studies, working as an intern with impossible hours at the hospital. Now his friends had passed on as he had outlived all of them, and it was this loss and solitude that had really prompted the move up north. He had become weary trying to explain to those who had known him in his youth why he was still alive when all the others had long gone.

Together, they explored the University of Melbourne where Gabby was excited to commence her own academic adventures.

They spent several days exploring lecture rooms and mingling with students, absorbing the lively atmosphere of intellect and social interaction. One day as they wandered into a large outdoor dining area, they noticed a crowd of students sitting around a raised podium.

Intrigued by the quiet, attentive atmosphere, they strolled across to see who everyone was listening to. A young man was standing on a small, raised stage, reciting poetry enthusiastically. It was a week for celebrating Australian bush poets, and this rendition was the well-known Banjo Patterson ballad 'The Man from Snowy River'.

His voice was deep and resonant, one that commanded attention above all others. He was a tall man with dark hair and attractive blue eyes, with full lips that curved up when he smiled and straight white teeth that gleamed in the morning light.

All of these details passed through Gabby's mind as she took in the scene. Joe sat down, so Gabby took the seat beside him and became enthralled in the rest of his recital.

They watched him build the tension until the poem came to the most exciting part, with the chase down the mountain, racing after the wild bush horses while the other riders stayed behind. Then his voice hushed as he told of their exhaustion on the trek homeward bound.

The crowd clapped and cheered when the recital came to its conclusion, then they broke up and all went their own way. Old Joe lingered because he hoped to meet the young man and discover more about him.

The energetic orator walked over and stared curiously at Gabby. Old Joe introduced himself and Gabby, and the young man shook hands with each of them in greeting. He said his name was Ben Giles. Breathing deeply, Gabby steeled herself to breathe normally. The old anxiety lurked under her surface of calm, always threatening to confiscate any feelings of pleasure or normality.

'What do you think of the university?' Joe asked the newcomer, covering Gabby's moment of dread with conversation.

'I really like it here. It's only my first year studying English literature but the lecturers are really supportive and the library is enormous,' he smiled encouragingly.

'Well, that's great as Gabby will be starting here mid-term, and it will be her first year as well.'

'Wonderful. What do you plan to study?' the young man probed.

'I want to do a science degree with a focus on global environmental change and environmental modelling,' Gabby offered as her course of choice.

'That's going to have some fascinating subjects and lots of field trips I imagine.' Ben smiled encouragingly.

'I hope so,' Gabby agreed.

'Well as far as the uni itself, I'm sure you're going to love it. I have a break in lectures now, so would you like me to show you around?' he kindly offered.

Ben took great pride in showing the visitors around the establishment, and it was obvious he didn't take this opportunity to study for granted. As Joe shook Ben's hand, he felt a strange inclination to keep him in their lives.

'Would you like to join us for dinner tonight, Ben? It would be our way of saying thank you for taking so much time out of your day to show us around.'

'Well, I don't have any pressing engagements or assignments due, so yes, that would be lovely, Joe.' Ben shook Joe's hand firmly in respect.

Joe gave Ben his address in Carlton, and they agreed on a convenient time.

For dinner, Gabby made them a delicious mushroom risotto with crusty bread. Sharing a meal was an age-old tradition that brought strangers together, building bonds of fellowship and friendship, and tonight was no different. After much laughter and storytelling, Ben felt very comfortable with this unlikely duo: a young woman so beautiful and fragile she barely seemed human, and probably the oldest man he had ever seen.

Before he departed, Ben offered to take Gabby to the zoo on the weekend if she was interested, glancing at Old Joe for his approval. He sensed that Joe was very protective of Gabby.

Joe nodded happily and reassured him it was a wonderful idea.

On Saturday, Ben was pleasant company. He told Gabby all about his dreams of becoming an English professor. He wanted to teach overseas at Cambridge University in England, going back to the very beginnings of Shakespeare and the great writers of past centuries.

He looked at her quizzically. 'Why did you choose science? Do you want to work in a laboratory or more as a field scientist?'

'Definitely not in a lab. Ideally, I would really like to work for an environmental wildlife rescue organisation, maybe Greenpeace if there was an opportunity.'

'Sounds like you're an adrenaline junkie.' He laughed as he jested.

'No, I just want to make a difference if I can.'

'Beautiful and noble. You seem too good to be true, Gabby.'

'Oh, trust me, I'm flawed. There are many parts of my life that I wish could have been different.' Shadows flitted over her face.

'Well, to the naked eye there are no obvious dents,' Ben teased.

Gabby did not want the conversation to delve any deeper, so she took hold of his arm and dragged him away from the lions to see the giraffes.

Arriving home exhausted, it was a treat to sit down to a bowl of hot, steaming spaghetti bolognaise that Joe had ready for them, over which he grated a strong cheese.

After the meal, they all sat sharing a glass of wine, and Joe quizzed Ben about his family.

'I don't really have any official family. You see, my birth mother was a crackhead junkie who relinquished my care to family services when I was just a baby. I have no memories of her, and the identity of my biological father is still a mystery.

'My whole childhood and early teens were spent in foster homes, some good, some bad and some ordinary. The worst is that you become reluctant to get too close to anyone. It hurts more to be moved if you have a strong attachment to the people who have taken you in.'

'It must have been tough having to re-adjust to a new family all the time?' Joe's face was a picture of empathy, his deep wrinkles even seemed to soften at the thought of Ben as a little boy without even one person to rely on.

'Well, it was all I knew so I didn't stress too much about it. But it did make me want more for my own life. I was determined to educate myself out of the system and make something of myself. Consequently, I worked hard to get good grades and win scholarships to further my education.'

Joe nodded in understanding. 'I was an orphan too until Gabby's family adopted me many years ago. So now we offer you the same, a place where you will always be welcome. Our door will always be open, and Ben, we want you to feel free to make yourself at home here in this little cottage any time of the day or night. Do you agree, Gabby?'

'Of course. I would certainly welcome a friend in this unfamiliar place.' Gabby nodded fervently to support Joe's kind offer.

'Really? But you don't even know me that well.' Ben stared at them both incredulously.

'I've been around a long time and have a knack of discerning the true nature of a person, and my heart tells me that you belong here. It's uncanny but I felt it as soon as we met at the university and sensed we may build a lifelong friendship with you.' Joe squeezed Ben's arm to show how much this meant to him.

'Thanks, Joe, meeting you and Gabby has been a lovely surprise. Your offer is very generous, but just to be clear, I didn't want you to feel sorry for me growing up in the foster system as I consider myself one of the lucky ones. There was always a roof over my head, and I was well looked after. But it just wasn't the same as having a family to call my own.'

Gabby did feel sorry for him. She could not imagine growing up without her family, to have no parents or siblings to share each day with. It would be so lonely and frightening to feel alone from such a young age.

Over the coming weeks, their friendship flourished, and Ben introduced Gabby to some other students who studied at the campus, which only made her more excited to begin her own course. Ben fell into a routine of visiting their cottage almost every night, and Gabby knew Old Joe enjoyed his company as much as she did as he was a great conversationalist with an intelligent, enquiring mind. The two men would discuss current affairs and debate their position on many topics, like the environment, the influence of world leaders, and historical figures like Shakespeare.

Gabby hadn't had any serious boyfriends. She'd had crushes on boys at school but these interludes had been very innocent. Until Andy's assault, she had never been intimate with anyone, and afterwards she had no interest in allowing anyone to get close.

Ben had casually asked if Gabby had left a boyfriend at home, and he couldn't miss the look that passed between her and Joe.

Joe's expression was one of concern, and Gabby's could only be fear. He wondered what they were running away from.

A couple of weeks later, they came home late from the movies, and before Gabby could say good night, Ben turned towards her and gently ran his fingers along a strand of hair that had escaped her pony tail.

Sitting so still and holding her breath, her heart was racing again and that same old choking feeling was back. Her hands convulsively clenched in her lap until the nails bit into her sweaty palms, leaving red lines across the soft white skin.

'Gabby, why do you hate it so much if I touch you? Am I really so repugnant that your skin crawls?'

'Ben, it's definitely not you. I have this condition that makes me uncomfortable with physical contact; it's a reaction I can't control.'

'Well, I'm prepared to wait until you get used to me. I don't care how long it takes. One thing my life has taught me is patience and the dividends of hard work.'

'No, Ben, please don't count on me. I don't think I will ever trust—, I mean be able to get close to anyone like that.' Gabby quickly recovered from almost blurting out the truth. 'I can be the best friend you ever had, but that is truly all I can offer you.'

'Gabby, it's too late for me to go back. Don't you see I am already in love with you, so whether you like it or not, my heart is in your hands now.'

'Ben, the last thing I want to do is hurt you. Truly, if I could give you more I would, but it's just not physically possible.'

The wood in Gabby's heart splintered when she saw the love in his eyes.

'It's okay, Gabby, don't get upset. Let's just stay friends for now and see what happens.'

'Friends I can do. I'm sorry, Ben.' She wiped away the tears with the back of her hand.

'Well, I am glad I get full marks for something.' He laughed to lighten the mood and hugged her in more of a brotherly fashion.

The thought of becoming intimate with any man made Gabby's skin prickle and sweat, and even someone as wonderful as Ben couldn't breach the wall built high around her heart. Deep down she thought that part of her life had died the day of the rape. Never would she be able to forget the pain and humiliation of her first sexual experience.

How would I tell a wonderful man like Ben about the scars inflicted by Andy Bolton and expect him to understand or still love me?

She was damaged goods now, and no man would want to stay with her once he knew the truth.

Eventually Ben approached Old Joe to find out if he knew about Gabby's affliction. Old Joe just shook his head. 'I can't say anything about Gabby or her feelings. I can only ask you to be her friend. Please don't push her on this.'

Ben sensed there was more to the story but knew he wasn't going to get anything more out of Old Joe. He would bide his time and wait patiently.

Watching from the sidelines, Josiel hovered close to Gabby, watching her lovingly as she picked up the threads of her former self. She felt so proud of Joe for averting the certain disaster that Gabby had been speeding towards. He'd become a perfect guardian for her beloved sister.

Smiling with happiness, she considered her own future plan. *How can I protect Gabby now that there are no curlews to watch over her? I'll have to groom another species for this sacred duty. What could offer constant protection against the dark forces?*

Josiel's guardians would prove to have flawless timing.

Eighteen

The day dawned when Gabby started her studies in a degree that she hoped would give her the accreditation and qualifications to follow her dreams.

Old Joe, ever the professor, still had a great love of science, and the cottage was quickly becoming a meeting house for young, thirsty minds from the university. Every night there were lively debates raging around the table, and like a vast tree in the forest surrounded by saplings, the old man thrived on their company.

True to his word, Old Joe organised for Gabby to fly home every three months to catch up with her family and to visit Eddie, who seemed to be adjusting to life in prison, noticing all the peculiarities and finding humour where it really shouldn't exist.

'It's so funny, Gabby, to see these tough-looking guys leap onto a chair if they see a cockroach running across the floor.' She laughed despite herself.

Gabby asked how he spent his days.

'To date, I've either helped the doctor with office filing or worked in the laundry. I don't mind the laundry days as Barry works in there, so at least I have his company. I've just been reassigned to work with Charlie in the carpentry sheds, but you should see him, Gabby. He's over six feet tall and covered with tattoos. Even his shaved head has Maori symbols all over it, but in spite of his size and the fierce markings over his body, he's a really good bloke.'

'Is he a prisoner too?'

'Many years ago, he got caught up in a pub brawl and hit someone a little too hard. Yet, when his sentence was done, he chose to stay here as an employee, one who does carpentry, but I think enjoys taking kids like me under his wing as well. It's his way of giving something back.'

'Eddie, remember when we were younger and you said you wanted to work with your hands to create things? Well, who would have thought it would begin here?'

Gabby told Eddie all about her life in Melbourne, and he smiled with happiness to see some enthusiasm returning to her face and voice. She could tell that her visits were a highlight in the drudgery of his routine. It was heartbreaking to see how his face lit up as soon their gaze met across the visitor's room.

The curlews got equally excited whenever she came home. They would surround her and hiss and dance around with their wings extended. Their antics resembled a courtship dance, and Gabby laughed and clapped her hands to encourage their funny little routine.

Eventually dropping to the ground, she would lie there in the grass with all of her old friends. The birds would crouch down in a circle around her making small clicking noises, and a wonderful sense of peace settled over her like a blanket.

Almost dozing off in the twilight, it was her mother's calls that roused her to come inside, and she knew there would be a night watchman on her window sill that night.

In spite of missing home, Gabby relished her studies and had already made several good friends. However, there was one girl who went to great lengths to avoid her. Miranda Newton shared some classes but always sat as far away as possible from her and would not even make eye contact when they passed in the corridors.

A quiet girl, pretty with long, straight black hair and unusual light brown eyes, she was one who preferred her own company to any of her peers. Those golden eyes watched everything and everyone. It was kind of spooky to feel her intent gaze. It bored into Gabby's shoulders every time Miranda sat behind her in lectures.

Knowing that everybody was entitled to their own space, Gabby stopped trying to befriend her after a couple of cool rebuffs and let it be. Miranda wasn't rude or nasty, just distant, and there was no crime in that.

Life continued on in a now-familiar pattern. Jacob and Thomas both came to stay and had a fantastic time enjoying all the highlights of a big city. They also loved the house and the constant flow of visitors and were able to describe it all to Kathleen and Frank when they returned home.

Gabby asked her brothers if her curlews still stayed close to the house when she wasn't there, and Thomas said that every night one still sat on the window sill in her bedroom. He wasn't sure if it was the same one all the time or if they were taking shifts watching for her to come home.

'So you're saying that some wild bird sits on the window of your house waiting for Gabby to come home?' Ben said in disbelief.

'Absolutely. Gabby has had these birds watch over her since she was a baby, and every time she stepped out of the house there would be a couple of wild birds following several metres behind,' Jacob explained nonchalantly as if this was completely rational.

Gabby blinked away tears as Jacob talked about her faithful little friends while Ben just shook his head in wonder.

Late one winter afternoon, Gabby walked home from university through a picturesque park, where the trees stood like bare sentinels with their branches starkly naked in the dwindling light. With her head down and coat drawn close against the chill, she didn't see the baby until she heard its cries.

The mournful sound was emanating from a bundle of blankets left on the timber park bench. Concerned to see it left there alone, Gabby approached the bench and bent down to gently move the blanket aside. There was a tiny infant, one that looked like a newborn as it wailed, naked and freezing in the evening chill.

With no parent in sight, it appeared to be abandoned.

'Poor little thing, where's your mother?' she crooned.

Carefully picking up the wriggling child, she held it to her chest and instinctively sang softly to settle it. The baby made snuffling noises and seemed to be trying to suckle through her shirt.

'Look at you, how could anyone leave you out here in the cold?' Compassion and pity welled up inside her, and she held the feather-light bundle close to warm it.

'I need to take you home to Old Joe. He'll know what to do.'

The night air became even colder, and her breath clouded the air. As she walked, Gabby kept looking wildly around for the child's mother.

Walking along the gravelled pathway towards the park's exit, she heard a loud growling coming from behind. Gabby turned towards the new threat and saw two massive dogs running towards her. They were snarling and baring long fangs that shone in the lights.

In panic, Gabby took off with the baby wailing in her arms, until one of the dogs leaped from behind and tackled her heavily to the ground. Unable to protect the baby as it rolled out of her arms onto the ground, Gabby screamed when she saw the attacking dog grab at the blanket and drag the baby away from her, just as the second dog also sank its teeth into the blanket.

'Oh my God, somebody help us,' Gabby screamed, reaching her arms out towards the child in supplication.

The baby no longer cried, and as the blanket opened up, she saw there wasn't any blood, even though the limbs had been ripped from the torso. There should have been blood everywhere.

Unable to move from shock, Gabby stayed frozen on her knees as the body parts strewn across the ground turned black and began to smoke. The smouldering increased until each particle became a soft dark cloud that lifted off the ground and floated away.

What on earth had just happened! Looking around to find the street deserted, Gabby's head was spinning so much she felt the world tilt with dizziness. Not even sure if her legs would hold her, she placed her hands on the ground and braced herself to stand up. She could hardly believe what she had just seen, and time seemed to move in slow motion. Gabby stood there, looking at the ground where she had seen an infant torn apart. If the blanket wasn't still on the ground, she may have believed it was all some kind of trick or a hallucination.

Ever so slowly, she backed away from the violent beasts panting before her, expecting them to rush forward and tear at her flesh. But as she moved away from them, they both crouched down on their haunches and crawled towards her, whimpering and softly whining.

'Go home!' Gabby tried to send them back to where they had come from. They only inched closer to her.

'Shoo, go home,' her voice stammered and broke. 'Please don't hurt me, just go home.' Once Gabby started crying, she couldn't stop.

She kept backing away with tears pouring down her face, the two dogs creeping along towards her.

Once she was in her street, Gabby picked up speed while constantly looking back to see where they were. Both kept a small distance but they were certainly stalking her.

Finally, she slammed the gate shut, keeping the two strange dogs locked firmly outside. Bursting into the house, she fell into Joe's arms and told the story between sobs and shudders.

'I still can't believe what I saw, Joe. There was no blood! What kind of being has no blood! I feel like a crazy person to say those ripped-off limbs disappeared in a cloud of black smoke. Do you believe me?'

'Of course I believe you, Gabby. Why would you make up such a story?'

He tried to reassure her while feeling secretly very uneasy.

'So how can we explain it?' she persisted.

'Sometimes everything is much clearer in the light of day, and as we have no answers tonight, and it's late, the best thing you can do is have a really hot shower and try to get some sleep. What do you say?' Joe suggested as he hugged her close to his side.

'Okay, Joe, but I don't know how I can sleep after this. It's more likely to be nightmares.' Gabby grimaced back at his concerned, wrinkled face.

Once he knew she had fallen asleep and the house was in darkness, Joe went outside to investigate the mysterious dogs. At first the street looked empty, until a shadow moved and came towards him. It was a huge dog, taller than a Great Dane, that stood before him on the footpath. Not long after, another stood before him at the first dog's shoulder.

Neither seemed vicious. They whimpered and licked Joe's hand as he tentatively held it out for them to smell his scent.

Feeling a bit more confident, Old Joe opened the front gate and let the dogs come closer to sniff at his trousers and shoes. After a few moments, one went to lay at the side of the front door and the other followed suit to lay opposite, like two sentinels guarding the house.

Old Joe closed the gate, and after giving each beast a tentative pat, he closed the front door and leaned his back on it in quiet consideration. What if these two dogs were not the perpetrators but the saviours in this supernatural phenomenon? They may have arrived to actually save Gabby from something far more dangerous.

The next morning, Joe explained that he had let the dogs in to the yard as they didn't seem to pose a threat.

Gabby looked out of the window to see the dogs were still crouching on either side of the front door.

'Who do you think they belong to?' she asked Joe, still not convinced they weren't dangerous.

'They're obviously well cared for, so somebody must be looking for them. We'll have to call the local vet and animal shelter and let them know that they're with us,' Joe reassured her.

Remembering how they had attacked that thing in the blanket, at first Gabby wouldn't go out of in the house unless Joe was there, just in case the animals became aggressive. However, over the next few days, her fear faded, and she came to see them as just two enormous brown dogs rather than violent beasts.

They became very excited every time Gabby appeared, almost as if she had always been their owner.

After exhausting all avenues to locate who owned the dogs, they never found the previous owners. It was if the animals had materialised that night when Gabby needed them, and they planned to stay. Just like the baby that wasn't a baby, the dogs became part of the unsolved mystery of a very strange night, one that Gabby and Joe decided not to mention to anyone. Who would believe them anyway?

The dogs walked Gabby to the university gates every morning, and when she finished, they would be waiting for her. Even if she left at different times during the day, they were there. It was like they had an uncanny instinct of when they would be required for guard duty. In honour of their size, she named them Samson and Goliath but her friends referred to them as 'the Titans'.

Josiel nodded her approval at them each time she visited the house. They were the perfect guardians, and what could be suspicious about dogs who were deemed to be 'man's best friend'?

Gabby's university years, or study years as she called them, flew past so quickly. She graduated each year with honours and found she was a popular student with professors and other classmates. Her outspoken beliefs labelled her as a greenie, a reputation she was happy to embrace. Ben was still her constant companion, and even the Titans became slightly friendly towards him.

A few times since his first romantic overture, he had tried to get closer to Gabby, but it was like catching a sunbeam. No matter how he tried, she remained elusive and out of reach.

There were many friendships made over these years, but eventually a few chosen ones became as close as family: Elisabeth Wright, Michael Tisch and Paul Montgomery.

Elisabeth was an outgoing girl who began to sit with Ben and Gabby between lectures. Their conversations and the topics discussed led to common interests and invitations for weekend activities.

Ben had brought Michael to join them for lunch one day, after which he seemed to settle comfortably into their circle.

Paul watched from a distance until he got brave enough to draw up a chair at their table and strike up a conversation with Michael. He had wanted to join their group for a while but had felt a little inferior; however, to his relief he found the group friendly and unpretentious.

At first, Gabby found his stares a little disconcerting but soon realised this was 'just Paul' and stopped noticing.

This group of five became best friends at university, each so different yet equally attached to the other.

Elisabeth had graduated as dux of the senior year at Toorak College before coming to Melbourne University. She was a tall girl with long, curly brown hair and intelligent grey eyes. So self-sufficient that unconsciously she scared most of her male counterparts, she didn't need another person to reinforce a belief in self. She actually scoffed at women who looked to a man for security or validation.

There was one topic that she loved to discuss for hours on end, her favourite subject: the law. Elisabeth thrived on all the various forms of legislation, and the rules and disparities in the legal system. She could debate any subject with such knowledge and determination that she made you question your previously firm position. She was definitely a good friend to have on your side if you ever found yourself in a spot of trouble.

Michael was of solid build and had Jewish blood in his veins. He was very astute with finances and had a huge crush on Elisabeth, but secretly believed that a girl with so much to offer would never consider an overweight schmuck like him.

Paul confessed that he wanted to associate with them because he was obsessed with Gabby. Once everyone got to know him, they understood that Paul loved beautiful things. He admired stylish sports cars, beautiful works of art and told her she was God's masterpiece of human art, which made them all laugh.

Tall and dark, he looked a little bit freaky, like a modern version of Dracula, and he was so serious about everything. It was his intensity that others found difficult to appreciate. He didn't seem to be interested in any one girl; he got more excited about a stunning piece of art deco than getting up close and personal with another human being. Paul just loved being a part of this crowd. He was studying cultural history and was an expert on many civilisations around the world. He could tell you about their belief systems, farming practices, architecture – the complete history of any civilisation from the Aztecs to Romans and Vikings. If you queried him, Paul could comprehensively give you a chronicle of any country in the world.

Every night they congregated at the Carlton Cottage. Joe loved having them there. He polished up his culinary skills and looked forward to the rich conversation around his table. The cottage became a second home to all of them, and each treasured this little oasis, a place to relax and express themselves honestly without judgement or ridicule.

Old Joe became a great-uncle of sorts, and his many years of experience provided a wealth of knowledge they were all able to draw from. They could only guess how old he really was. He talked constantly about the world he had lived in, and if their calculations were close, it would make him around ninety years old, which surely was impossible when they considered how active and fit he was.

At times, Gabby felt guilty that her future shone so brightly while Eddie was still locked up behind bars. When she confided these feelings to Old Joe, he told her not to be so foolish.

'Do you think Eddie would be happier if he knew you were miserable and unhappy in the free world? It would only make him feel even worse about his incarceration. Trust me, Gabby, your happiness would be a small light in the darkness that Eddie is enduring; otherwise, his sentence would be even more difficult to bear.'

A small voice in her head had other ideas. *I try to see it this way but deep down I still felt horrible that I'm getting on with my life when my childhood friend is locked up like an animal, because of a terrible mistake after trying to defend my honour.*

In spite of her momentary down times, life in Melbourne was fun. They had pasta-making nights, where the guys kneaded the dough, rolled it out and then put it through the machine. While they worked over the pasta, the girls made the sauce, one vegetarian that Gabby now preferred and another made with meat for the rest of their group.

There was a lot of amusement to balance out the hard work of study. They were young and loved nothing better than socialising and having a few drinks, and as a group they loved going to pubs and listening to live music.

Another group activity was church on Christmas Eve and Good Friday. Paul was a devout Catholic and insisted they all come to church on these two occasions.

Father Gerry was his Irish priest, a big robust man with an accent so strong it was a challenge to understand what he was preaching during his sermons, but his congregation wouldn't have him any other way. He was a man for all seasons, and they all loved him for it.

He would often come over to their house for dinner to sharpen his mind against Old Joe's. These two became great friends, catching up for a coffee during the week to discuss world events.

Many nights were spent around the dining table in lively debate over a range of subjects. From religion to politics, nothing was off limits, and everyone's opinion was respected even if it was contrary to another. Father Gerry kept an open mind and loved to hear what this generation believed, even if sometimes it conflicted with the traditional teachings of his church.

One night he asked Gabby if she believed in God.

This was a complicated and sensitive topic, and she hesitated slightly before responding to his question. The group watched her face take on a thoughtful expression and waited for a response.

'Well, I don't know a lot about God but I do know about angels.'

'Are you serious? Angels?' Ben mused sardonically.

'Yes, Ben. Angels. When I was little, I told everyone my guardian angel was called Jo Jo.' She tried to be serious, but he kept laughing at her.

'Jo Jo, what kind of name was that?' Michael was laughing now too.

'I don't know, but that's how it was. She told me all about angels, where they lived and what they were like.'

'Are you at liberty to share this privileged information with us Philistines?' Ben persisted.

'What would you like to know?' She arched her brows at his challenge.

'Do they have wings? Elisabeth asked.

'Of course they do. Magnificent wings, and they sit high above their shoulders like a butterfly.'

'Okay, I can play this game too.' Michael smiled mischievously. 'Do they all look the same?'

'Their created form is spiritual, more etheric; however, when they choose to reveal themselves, it is in a form that we recognise. But in saying that, they each have a unique identity that sets them apart from each other, even if you may not believe me.' Gabby smiled at the doubtful expressions all around her.

'Tell us more, Gabby,' Father Gerry gently prompted.

'Well, they all have the same massive wings but with different coloured hair and eyes, like us, and the edges of their wings match their hair colour.'

'Are they male or female?' Ben asked her.

'Once again, when they take on a human form, they don't have any, hmmm, sexual features, but they do have the other gender qualities that speak of being attached to either a male or female creed. So amongst themselves they're seen and greeted as a sister or brother, but without having any of those.' She glanced pointedly at Elisabeth's ample breasts and laughed along with everybody else.

'Where do they live?' Paul asked seriously.

'Their home is called the City of Angels or Silver City, and my angel friend said it has golden gates with statues of embracing angels all along the borders of the city walls. I'm not sure why, but I get the feeling you are all laughing at me, so you only get one last question. Anyone got one?' Gabby humoured them all a little bit longer.

'Do they work or just play harps all day?' Michael quizzed.

'They are very busy indeed. Everyone has a job to do, and only those talented enough get to play harps. I think I still have a couple of Jo Jo's feathers if anyone is interested?'

A chorus of voices all declared they wanted to see.

Gabby left the room and soon returned with two exceptionally large feathers resting in the palm of her hand. They were faded slightly yellow with age but the dark edging had everyone fascinated.

Father Gerry said nothing but thoughtfully rubbed his jaw and closed his eyes. Opening them with intent, he turned to Gabby to make his own enquiry. 'So if you believe in angels, you probably also believe there is life after death?'

'Yes.' Gabby interlocked her fingers and leaned forward towards him. 'Which may seem contrary to a scientist who always looks for proof, yet my heart tells me, or maybe it was my angel, that there is definitely another dimension to experience beyond the one we presently dwell in.'

'Or is it just wishful thinking? That life is more than this?' Ben added his own doubts.

The conversation went round and round the table as each of the dinner guests expressed their own version of faith in God and the afterlife.

'What about you, Paul? We all assume you have a strong belief in religion?' Elisabeth asked him.

'Well, as you are all aware, I was brought up Catholic and I have never felt the need to search for another truth. I'm not saying that this is the only path to God and eternal life, but for me it makes perfect sense. The bible only reinforces Gabby's beliefs about angels, maybe not in such graphic detail, but Father Gerry would be the expert on those specific scriptures. For me, all the answers are in the holy book; however, I would never assume that I am right and everyone else is wrong.'

Michael waded into the conversation.

'Okay, guys. Just imagine my upbringing, which as most of you know is Jewish. You can imagine how I was influenced to put a lot of faith in the Old Testament, but not so keen on the message of the New Testament. I ask you, "Who do you believe when there are so many conflicting views around the world on the same deity?" Every culture has its own version of "the truth".' He dropped his head into his arms and shook it in mock despair.

Elisabeth waded into the topic and said her parents were agnostic and had decided that she should make up her own mind once she had grown up.

'Well, Elisabeth, are you grown up enough to have an opinion?' Michael asked cheekily as he raised his head.

'I can't say that I knew my guardian angel like Gabby, and I'm not sure if you have noticed that I am now quite grown up.' She raised her eyebrows in challenge at him. 'However, in spite of my new maturity, I'm not sure if I've worked out the answer to the big questions yet. My mind is of a practical nature, so I am always looking for proof, which doesn't necessarily fit too well with faith. Does our time here count for anything? If this is it and all we have, I would like to think that my life is going to have purpose and do some good. So I guess for now, I will try to remain open and consider all of your views, but I think I like Gabby's story the most, for now anyway. This may change as I become more grown up, particularly if I ever become as grown up as Old Joe.'

Laughter erupted around the table at Elisabeth's reference to just how old Joe could be. He would never tell them his birthday, so they had to suffice with guessing.

'So Joe, what are your thoughts on this heavy subject matter?' Father Gerry thoughtfully voiced what everyone was thinking.

'Well, I have died once already.'

This caused quite a stir around the table as each one expressed their disbelief and surprise. Once the ripple of shock settled, he continued his story.

'It was many years ago. I was quite young then, not yet in my sixties when cancer struck. First in my pancreas, then my liver, and finally it settled into my bones. The doctors knew I was dying, so I went home in the care of a nurse, Jocelyn, a sweet, gentle lady. The disease progressed as diagnosed and eventually death came to ease my pain and suffering.'

'How did if feel? Did you see the light? Did any of your deceased loved ones come to meet you?' The questions fired from everyone at once.

'I do remember that just before I stopped breathing, I began to feel lighter and lighter, as if I was a feather gently lifting and leaving my withered and shrunken body. The pain that had been consuming me lost its grip as I floated up and away. I remember that 'relief' was the overwhelming feeling at that time, being released from the heavy burden of pain.'

'And?' they all cried, captivated by Joe's experience.

'That was it. Light as a feather and no more pain. That is all I remember until I was back in that body.'

'But what happened to the cancer that was killing you?' Michael queried.

'That is the mystery, for when I came back, the cancer was gone, and I made a full recovery. No doctor was able to offer a medical explanation, so I guess it just wasn't my time yet.'

Elisabeth was curious about Jocelyn the nurse.

'What did the nurse do when you suddenly came back from the dead?'

'Poor thing, she almost died of a heart attack.'

They all laughed at the irony of Joe's story.

'So, how long ago are we talking about, Joe? If you were almost sixty then, how old does it make you now?'

'That is for me to know and for you to keep guessing, Michael.' They just laughed, but he didn't intend to shed any light on his age.

Nineteen

The final semester of university arrived, and life in the real world was looming closer, teasing them with its upcoming freedoms and responsibilities. One particular afternoon when Gabby went into the bathroom, she could hear whispering coming from one of the cubicles. It sounded like someone talking to themselves, with bursts of swearing and then a whimpering, sometimes harsh and raspy, then soft and sad.

'I have to do as I'm told. There will be consequences if don't. But I don't want to become like them, not now especially. They will kill her anyway, and whether I do it now or not, she is already dead. Why should I protect her and not myself? What would Rowan do? Rowan, help me. I am lost in the dark and can't decide what is right and wrong anymore.'

The sobbing that came from deep within touched Gabby as she stood there mesmerised by the dialogue, uncertain to intervene but sad for the suffering.

As she moved towards the door of the cubicle, the hair on the back of Gabby's neck stood on end, her stomach began to churn and her heart raced. Wiping her brow, she was surprised at how clammy her skin was.

'Are you alright in there?' She knocked lightly on the door.

Silence greeted her and then a small burst of whimpering seeped out of the space.

'Do you want me to get someone to help you, a counsellor, or maybe I can take you to a doctor or home if you're not feeling well?' Gabby got no response at all, so after a while she reluctantly left the bathroom.

Standing just out of sight, Gabby hovered close by to see who came out.

The only one who came out was Miranda Newton.

Poor Miranda! Was it drugs or a mental illness?

Raking her brain, Gabby tried to think of how she could help but knew that Miranda would only reject any attempts of friendship. She was at a loss at what to do.

That night, she talked to Joe to get his insight and advice. 'What she was saying was nonsensical, but I just don't know why my body had such a physical reaction to the conversation she was conducting with herself.'

Joe replied thoughtfully. 'It's the same reaction when someone tells you a story about a ghost or something of a spiritual nature. The body senses the otherworldly information is not of this dimension and gets uncomfortable about confronting something the mind has decided doesn't exist. I've seen many cultures in my travels, and there is always a belief system in place. It can vary significantly but the underlying message is often the same. There is more out there than we know, more than the eye can see, and only those who seek the truth discover the unseen.'

'That's pretty deep, Joe. I never realised you believed in the layers of dimensions and the spiritual world.'

'I would be a fool not to, Gabby. I wasn't entirely frank when we were discussing the way I died many years ago. There were many experiences when I left my body behind, and to be honest, I still cannot make a great deal of sense of what I saw and heard. Only that I know our journey doesn't end with death.'

From that time onwards, Gabby took special notice of Miranda, noting the dark circles around her eyes, and that she seemed even more introverted than before, never participating in class debates or forums.

Not too long after this encounter, Miranda stopped attending any of their classes, and Gabby politely asked the student council representative if Miranda was still studying at the university.

He said he couldn't divulge personal information about students and suggested she check with her friends; however, to her knowledge Miranda didn't have any friends.

Gabby tried not to dwell on Miranda's problems but couldn't deny the urge to find her and help if she could.

That night she had a vivid dream of Miranda drowning in murky dark water. She was calling out for help, but nobody came.

Joe and Gabby checked the local directory but there was no listing for an M. Newton so they had no address, only her name.

'Maybe I should hire a private investigator? They would know where to look and should be able to find something as simple as an address.'

'If you could, Joe. Maybe I'm overreacting but I can't shake this feeling that something is very wrong.'

'Gabby, you should always trust your instincts. If you can sense trouble, it is surely hovering close by.'

It was at this time that Joe called each friend and made sure they would be at the cottage for dinner that night.

It was a bad night to be out, a stormy summer night, and the rain was lashing the windows as each one arrived under cloaks or umbrellas. They shook the water off and laughed about it raining cats and dogs while they had driven over to Carlton.

After dinner, Joe began to speak. 'I would like to thank you all for coming out on such a wet, windy night. There is something on my mind and in my heart that you all need to know.'

A few worried looks were shared around the table, some fearing bad news from their much-loved elderly friend. Maybe the old man was sick and had bad news to share? This thought was unconsciously going through several minds at once.

'Your time at university is drawing to a close, and I must make my case before you all scatter to the winds following your chosen professions. I see many skills amongst you, that when combined, would make a force to be reckoned with. As such, I have a feeling that your association was not by chance. It is my belief that destiny has handpicked each of you for a reason, and tonight is the best time to explain what I have in mind.'

He intently watched each face around the table and could see he had roused their curiosity, but none interrupted. Each one sat quietly and waited for him to go on.

'I have saved a sum of money for a rainy day,' he began.

Everyone laughed as the wind threw the rain against the window panes with an extra hard gust.

'Gabby and I have already spoken of where we go from here, and we want to start our own environmental agency that tackles issues relating to our time. Climate change, endangered species, and the unrelenting fact that we desperately need to change our disposable society.' Joe had their full attention now.

'The catch is, to be successful, we cannot do this all on our own. We need a group of trusted associates that will work with us every step of the way. A few good men and women who have the skills to run an international organisation, one that has activities in many countries. We need legal advice, financial guidance, a voice that can reach out and touch people with words from the heart, someone who is educated in other cultures, and one who could provide advice on how a country manages their affairs. Do you see how well each of you would fit into this plan?' Everyone nodded, a bit dumbstruck.

'The question I ask you tonight is: What will you make of your life? If you join us, the wage will be minimal, the working hours long and never-ending, and sometimes there will be backlash from the media when they disagree with our moral compass. One thing that is guaranteed is the huge amount of satisfaction that comes with the knowledge that your life has not been frittered away but has been well lived.'

'What say you to my offer?' Joe smiled mischievously at each of the loved faces around the table.

'There is no doubt in my mind that this is meant to be, so you can count me in.' Ben grinned with excitement.

'Me too.' Michael did not hesitate.

'I am honoured that you have considered me worthy to be a part of your mission.' Paul dramatically placed his hand on his heart as he accepted Joe's offer.

'It is obvious that you need one level head operating amongst this sentimental bunch, so I will have to accept, out of necessity it seems.' Elisabeth smiled to take any sting out of her response.

'How do you feel about calling our agency, 'The Greater Good'? These were the first words Gabby had spoken since Joe had put his offer on the table. They all concurred and The Greater Good was born on this wild and stormy night.

Michael and Elisabeth both came from affluent backgrounds. His family worked in business investment and finance, and Elisabeth's parents were both medical practitioners.

The Tisch family expected Michael to follow in their footsteps; however, even though he had inherited the skill and understanding of financial matters from his family genes, his mind now lay with Gabby and Joe. Their offer had sung to his heart, and he had no doubts that this was what he was born to do.

He looked at his mother's proud features and loved her more than he probably could ever explain, and he also knew his father was not going to accept his decision by the stubborn set of his jaw. They were good people, and he didn't want to disappoint them, so Michael put his best arguments forward to explain where his convictions lay. However, both of his parents thought he had been brainwashed by free-thinking radicals from university and demanded he reconsider his decision.

They had no success at all.

'Listen here, son, don't come running to me crying that you don't have a cent to your name. Principles won't feed you and provide for your retirement,' his father shouted angrily at him when he wouldn't change his mind.

'Dad, I'm the one who has to live with the consequences of this decision, and I just don't want to waste my life chasing material gain. We need to start thinking of the environment and what society is going to look like in fifty years' time.'

'Oh, rubbish, Michael. Don't be so naïve! These crazy people have been predicting the end of the world for the last two thousand years and trust me, they will still be spouting the same lies into the next millennia.'

'Dad, I know you believe what you are saying and Heaven knows it may be true, but I don't want to get to the end of my life and ask myself, "What was that all about?" I want to live with purpose and look back and see it all counted for something.'

'You don't need to listen to these hypocrites, Michael! I can tell you what your purpose is: It is to work with your family and be successful.'

'Dad, that is your path but not mine. I am sorry to disappoint you.'

Walking out of the house was one of hardest things he'd ever done. To turn his back on those that he loved was the first sacrifice he was called to make. It hurt, but he still knew that he didn't want to go back, only forwards from now on.

Elisabeth didn't get any opposition from her parents. She put up such a convincing argument they were gratified to see her placing value in her life's work.

They both hugged and kissed her and said how proud they were of their daughter. They expressed an interest in donating a significant amount of money to her new project.

Paul's parents had divorced several years ago, and he hardly ever heard from his father anymore. He had apparently remarried and started a new family and did not make time or effort to see his old one. His mother had worked long hours as a supervisor at a hosiery manufacturer to support Paul and his two sisters, and had even managed to make sure each of them had a university education. Paul was the youngest, and his mother did not put any demands on his choice of career.

'Paul, all I ever wanted was for my children to be happy and have a good career. If you think this is the best option and will be happy then I'm happy too. I am very proud of you, son.' She hugged him close.

'I love you too, Mum, and no matter what happens, I'll look after you.'

Paul secretly thought that the poor woman was just too worn out to even uphold an argument. He loved her dearly and appreciated all the sacrifices she had made for her family. He knew she had done her best so that they could have a better life, and what more could you ask of anyone.

His eldest sister, Deborah, was an accountant, and Sara a lawyer. Both of them had moved overseas to work in London and seemed settled there. But Paul knew he would always be there for his mother. She could count on him to look after her once she retired from her job.

Twenty

Two weeks passed with no word about Miranda Newton. During this time, Gabby was kept busy with the other associates as there was much to do in establishing The Greater Good society.

Finally, Joe got a report from the private investigator with an address for Miranda. It was an old house inherited from her grandmother.

The house was situated in North Melbourne, not that far from where Old Joe and Gabby had lived for the last few years, and she could have walked there in about twenty minutes. The next day, Gabby went to see her. She parked the car in front of Miranda's house and opened the gate. It was an old white house that looked abandoned. The paint was peeling off the walls, and the garden had long given up any pretence of looking orderly. The grass had grown so long it brushed higher than her knees. Knocking on the front door, she listened for any movement inside the small house, and after a while, Gabby called out.

'Miranda, are you home?' But once again there was no response. As she walked back down the path to the gate, the hair on the back of her neck stood up, and she quickly turned around to see the curtain drop back into place.

So Miranda was in there but refused to see her. It was really hard to keep walking away. All of her instincts were urging her to go back and grab that poor girl and get her out of there. With a heavy and troubled heart, Gabby asked herself how she could break down these barriers and see Miranda. She only wanted to talk to her and make sure she wasn't going to hurt herself.

To show how much she cared, Gabby began to drop in to Miranda's house every day at random times, hoping she could wear down Miranda's refusal to see her. Even after two weeks of no response, Gabby still kept calling, until the afternoon when that wall came crashing down.

It was a hot Wednesday afternoon in late January. Melbourne was in the middle of a heatwave with temperatures soaring to forty degrees.

Inside, Miranda sat dispiritedly at her grandmother's antique dressing table and stared at the fuzzy, distorted image looking back at her. The face she saw looked tired and drawn, even without the sharp resolution of modern glass, and in the reflection she noted that the sores were getting worse. As soon as *he'd* arrived, her skin had begun to crawl and burn with a belligerent itch.

Her nails ripped away the skin until the weeping sores covered her face, arms and legs. Infection was spreading, and fevers made her feel either stifling hot or freezing cold. Looking again at that haunted face in the mirror, her thoughts strayed to the ever-present question: Would it hurt to die?

Obviously, death was a natural process, but how did it really feel? Was it painful? Was there any life after death? Did you feel your spirit leave or was there just nothing but emptiness as the opposite to the fullness of life?

Rowan, I wish you could come back to tell me what is going to happen.

Rubbing her hands over her face, which smeared blood across her cheeks, she thought back to the time when her life changed. In fifth grade, a traffic accident had killed both her parents, and if she closed her eyes, she could still see the school principal's mouth saying the words that refused to sink in. His voice sounded warped and distant as her young mind tried to come to grips with this news. Her beautiful mother and fun-loving father were gone, forever gone. There was no time to say goodbye or hug them one more time.

Miranda resembled her Chilean mother, with the same long black hair and golden eyes. Before the accident, they had lived a big life, and their home was happy and filled with friends, loud in conversation with spicy food and salsa dancing. This was in stark contrast to the quiet, conservative home Rupert Newton had grown up in, so like a moth to a flame, he was captivated by Katarina's exuberance, and such opposites found a love that was the envy of many.

To leave this vibrant, happy environment and move in with Gran was like taking an exotic orchid out of its habitat and trying to replant it in the desert. She had withered away without her parents' love and affection to a quiet, lonely little girl, one who longed to have a family of her own. To have sisters to argue with and brothers to play rough and tumble. Instead, she learned to look after her ailing grandmother, standing on a chair to cook them a simple dinner, mostly eggs or beans on toast, but her palate longed for hot empanada's while her body forgot how to dance.

During her studies at university, Miranda met Rowan at church, not a traditional place of worship, but an eclectic group of people seeking another path to enlightenment, one that would change their lives forever, even tragically. Rowan was zealous about his beliefs, and it was this emotion that attracted Miranda. His strong feelings filled the void within her.

From the first kiss, Miranda's world righted itself. Rowan was the missing piece, and now she had her own special person. There was purpose in her step and a new sparkle in her eyes as he taught her the true power of love, and the gift of pleasure was bestowed upon each other. Laughter bubbled up spontaneously as happiness filled all the empty spaces.

However, this could not last, for the same passion and zealousness that initially attracted her would bring about his demise, and the thought of Rowan's death brought her face to face once again with her own. She didn't consciously feel frightened to die, just a little scared of the process of getting from life to the state of death.

In some ways, Miranda just wished he would finish what he had started. The waiting and the itching were driving her mad; let him just get it over and done with.

Then she heard the growling dogs.

Gabby had Ben's Ute so she had taken the dogs for a drive to cool them down. It was so hot that Gabby dropped by Miranda's in a pair of denim shorts, a brightly striped singlet and some open sandals.

The dogs began snarling as soon as they walked through the gate. The hair on their backs stood straight up, and their ears flattened against their heads.

They drew back their lips to reveal long, sharp canine teeth.

Gabby reached out to touch Samson, who was closer, and used her mind to calm them. She had no idea how she was able to use telepathy with the animals like this, but for some reason it seemed as natural to her as breathing.

'Steady boys,' she soothed them. They positioned themselves on each side of her as she stood at the dark green front door and knocked.

'Hello. Miranda?'

The door was flung open so suddenly that Gabby stumbled backwards, reeling with surprise as she looked at the tall, brown-haired man standing against the gloom. The dogs immediately crouched forward, hackles standing high, muscles quivering and ready to launch.

Before a word was spoken between them, the stranger raised his arm and Samson was thrown down the steps, knocking Gabby sideways as he flew past her. Goliath howled with rage over the treatment of his brother and threw himself at the man. Such a huge beast should have knocked the man off his feet but just as Gabby staggered upright, she saw Goliath go over her shoulder and skid through the long grass.

The man in black snarled, 'Call off your dogs before I kill them both. They can't help you now.'

Rushing back to the front yard, she checked the dogs. Samson couldn't stand on his front leg, and Gabby thought it looked broken. Goliath was crouched and ready to fight again; he wasn't going to give up on her or Samson.

She immediately reprimanded him mind-to-mind. 'No, Goliath. Stand down.'

Whining at her in confusion, his instincts girded him to protect her, even to the death if need be.

'No Goliath. I said stand down.' In her panic, she spoke harshly to him.

Reluctantly, he went to crouch beside Samson, growling at the stranger at the top of the stairs.

'Very good, Gabrielle. I could hear you send that message. You are growing up,' the stranger said.

'Who are you and where is Miranda?' she turned and demanded.

The stranger crowed. 'Miranda is being punished for her disobedience. Please come in and let's see how much you want to help your poor little friend.'

So many thoughts were going through Gabby's mind. *Who was he? How did he know her name? Most importantly, what did he plan to do now?*

When she looked back at her two friends in the front yard, she couldn't believe how quickly he had disposed of her strong protectors.

God help us now.

Praying to her angel, she took one step at a time walking to this stranger. With her heart pounding so hard that it felt like it planned to leap out of her chest and run away, she desperately wanted to get her dogs into Ben's car and get out of here. But if Miranda was somewhere in this house, she needed to help her. Gabby couldn't turn away now, she had to see this through to the end.

As she entered the house, the first two things she noticed was the dark interior and the stale air, along with the smell of death that made her gag. The next impression was the temperature. It was so cold compared to the hot day outside.

'Miranda, are you okay?' she shouted, looking out for a sign that her rescue wasn't in vain.

'Gabby, you shouldn't have come here,' Miranda whispered hoarsely as her face peeked around the corner of a bedroom.

Gabby tried to hide how shocked she was at her appearance. Miranda's hair was unwashed and awry, and her dirty face was streaked with tears and blood. Much thinner than last year, she seemed about to collapse as she held on to the doorframe, and there were dreadful oozing sores all over her face, arms and legs. One had burst on her lip, and it trickled yellow pus over her tiny pointed chin.

'It's going to be alright, Miranda.' In spite of the obvious, Gabby still tried to comfort her.

The stranger moved across the small living room to sit on the sagging old couch and motioned for her to sit opposite him. Miranda started sobbing and shaking her head at Gabby, desperately trying to warn her to get out of here before it was too late.

'Go back to your room, Miranda. I will deal with you soon enough,' he whispered menacingly, and she scuttled back to her bedroom.

Poor Gabrielle, now he has her as a prisoner too. I tried to avoid her but she was persistent and wouldn't listen. If only she'd lost interest in me and let darkness take my soul.

Unable to stop him, Miranda sat on the side of her bed and let the tears fall. She couldn't stop shaking with fear and loathing. Knowing what this monster was capable of, it would be her fault that an innocent person got murdered here today.

She sat holding her head between her hands and rocked backwards and forwards in misery.

In the living room, Gabby gingerly sat down and began to shake. There were goosebumps breaking out all over her skin from the temperature and shock. She couldn't stop thinking,

Please don't let this be another rape. I can't survive that again.

Staring at the man opposite her, she tried not to show how terrified she felt inside.

'You see, Gabrielle Harrison. Oh, don't look so surprised. I know all about you, far more than you could imagine. You have no idea, do you? So cruel that they left you here defenceless. How your old comrades must cringe at the notion.'

'Stop talking in riddles,' Gabby's voice hissed in frustration. 'Comrades and nonsense. Tell me who are you and what you want with us.'

'Don't get anxious now. It will all be explained in good time. Your little friend Miranda was assigned a task last year, but somehow you appealed to her conscience and she refused our commands.'

'More riddles.'

'She was meant to dispose of you. Permanently.'

'Why would anyone want to do that!' Gabby clasped her hands tighter to disguise how much they were trembling.

'Among other things, your presence here is forbidden,' he sneered. 'It would probably also surprise you that Miranda was not the first person who has worked for our cause.' Gabby just stared at him, her mind uncomprehending what he was saying.

'Have you ever wondered why Andy Bolton hated you so much? His whole life, he harboured such malice towards you without even knowing why. We fed it and kept it going until he was old enough to act. He was commanded to leave you damaged but still alive. Andy was born with a susceptibility towards cruelty, so it wasn't difficult to corrupt his soul.' Gabby shrank back into the couch in horror.

'Then your friend 'Old Joe' finished him off, with his magic tricks. Gabrielle Harrison, don't you see these attacks are not random? They won't stop until you leave this realm and return to face the retribution that is surely awaiting you in the Silver City.'

Gabby's mind was moving too fast. There were so many questions. What did he mean Old Joe finished Andy off? And that Miranda had been told to murder her but refused? Why? And Silver City, what on earth was the stranger ranting about?

The stranger smiled with such smug assurance.

'Gabrielle, I can enter your mind and can control your every thought, your every sensation. You will experience my powers first hand and realise that it is useless to fight your fate today.'

She could not take her eyes off those thin lips as a feeling began to wash over her, from the top of her head through to soles of her feet.

Such an exquisite awareness started deep in the pit of her stomach, the pressure increasing to the point of no return. Blood bubbled through her veins, making her feel hot all over, and her hands went to grasp her crotch to stop the sensations, but she couldn't do anything but get swept along. She was out of control, riding a wave higher and higher towards something unknown and frightening. She begged him to stop, knowing this was wrong but unable to fight the sensations.

Then finally when she thought she couldn't bear such ecstasy any longer, her whole body shuddered over and over again, and her gasping breaths filled the room as she tried to understand what had just happened. Her mind was distracted and unfocussed and would not function in a rational fashion. It had almost shut down, floating along on a sea of pleasure.

'Look at you, those celestial eyes have opened wide with wonder that your body could ever feel so good. That was an orgasm, dear child. Good, isn't it? A shame young Andy didn't take the time to give you some pleasure when he took you, but he was just a boy after all and in such a hurry. You know they really don't have much idea. He just rushed in and made a mess of you.'

Any response was beyond Gabby. She was now lying on the couch in a dazed stupor, and her limbs felt soft and dislocated.

The stranger laughed at her glassy eyes. 'Now let's explore the opposite to pleasure. Pain is actually the element I excel in.'

With the same sudden onslaught, Gabby began to scream in agony. Every one of her muscles tightened to the point of snapping, going from relaxed to as tight as a bow. She rolled off the couch onto the floor, trying to break his hold on her but it made no difference. If anything, the intensity only increased, and she threw back her head and clenched her teeth so tightly she could hear them grinding. Her body was tightened past the point of no return. It was arched like a distorted rainbow, putting so much strain on her spine that it must surely snap from the pressure.

'Please, please stop,' she begged him through clenched teeth.

The dogs were howling at the front door. Goliath threw himself again and again against the timber. As if from far away, she heard the wood tremble and begin to split but it held its place, keeping them out, stopping them from saving her.

The vessels burst in Gabby's eyes and welled tears of blood. Her tongue split so blood seeped out of the corner of her mouth, and sweat poured off in great rivulets until her clothes clung to her wet skin. A painful force was taking over her body, like an intruder pushing a door against her mind. And no matter how hard she pushed back, it kept creeping open until it felt like *she* was about to burst open from this trespasser. It was a dark shadow, malevolent to the core and about to steal her life away.

Moments later, her mind and soul felt disorientated and began to disconnect from her body.

Gabby knew she was close to shutting down. She could feel each beat of her heart, squeezing tighter and tighter and slowly losing its rhythm.

The stranger felt her mind shutting down and smiled at his own cleverness.

'Soon the shackles of man shall fall away, and you can leave a world that you never belonged in.'

For some reason, those gloating words made her burn with anger. A fire began to smoulder in her belly, and suddenly she was no longer the victim. Her strength grew like a vine, sinuously sweeping through her veins until she slammed the door to her mind in his face.

A power, a combustible force, was rising like water in a well. Her feet burned, her legs burned, her torso burned, her arms burned, and then her mind was on fire. It was exhilarating to be a passenger on this rush of light that was so blindingly bright it devoured her being.

His eyes squinted in surprise at her expression as she rose from the couch, and he took a step back to move away from it. Stalking like a cat, the hunter became the hunted. Stepping forward quickly, she caught hold of his throat and somehow it was easy to lift him high and squeeze the life out of him. Hands clawing at his throat, he tried to dislodge her grip until a small puff of grey smoke huffed out of his mouth. The tighter she clenched, the more the smoke drifted out of his nostrils, which ignited a flame across his face. Gabby held tight as his eyes melted away.

Before the fire could spread across his body, he began to shimmer and lighten in her grip. Suddenly, as real as he appeared, he was gone. Only the smell of smoke and burned flesh told them the experience hadn't been conjured.

'Oh my God! Gabby, what just happened?' Miranda screamed as she rushed into the room.

'Come here, Miranda. Stay close to me.' Gabby tried to reassure her as she sank to the floor.

'You killed him?' Miranda was too frightened to hope.

'I think so.' Gabby's voice had lost its authority and sounded small and squeaky.

'How did you do that to him?'

'I don't know?' she whispered.

'Who are you, Gabby?'

'I don't know,' she whispered, even softer.

In what seemed only an instant, Josiel was suddenly not alone. This time, Gadriel didn't wait to get sanction for his flight. Instead, he made the journey through the portal as soon as he felt Gabby draw on her divine powers. His friends needed him.

On this day, in this moment of time, they stood together and considered the tragic scene before them. Gadriel was not only worried about Fallon, but now knew that Josiel's actions to support Fallon would be considered traitorous to their ethos.

Fallon was living as a human but had destroyed an enemy with supernatural force. It was as bad at Puriel had predicted it would be. What if her actions tore apart the veil and their unseen world became known to those who were oblivious to their presence? What if they knew how often the celestials walked by their side, not only in their dreams?

Gabby and Miranda lay entwined on the floor where the acrid smell of smoke still lingered in the air. Gadriel paced around them, unseen but definitely unsettled. He turned to Josiel in consternation at this current quandary.

'Josiel, what have you done! We were supposed to keep a low profile and not draw attention from the council.' Gadriel's brow furrowed as he sought answers from his trusted friend.

'What did I do? I did the right thing, Gadriel! That evil monster was destroying her, making her own body turn on itself, and I wasn't going to stand by and let her die.' Josiel's aura flashed red with defiance.

'Fallon has been dying from the moment she became human, and as Gabby is not immortal, the time she dies is irrelevant.'

But Josiel was resolute. 'Not today, and not like this. She doesn't deserve this kind of death.'

'Tell me what death is good then, as it's always a parting of what they know and a step into the unknown,' he argued.

'This angel-child doesn't deserve such a violent and helpless end to her existence.' Josiel begged for his absolution and understanding.

Gadriel grabbed her arms, trying to make her understand the gravity of what she'd done. 'This empathy, this compassion of yours, has caused a great commotion in the City of Angels. The council is demanding you be arrested and brought before them for violating their orders. There will be punishment wreaked upon you for what you've done today. You may be imprisoned or at the very least could have your access to the realm of men revoked.'

Josiel pulled away from Gadriel's grasp and paced in agitation. 'I no longer care about the council and their apathy; they strut around full of importance yet do nothing. I have served and scouted for them over a millennium, and since I have witnessed Gabby's life, I don't understand why we stand aside and let Lucifer and his demons get away with murder. Why should mankind suffer because of our fallen brothers and sisters? These demons keep violating the treaty over and over again. Do we not have the power to stop them? Instead, we keep watching, listening – but doing nothing. Fallon used to at least rescue humans from their demonic clutches. What do we do? It's not good enough that we are scouts for information, in the hope of keeping them out of the Silver City. Look at what they're doing in this realm! Enough is enough!'

'Your words sound traitorous, Josiel, and you know what happened the last time our kind rebelled. I fear you've become too involved with this human version of Fallon.' Gadriel's eyes shone with concern.

'Yes, most likely. Before that, I didn't see the pain or feel the suffering that our fallen comrades inflict on so many, day after day, and year after year. Now I want our leaders to intervene and protect the sons of man from Lucifer and his hosts!'

'You sound so much like Fallon. She also chafed at the lack of action from our leaders.' Gadriel's mind was racing with notions about what to do next.

'I know she did, and I was always the one counselling her to be patient and trust the wisdom of the council. However, now I see the world from her viewpoint. Now I agree that we don't do enough.' Josiel's contempt was evident.

'How did Gabby know she had such power at her disposal?' Gadriel took hold of Josiel's shoulder to stop her moving and turned her to face him.

Josiel pulled away from his hold and crouched down close to Gabby, wishing she could stay but knowing she would soon have to go, and probably for good this time. 'I made her angry, so angry that an inferno built up within her. It became a power that could not be contained, until it burst out of her and consumed that vile agent.' Her countenance lifted with pleasure at the memory.

'Did you consider the consequences of this decision? Do you understand you may no longer be able to provide her with any more protection?' he warned.

Standing again and facing Gadriel, she saw the conflict in his eyes. Josiel knew he was torn between protecting his friends and following orders. 'There wouldn't have been any further protection needed if Gabby had died,' she countered his reasoning, clasping his arm to make him listen. 'In fact, I have to confess to you that it actually felt good to push evil back a step, instead of us always retreating. You must understand, Gadriel, that I did it not only for Fallon but for the greater good.'

'Well, it's only reinforced the initial opposition we had to leave Fallon to live this life on her own. Now those who objected in the beginning have raised their voices so loud the disturbance has reached the council. You can't go home, Josiel, because the same wise leaders who relied on your intel are now head-hunting you instead.' Gadriel's aura was intensifying as he spoke.

Josiel turned away and sighed with resignation, knowing there would be dire consequences for her actions this day. 'There is nowhere to hide, not in any realm, so I may as well go back to face the consequences of saving Gabby's life.' Josiel looked sadly at the sleeping women, knowing she would miss this person Fallon had become.

'No, you can't go back, Josiel. You of all messengers would know there are many places where you could conceal yourself. You have been a scout for aeons and know every corner of this realm, the surface and below.' Gadriel prompted her to think of a safe sanctuary. 'At least until the commotion has settled and the council can see clearly that this is not the disaster they all believe it to be. Think, Josiel, where is a place no one would think to search for you, somewhere safe from our kind and the fallen angels?'

'The best place to hide is actually within sight, Gadriel. The most invisible place is usually right in front of you.' Josiel looked around the gloomy room as if she was imagining a hiding place, until an idea began for form, an ideal place to be invisible. Turning to Gadriel she pitched the concept. 'Maybe I could stay within the Vatican in Rome as nobody would imagine I would be bold enough to hide within sight of all who do not really see.'

Smiling at her ingenuity, he agreed it just may work. 'I understand your reasoning. The best place to conceal yourself is in the least expected. It is also for the best that it's on the other side of this world, as messengers will expect you to stay close to Fallon.' Gadriel placed his arm around Josiel to soften the blow of what he was about to say.

'Dear sister, you must accept that your time of watching out for Fallon is over, at least for her foreseeable future.'

'At least now she has a future.' Josiel looked up at him as she crouched down again beside Gabby and Miranda. They were both oblivious to her presence, so Josiel took a moment to commit to memory the features of her much-loved sister, to hoard this small treasure for the time to come.

'How long do I need to stay invisible within the Holy City,' she asked Gadriel before they parted ways.

'As long as it takes, Josiel,' he warned her.

Becoming conscious again, Gabby held Miranda tightly against her chest. But she was now so weak that she couldn't even muster the strength to move. The dogs were whining at the door and scratching the timber to get inside. So much pain, every part of her body felt crushed and broken. They remained there motionless, wrapped up in each other's arms until Gabby recovered enough to grab Miranda's shoulder and weakly shake her.

'Miranda, we have to get Joe and Ben to come and help us. Do you have a phone?' Miranda shook her head.

There was a phone in Gabby's bag in the car, but she couldn't even crawl down the stairs and out to the car.

Samson and Goliath still whimpered at the front door. They could feel Gabby's pain and wanted to get into the house.

Gabby reached out and touched Goliath's mind. 'Samson, stay! Goliath, go home and bring Joe.'

Barking in response, she heard his claws clicking down the steps as he ran away. Slumping back down on the floor, she could hear Samson still whining at the door.

They must have fallen into a state of semi-consciousness until a car screeching to a halt out the front of the house stirred them. Gabby could hear voices calling out as they tried to break into the house amongst a lot of frenzied barking.

Ben and Joe threw their weight against the door, and after several attempts, it crashed inwards.

Miranda got up from the floor and crawled nervously to the other end of the couch, distancing herself from Gabby's bloody, broken body. She didn't know how these men were going to react to the state they were in.

'What have you done to her!' Ben yelled as he kneeled beside Gabby's prone form.

Opening one bloody green eye, she whispered, 'Miranda is hurt too. Ben, please get us to a hospital.'

Old Joe sniffed and pulled a face at the smell, smoke mixed with a residue of evil that still lingered in the air. His mind was still playing catch-up, trying to work out what could have happened. It was like a war zone, but with no obvious enemy in sight. He examined Gabby's body and couldn't believe the damage inflicted. There was blood trickling from her eyes, ears and nostrils. Pools of blood sat beneath the skin all over her body. She was haemorrhaging everywhere.

'Gabby, what on earth happened here today?' He cradled her in his arms.

'Later, Joe, later,' she slurred, and slipped back into the softness of oblivion

An ambulance was called and the two male officers didn't waste a moment to put Gabby and Miranda into the vehicle and sped off to the hospital with the siren wailing. Joe went with them. Ben agreed to meet Joe at the hospital then did his best to make Samson comfortable in the back of the Ute. The dogs were too big to squeeze into the cab with him. Driving carefully so that they wouldn't slide around, he took Samson to a veterinarian to get treatment for his injured leg.

Once the girls were admitted to emergency, it was obvious that Gabby was in a critical condition.

'The next twenty-four hours will be the most dangerous.' The doctor told Joe to call her family just in case. After they had completed all the scans and X-rays, he was able to sit in her room while the intravenous catheter slowly dripped fluid into her traumatised body.

Watching her slow breathing, he was glad that she remained unconscious while her body healed. He couldn't believe he had failed her again.

Twenty-one

Ben's mind was racing as he drove the dogs to the veterinarian. Who could have hurt Gabby and the Titans so badly? Were there several assailants that escaped from the back of the house? None of it made sense to him.

Ben had to ask the vet to help him get Samson from the Ute to the examination room, and as they staggered under the weight of the huge dog, he explained that Gabby and Samson had been in an accident.

The X-ray revealed a decisive break in Samson's radius and ulna bones in his front leg.

'I'll have to operate and pin both bones so that he can carry his weight and move without a limp,' Jack, the vet, explained.

'Do whatever you have to, Jack, to make him new again.' Ben authorised the procedure while he took Samson's big head in his hands and whispered 'thank you' for putting his life on the line for Gabby.

The vet offered to keep both of the dogs at the surgery until Ben was able to collect Goliath.

'Thanks, Jack. We'd really appreciate that.' Giving both dogs a final pat, he raced to the hospital and sat with Old Joe in a vigil beside Gabby's bed.

Joe had called Kathleen and Frank and did his best to explain how Gabby had been hurt. It was difficult for he really had no idea what had transpired. All he could do was ask them to come as soon as they could get flights.

There were so many questions running through their minds. Who the hell had done this to Gabby and Miranda?

At some time during the night, Joe went to Miranda's room, which was on another level. He wanted to check on her well-being and see if she could answer some questions.

The doctor had diagnosed a blood infection and dehydration, so they administered antibiotics and fluids by an intravenous line. Her lesions had been treated and were no longer weeping fluid, and Joe was relieved to see Miranda open her bleary eyes when he sat on the side of her bed.

'Miranda, can you talk?' Joe asked.

Miranda nodded her head and waited for him to begin.

'Who did this to Gabby?'

'There was a man at my house today when she called to check in on me. He is a cult master, and he came to punish me.'

'Punish you for what?' Joe pressed for more information from her sluggish mind.

'It's a long story, but Gabby became a victim of his as well. He used his mind to hurt her.'

'How can a mind hurt you, Miranda?'

'By entering your mind, he can destroy your body from the inside, and that is what he did to Gabby today.'

'Where is he now?'

'Somehow, she destroyed him. I am not sure exactly what happened but there was a struggle and then he was gone. All I know is that my life would be over now if she hadn't called in to my house, and I don't even know why she cares about me. I'm not her friend. Nobody else would take an interest in someone like me. Most people would just say it was my fault for getting into something that I couldn't handle.'

Miranda started crying again, and Joe took her hand to offer some comfort.

'Gabby has been worrying about you for a while. She sensed you may be in trouble and didn't hesitate to help. That's just who she is.'

'I don't deserve her concern.' Miranda sniffled as her nose began to run.

'You had better rest up and get strong again so that you can be the same kind of friend to Gabby once she gets better.'

'Do you think she's going to pull through?' Miranda asked him tearfully.

'Yes, I believe she will come back to us. She has to, and her first thought will be of you, Miranda. I can assure you that it will provide an enormous amount of joy that she got there in time to save you.'

Miranda smiled her thanks then her eyes closed in exhaustion.

Joe went back to Gabby's room and explained to Ben as best he could what the girls had suffered that afternoon.

Ben asked a lot of questions about the man who had initiated this assault on Gabby, and Joe told him as much as he knew, but there was no earthly explanation for such an outcome. The assailant had supposedly caught on fire but there was no body or evidence of such.

Joe tried to explain what he knew about astral travel and how you could leave the body and project your being long distances away. But even in all his long years of life, he had never heard of such force from an out-of-body experience. How did this unknown person inflict such suffering?

Old Joe knew there were many unexplained mysteries in life. Free will granted mankind a banquet of choices, some good and some definitely bad. Usually, it was balanced, but sometimes in history the equilibrium got disturbed and this had cataclysmic consequences. The holocaust was a prime example of mankind embracing evil.

Ben got a call from Frank Harrison to advise him of their arrival time, so Michael was organised to collect them from the airport the next morning.

The hours passed with the monotony of a dripping tap. Old Joe and Ben dared not close their eyes in case Gabby regained consciousness. They trudged a path from the room to the coffee vending machine, hoping caffeine would keep them awake. To fill the time, they spoke of many things, the concerns of the present and hopes for the future.

The morning brought no change and while Joe's face looked even more wrinkled, it was Ben who looked worse for wear.

'Find a bed, Ben, and get some sleep. I promise to wake you if anything happens.'

The nurse kindly found him one in a quiet corner of the ward and he was asleep as soon as his head settled onto the pillow.

Old Joe remained at Gabby's side, talking quietly of all the things they had done together and making plans for the future. His eyes closed with tiredness, and the emotional strain etched deep into his creased face, yet still he refused to accept that Gabby might die. The doctors came around to check on her and advised that nothing much had changed. They kept her sedated with intravenous antibiotics and anti-inflammatory medications to assist with her recovery.

The next morning, Miranda was released with oral medication and joined the two men. She sat in the corner of Gabby's room on the floor and dropped her head onto her drawn-up knees. The nurses had re-dressed all of her wounds on her face and arms.

Ben woke and went outside to check the messages on his mobile and answered the worried calls from their friends. He was very sketchy on details as he had difficulty explaining what had actually happened. He reassured everyone that as soon as there was any change, he would let them know.

When he got back to the hospital room, he found two police officers asking Miranda questions about the assault. There wasn't any rational explanation for their attack. How could they understand the supernatural if they had never experienced this or another dimension? In the end, all she could do was to give a description of a home invader who had attacked both of them. She already knew they wouldn't find anything. The occult had ways to avoid any penalties with the law, but at the moment she was too worried about Gabby to care.

Miranda settled back into the corner. Ben offered the chair but she shook her head and dropped back into the same position.

Time passed by as sluggishly as the Ganges River and only rippled with disturbance when Gabby's parents arrived before lunch. Kathleen cried out with shock when she saw all the bruises under Gabby's skin. Frank pulled up a chair beside the bed and gently pressed his face into her side, and they could see his shoulders shake as he sobbed quietly.

'Oh, my poor girl, not again,' Kathleen whimpered over and over again as she took Old Joe's place and wrapped both of her hands around Gabby's pale white hand.

Ben noticed Miranda slip out of the room and joined her at the coffee machine.

Miranda turned her dark, tortured eyes to Ben.

'This is my fault. If she hadn't tried to save me, she wouldn't be here.'

He felt a little bit more empathetic towards her when he saw how genuine her remorse was. Placing his arm around her shoulder, he led her across to sit on some plastic corridor chairs to offer comfort. After a while, Old Joe joined them. He wanted to give Frank and Kathleen some time alone with their daughter.

The three sat there quietly talking for several hours. Old Joe questioned Miranda some more about her Satanic church, like who was the leader and where did they meet?

Miranda explained the rituals they practiced to worship Satan and told Joe the location always changed so that they left no traces for anyone to follow their secret activities.

Ben interrupted. 'Why in God's name did you want to join a Satanic cult?'

'Rowan and I were finding it hard to fit in, and these people gave us a place to belong and a sense of purpose. They didn't judge us like other religious institutions.' Miranda tried to justify the decision.

'Where's Rowan now?'

'He's dead; they killed him.' Miranda bluntly dropped the bombshell.

'Bloody hell,' was all Ben said as he shook his head in disbelief.

Old Joe just watched and listened.

Eventually Miranda's head settled against Ben's shoulder, and she fell into unsettled slumber. Equally exhausted, he leaned back against the wall and let his eyes rest in a little doze. Even Old Joe slipped into an uneasy sleep.

Still unconscious, Gabby dreamed.

In this dream she was transported to a place so foreign and yet so familiar. Standing under an enormous tree, she looked up in wonder at the reach of its branches and how far the canopy spread across the land where it stood.

Surely this must be the oldest tree in the world, she thought to herself, with its vast trunk and the network of roots entwined around the base. It looked ancient, like it had been there since the beginning of time.

Her exhausted mind tried to remember where she had seen this tree, where she had held the red star-shaped leaves. It was there at the edge of her consciousness yet slipped away each time she tried to grasp the elusive truth.

As she stood there marvelling at the sight and searching her mind for the tenuous memory, a thrum began to reverberate in her being. Turning her head to the side, Gabby tried to determine where the vibration was coming from, until it dawned on her that the tree had a heart not unlike her own. It too had blood pulsing through its leafy veins, and somehow her own heart adjusted to beat in rhythm with this strange phenomenon.

Entranced by this revelation, Gabby took one small step, then another, until she reached out to touch the mighty tree. Looking at her hand, she was shocked to see it so bruised, so discoloured, black with blood pooling under her skin, and her body felt heavy with pain. Even her heart felt heavy, and each beat felt more strenuous than the last.

How on earth did she sustain such injuries, and who could have inflicted so much pain? In this dreamlike state, she had no recollection of what had happened or how she had stumbled into this dream.

'Come closer, Fallon, my dear friend,' the tree seemed to whisper. 'Come closer so that I may take away your pain.' Why was the tree calling her Fallon? Her mind reached out to grasp the significance of the name, as it was hauntingly familiar, but the meaning remained just beyond her grasp.

When her hand made contact with the tree, a warm flush of red light began to move up her arm and into her chest to embrace her weary heart.

Staggering from the force flowing out of the tree and into her body, she stumbled until her legs could hardly hold her up. Moving closer, she leaned all of her weight against the trunk and pressed her face into the gnarly bark.

Slowly but surely, the pooled blood from her injuries began to disperse as the tree's strength flowed through her. The pain was also being taken in by the tree, as crazy as it sounded. The tree was taking her suffering and replacing it with its own power.

As her body drew away from death and advanced towards life, Gabby kept whispering 'thank you' over and over again as the Blood Tree healed her body and renewed her strength.

Everyone woke with a start when Kathleen shook Old Joe awake.

'Come quickly, Joe. Gabby has woken up.' They all leaped up with excitement and rushed back to her room to find Gabby lying there with her beautiful eyes open and gazing around the room.

Frank had tears of joy, and he kept squeezing her hand and stroking her hair off her forehead.

Ben's eyes brimmed with tears when he saw that she had turned the corner.

Kathleen stood at the back of the room with a huge smile beaming across her face. Old Joe, Ben and Miranda gathered around her bed, and everyone began talking at once.

Gabby just smiled and shook her head as her eyes drifted closed again. They all hushed as the nurse came in to check her pulse and blood pressure. After this, she spoke to Gabby's parents and said her return to consciousness was a good sign. They would page the doctor to let him know. Gabby slept the remainder of the night, and in the morning the doctors asked the nurses to take her off the intravenous drip.

Gabby was awake and was ready to answer all of her doctor's questions with a clear mind and articulate all the correct responses. She told him she still felt exceptionally tired and sore but otherwise there was no severe pain. A dream about a giant tree flitted across her consciousness, but as quickly as it arose, it disappeared.

The medical staff told everyone that they still had to run some tests but felt that her prognosis had improved dramatically, and if their patient continued this way, they could expect to send her home in a couple of days.

Old Joe finally went home to get some sleep, and he took Frank and Kathleen with him. Ben offered to give Miranda a ride home but she couldn't return to her grandmother's old house. Instead, she slept on the couch in his apartment. He had promised Gabby he would go and check on Samson and Goliath the next morning to make sure they were also recovering.

After lunch, Elisabeth, Paul and Michael took over the bedside vigil while the others were off catching up on sleep time. Although they were shocked at Gabby's appearance, they put on a brave face and pretended nothing was amiss.

Gabby didn't want to talk about what happened until she could fill in the missing pieces with Miranda. She just told them that both she and Miranda had been assaulted and would explain when she had more information.

'We have been worried sick about you, Gabrielle. Please be more careful in future. If anything happened to you—' Paul didn't elaborate but grasped her hands tightly in his.

Elisabeth's brave face slipped as soon as they got out into the hallway, when she turned to Michael and burst into tears. Michael wrapped his arms around to hold her close, murmuring words of comfort. It felt good to have her in his arms but he wished for another excuse to hold her close.

There was another visitor late that night when all her friends and family had gone home. Gabby opened her eyes to regard a middle-aged female doctor sitting at her bedside. With thick dark hair and streaks of grey framing her intelligent, caring eyes, she seemed vaguely familiar.

'Hello, Gabrielle. How are you feeling now?'

'Much better, thank you. Are you looking after me now?' she queried.

'No. My name is Dr Scarlett Jones.'

'Why are you here if you're not my treating doctor?'

'I had to see if you remembered me?'

'No, I'm sorry. I don't think we've met before.'

'Oh, but we have,' the strange yet familiar woman replied.

'When I saw your face, it took me back many years. However, I wasn't sure until I looked into your eyes, for that is my strongest memory of our first meeting.'

'I think you're mistaken as I feel fairly certain we haven't met before,' Gabby insisted, while something stirred in the depths of her mind.

'Oh, but I am quite sure you are the one who saved me. Let me take you back to that day.' Gabby stared at her in confusion.

'Just when I was about to complete my medical degree, I was abducted and assaulted by a monster who consumed my flesh as I bled to death. Just when I was about to surrender to my fate, a beautiful angel appeared and somehow destroyed the beast who had me bound and gagged. Miss Harrison, I don't know how, but that angel looked exactly like you.'

'I'm sorry, but I have no idea what you're talking about,' Gabby stammered.

'I understand it is an unlikely tale, and one that makes no logical sense, but somehow this angel who looked just like you helped people in trouble like me.' Scarlett squeezed her hand to encourage Gabby to see this truth.

'It sounds like a fairy tale more than real life.' Gabby smiled weakly back at the stranger. She seemed like a lovely lady even though her story sounded more like make-believe.

'Well, this may trigger your memory a little, as you left this behind when the demon broke it that fateful night.' Scarlett took a shimmering piece of red metal out of her white doctor's coat.

Gabby held the piece to the light, watching it sparkle with a life of its own.

'That's unbelievable! I think I have the other piece of this star,' Gabby whispered as she marvelled at the half-symbol of the Blood Tree leaf.

'Of course you do. It was yours, after all,' Dr Scarlett whispered reverently. 'Ever since that night, I understand there is another world unseen to us mere mortals, a world that can be violent or kind and beautiful. I'm just thankful you heard my pleas that night and saved me.' Scarlett looked at Gabby holding her red star with wonder in her eyes.

'I do believe in angels,' Gabby murmured.

'Not many people believe me. But I also have this keepsake to remind me. This is what he did that night.' The doctor lifted her fringe to reveal a scar that followed her hairline, and then she lifted the sleeve of her scrubs to show a deep scar along her forearm, indented where the flesh had been scooped out.

Gabby frowned as a whisper of recollection flitted across her mind. She had seen these wounds before, but how? And when?

'I'm sorry. I didn't mean to frighten you with such horror. I just had to come to you and say how thankful I am that you intervened. And to let you know that I have never forgotten what you said: "Scarlett, make your life count; don't waste a moment," and I did. After my rehabilitation, I finished my degree and have used that knowledge to serve my fellow man. I have saved many lives at this hospital, all because of you.'

'I don't know, maybe this is a dream.' Gabby sighed from the exhaustion of trying to concentrate so hard.

'Sweet angel, now you need your rest. I know Heaven has sent you here to do something very special, and I hope we meet again someday.' Scarlett leaned forward to softly kiss her on the cheek.

Gabby smiled uncertainly at her curious visitor as she pushed through the heavy hospital doors back into the ward.

Holding the cool metal tightly in her hand, Gabby knew it was the same as the piece she had found on the beach those many years ago at San Remo. It was made from a material she had never seen since, and the coincidence was not lost on her.

However, it was a big leap to say that she was some angel who had saved the doctor. But then the stranger at Miranda's had said Gabby had no idea who she really was.

Who was she?

Or what was she?

With her head pounding, Gabby decided to stop trying to solve the puzzle and just accept what she knew and let go of what she didn't. She knew her life was surrounded by good friends and family and that they were doing what they believed in. For now, that was enough to allow her to drift into a peaceful sleep.

The next morning, if she hadn't had the memento as proof, she would have blamed the whole experience on her opiate-affected state. With so many unanswered questions, she hid the piece of metal away and didn't mention her visitor in the night.

Twenty-two

Three days later, Gabby was released with strict instructions from her doctor to take it easy until her body had fully healed.

The dogs were so happy to see her; they howled with pleasure and declared to the whole world that she was back. She gently hugged each of them and stroked their beautiful coats. Samson had his front leg in a half-plaster cast and had to hop around on his other three legs, holding that stiffened leg off the ground. A shudder passed through her as she was reminded of that day and how close they had come to death.

Ben explained that the vet wanted to leave the cast on for about four weeks to make sure the leg healed completely. Gabby allowed her mind to touch the dogs'. It was strange, the connection she had formed, as now she could sense what the dogs felt, and they could also sense what she was experiencing. An unusual phenomenon, but one that felt completely natural between these three. Today, they were all happy, especially now that she was here with them. Gratefully, she passed them a message of love and thankfulness for their protection.

They both whined and barked as if they were trying to say something.

There was a party waiting inside. Kathleen and Joe had cooked a feast of her favourite food, and they all gathered around the table to celebrate her return home. After only a nibble or two, she had to retire early due to overwhelming exhaustion, so excusing herself, she went off to bed. Kathleen followed Gabby to make sure she was comfortable, and hovered near the door when Miranda poked her head around the corner.

Gabby was relieved to see the blisters on her face had almost cleared now that she had stopped picking and scratching at her skin.

'I just wanted to say I am so grateful for what you did for me, Gabby. I am sure you agree that I wouldn't be here if you hadn't come over that day. I owe you my life.'

Shaking her head, Gabby told Miranda there was no debt. 'When I'm stronger, we need to have a really good chat about what happened, certainly as soon as I can keep my eyes open for at least a couple of hours.' She smiled contritely.

Miranda nodded her black tresses in understanding and quietly closed the bedroom door.

In the darkness, Gabby closed her eyes to rest but strange memories kept flashing through her mind. Memories of seeing people suffering terrible injuries, of cruelties more dreadful than her exhausted body could ever sustain.

'Stop it!' She scolded herself to let go of this internal torment. Where did all this come from?

It had started as soon as her consciousness had returned in hospital, and now it seemed she was being bombarded with images of another life in another time. Not even a life as a human, as this being could never have witnessed so much in a normal lifespan.

The visions were of the sort that historians only dreamed of, and now it seemed her mind was the storage bank that these memories had been archived within.

How was she going to live as she had before with all these images running through her head?

Eventually her mind must have surrendered to fatigue, and sleep came, only to be replaced by the wildest of dreams. One that Gabby couldn't forget was descending through this swirling cloud tunnel and knowing she had to follow the light for a safe passage.

Miranda had asked if she could stay with them at the cottage, just in case someone else tried to attack her at home again.

Kathleen had also decided to stay on to spend some more time with her daughter, and to make sure her recovery continued under a mother's watchful eye. Frank had returned to Cairns to reassure Jacob and Thomas that Gabby was recovering. They called daily but hadn't been able to get time away from their jobs to fly down.

Before Gabby could talk further with Miranda, she spent time with Joe to discuss what had happened to them that afternoon. A week later, while sitting on a secluded park bench with Goliath beside her, Gabby broached the subject that sat heavy between them.

'What's going on, Joe? Suddenly the world I thought I knew looks totally alien.'

'Alien is a good word to describe what you experienced at Miranda's house. I have never seen anything like that in my rather long life, Gabby. It seems we are caught up in something that we don't understand, and all I can suggest is that we seek advice from those who might.'

'Who would know of such things? Until last week, I was completely ignorant of these people and their abilities.'

'Father Gerry would be a good place to start. That man is much more than meets the eye. He may understand what has happened and tell us how to avoid any further altercations with these dangerous people in the future. Can you tell me more about what happened that afternoon? Exactly what did that man do to you, Gabby?'

'At first he made me feel things that I never knew. Sexual things.'

'Did he sexually assault you?' Joe raged at the thought.

'Only with his mind. Then he hurt me so badly that I almost died, until I got angry with him. Do you remember what happened the last time I got angry?'

'Oh, yes. You threw me across a room, through a door and almost knocked me out.

'Why does this happen, and how can I be that strong? I mean it is insanely strong when it happens.'

'I'm not sure, Gabby. You have many attributes that are unexplainable. For instance, how can you communicate with your dogs without speaking?'

'You've noticed? It's a connection of the minds that has been getting stronger for a while. This is why I stopped eating meat. It seemed wrong to understand an animal's thoughts and then eat it. I know it's strange, but it's true.'

'Is it all animals or just the Titans?'

'When I concentrate, I can make that connection with any animal, but not humans. So I am still not as strong as that cult master, you mentioned that's what he was, who got inside my head.'

'It is certainly strange times,' he sighed.

'Joe, there is another thing I need to ask you, and I need the truth.'

'What do you want to ask?'

'That stranger who attacked us said some weird things. First-ly, he said you had disposed of Andy Bolton.' Her finely arched brows rose in question.

There was a long silence as he weighed up his options. 'That's true in a sense. I was instrumental in his fate, but the outcome was his doing and his alone.'

'That is not a sufficient explanation, Joe. As much as I hate to relive that day, please tell me exactly what happened.' Her green eyes darkened with pain at the memory.

'We have never spoken of that day. You cannot imagine how it felt to find you lying broken and bloody on that dirt track. I thought my heart was going to break, Gabby, and what he did to you cried out for retribution. As soon as I knew you were out of surgery, I went home to get what I needed. Track-ing him through the scrub was easy, and I almost choked on bile when I saw your blood drying on his face and knuckles.

'I dispensed justice in the fairest way that I knew how. Spirit Ants can determine just how dark a soul really is, and if there is no hope of redemption, they will dispose of the wickedness. Andy had his chance but he was beyond saving and met his fate exactly the way he deserved.'

'Spirit Ants? Joe what are you talking about?' Gabby was aghast. She reached down to stroke Goliath's smooth coat, needing a physical reminder of a positive supernatural occur-rence.

Joe took his time to describe the tribal life he had shared with the Aborigines and the intuitive abilities of the Spirit Ants. 'This was the best way, and I believe the fairest way, to treat him after what he did to you.' He sat back and waited for her to respond.

'It would be a terrifying way to die. Joe, I cannot condone your actions, even if I understand your motives. Why didn't you tell me about this before?'

'I promised to keep their identity a secret. It is part of the oath I swore with the elders of my tribe, and I would never have told you about them if you hadn't been informed of Andy's demise.'

'There are so many strange happenings at the moment. The existence of Spirit Ants that can be judge and jury, and then the man who hurt Miranda and me. It feels like the world I thought I knew doesn't really exist, but instead I have fallen down a rabbit hole and wandered into a nightmare. Where are they now?'

'Where are what?' Joe said.

'The Spirit Ants, Joe. Surely you don't just leave them running around!' Gabby said incredulously.

'Of course not. They were retrieved after Andy's verdict, and I have sent them back to the red land, to their traditional people.'

'My head is spinning with so much to process that I don't know what to think. Who am I, or maybe I should ask, what am I?' Gabby glanced sidelong at Joe through a curtain of blonde hair.

'Who or what you are doesn't matter. You belong to us and we belong to you and that is all that matters. The rest of this uncertainty can be faced together, and I am sure that one day it will all make sense. We're just not there yet.'

'This is why you are my dearest friend, Joe. One I can always rely on for wisdom and unconditional love.'

With arms interlocked they left the park and started for home.

But Gabby never mentioned her visit from Dr Scarlett Jones, not to anybody.

A couple of days later, Miranda and Gabby sat just outside the cottage. They spread a rug on the lawn in the shade of the Jacaranda tree with a jug of freshly squeezed lemonade to enjoy.

'Miranda, if it isn't too painful, can you tell me how this all began?'

Miranda hung her head in shame. 'Gabby, it all started with a desire to be accepted. My parents died in a car accident when I was little, and all I had left was a very elderly grandmother, who loved me in her own way until her health began to fail. Most of my life was spent looking after her as best I could.' Gabby reached out and took Miranda's hand in hers as her tears began to fall.

'Growing up, I used to watch other children so intently, resenting their loving parents and siblings, wishing the same for myself. Then in my teen years, I felt so abandoned by God that I turned in the opposite direction, reading books about the occult and the dark arts until one day two years ago, I met Rowan at our church.

'He was tall and fair, a good-looking guy who seemed a little shy like me. His eyes were like the sea on a calm day, and his cheeks hinted at dimples when he smiled. The connection between us was instant so I didn't hesitate to accept his offer of a coffee catch-up. We ordered coffee after coffee as we sat talking for hours and hours. I could hardly believe he was interested in me, and after this prolonged coffee date we spent almost every day together.' Gabby squeezed her hand.

'Rowan had a very volatile relationship with his father, a cruel and domineering man who constantly criticised him. No matter what he did, it was never good enough, so after another night of fighting, he couldn't stand it anymore and moved in with me instead. We became even more involved in the Satanic church after this and attended meetings at the local charter. Each initiate gets a tattoo on the arm with their very own identifying mark.'

She lifted her sleeve to show Gabby a large tattoo of a red rose dripping with blood amongst a nest of black thorns. It covered the entire inside of her forearm and one can only imagine how much this would have hurt.

'That would have been very painful, especially here,' Gabby murmured as she ran her finger along the symbol of oppression.

'Rowan's tattoo was the same size, but instead it was of a goat standing on a rock.'

'How does the hierarchy work in this organisation?' Gabby wanted to know.

'Well, there are cult leaders and priests, some are male and some female. There are also cult masters, and the most powerful of all is the magician. On a local level, we would only have contact with the priests and leaders. The cult master is too important, and the magician, well, he is always spoken of in a hushed voice and I think he is based in Rome or somewhere like that. The cult leader told us he would soon be making a momentous decision and that it would change the whole focus of our worship.'

Gabby's skin started to crawl, but she nodded to encourage Miranda to continue.

'The big announcement was that at the next black mass they would be making a human sacrifice. The leader told us all of the names of our coven would be considered and that one vastly fortunate member would be selected to give the ultimate gift to our dark lord.'

'You mean they meant to kill someone,' Gabby asked in shock.

'Yes, but they spoke of it as a great honour to offer your life as a sacrifice.' Miranda struggled to explain the power of extremism and the sway it held over a life.

Any rational person would have bolted at the first hint of human sacrifice, but she and Rowan had been brainwashed by those crafty in the dark arts.

'Miranda, where is Rowan,' Gabby asked with a sinking sensation.

'I'm getting to that part, Gabby. I just hope you can understand. When this announcement was proclaimed, I felt sick inside. As much as I valued being a part of something greater than myself, I was in love and didn't want to die.'

'Of course you didn't, and no faith should ask such a price.' Gabby clasped her hands in support as the tears were now streaming out of Miranda's eyes.

'Rowan was different; he didn't have any such traitorous thoughts. Instead, he became so excited. He relished the thought that he might be chosen to be a worthy sacrifice for the Prince of the Earth. I didn't want him to die. Deep down I wanted to get married and have children and raise them in Granny's little house, but it would have been sacrilegious to even voice these foolish longings.'

'What happened to Rowan?' Gabby whispered.

'I think I always knew that Rowan would be chosen, and right until his last breath, he gave his life without hesitation. I begged him to run away with me. I was so scared as this was no longer a safe harbour to find acceptance and purpose. It had become much more sinister than I had at first believed. But he remained determined to offer his life as a token of his faith and love for a prince he thought was worthy of the sacrifice.' Miranda was openly crying as she spoke.

'I'm so sorry, Miranda.' Gabby had tears coursing down her cheeks as well.

'I'll never forget that night. I had to attend even as my heart was breaking to lose my love, and at that moment, I hated them all. I realised they had taken advantage of our innocence but there was no turning back now, at least not for Rowan.'

For a while there was silence as Miranda seemed lost in the memory of the tragic event that had snatched away her happiness.

'I understand if it's too painful, Miranda....' Gabby squeezed her hand again.

Miranda seemed not to hear, and even her voice seemed to come from far away as she whispered. 'At the black mass, they gave Rowan a sedative to take away any fear, and he was laid out on the pentacle. He seemed at peace, but I wasn't sure if he really felt this way or if it was the effect of the drugs. I had tears pouring down my face but I couldn't even cry out loud as this would be seen as an act of defiance. As we circled, chanting, I looked deep into his eyes and tried to convey as much love as I could. Then they slashed him across the throat, and while he was dying, the priests collected his blood with a golden chalice and placed it on the altar.'

Gabby shuddered with revulsion. Did these people know no end to evil?

'After this, they began another prayer, a chant that got louder and louder until everyone fell to their knees to sway, holding shoulders and singing loudly. All the others kept their eyes closed, but I wanted to see what we were praying to, and then it came. There was the beating of wings, great heavy wings, much louder than any bird, and to my shock, a beast came through the ceiling. It moved through the solid timber like it was nothing and hovered over the altar. The air from those wings made the blood ripple and move like a living thing. The creature's flesh was pale and insipid as it settled onto the floor, stretching its long neck like a cobra about to strike. It had a face with fleshed pulled back so tight that it warped all its features, and when our gaze met, it growled with displeasure.'

'Miranda, did you actually see this demon?' Gabby asked, as the description matched some of the nasty memories locked in her head.

'Yes, Gabby. I swear my eyes were open wide. It wasn't some drug-induced hallucination.'

Gabby's sense of dread intensified. 'What happened then?' She wanted to know more about what they were potentially going to have to deal with.

'Settling before the chalice, the creature's long tongue flicked into the blood over and over again, savouring it until it infused the demon's insipid flesh with a soft red glow. I closed my eyes for just a second, and when I reopened them, the creature was gone. To finish the ceremony, the priests passed the chalice around the room for everyone to drink the blood of a martyr and share in the blessings.'

'Of course, I let it pass by me. All I could see in this cup of misery was the bleak future ahead of me without Rowan. Oh my God, if only I could turn back time and have him with me again.'

Miranda couldn't continue. She sat hunched over so far that her head was almost falling into her lap, and Gabby could see her shoulders shaking. Sitting closer, Gabby placed her arm gently across her shoulders and whispered that she understood the burden of grief.

After a while, Miranda looked at Gabby with tears still clinging to her long black eyelashes and cried out her pain. 'Do you know what hurts the most? It's that I didn't even try to save him, Gabby. Those bastards killed him; they slashed open his throat, and I just stood there like a statue. I didn't cry out for help, didn't make a noise, even though I was screaming inside, knowing they would kill me if I showed any sign of resistance. So I just stood there.

'After that, I tried to withdraw but they kept calling, dropping by, knowing they could not lose control of someone who knew their secrets. That is about the time you came into my life. You were like the bright sun in a dark room, and it hurt me even to look at you.'

'I'm so sorry, Miranda. I had no idea what you were going through. I wish I could have done something earlier, anything to save Rowan and prevent what they've done to you.' Gabby's whole persona was full of regret.

'Well, my first impression was that you couldn't really be that good, so I waited to see if you were as shallow as my own faith had become. But, of course, you weren't a fake, and like moths to a flame we all drew closer, even if it was against my will.' Gabby smiled at her.

'Until one day the priest from our coven came to my house to see me.'

'Why did you let him in the house? Surely after Rowan you cut all ties with these extremists.'

'It's not that easy, Gabby. Most people who want out just disappear.' Miranda shook her head in despair.

'Placing a black cloth on the table, he told me to take it. I hesitated until he laid his hand upon my back and put a compulsion upon me. Unable to fight it, like a zombie, I then stepped forward to unwrap an evil-looking dagger with inscriptions on the blade. The writing was in a strange language, and it whispered to me, "Plunge me into the heart of our enemy and wash the sin away in her blood."'

'I tried that day in the bathroom, and it took all of my willpower to resist the compulsion placed upon me. But in my heart, I knew that if I stepped over that line, I would be forever lost. To make it worse, you were right there offering to help me, never knowing that I was planning to take your life. A bizarre twist, wouldn't you say.'

Gabby would never forget that day either.

'After that, I stopped going to uni. I thought that if I didn't leave the house then I could resist the power they had over me. I heard you each time you came over to offer me a lifeline, but I was too scared that if I let you in, I might be overcome and try to attack you. So I just locked myself in the bedroom and re-fused to respond.' Gabby looked at her in sympathy.

'Then another made a house call. The cult master is a priest more powerful than anyone I had ever met before. As you know, he can inflict suffering using only his mind, and my an-guish was the bait to draw you in.'

Gabby shuddered at the memory but offered Miranda a sil-ver lining instead. 'Somehow, we overcame him, and now you have friends, Miranda. You never have to face them alone again.'

'Evil won't stop here, Gabby. They will attack with even more force next time, so I still fear for our lives.'

'That is why Joe and I want to meet with Father Gerry and see what he knows about cult masters. Are you comfortable to retell your story?'

'If you think he can help us, then yes, but I don't want to put any of you in this kind of danger.'

But both were heedlessly running full speed towards danger, whether Miranda wanted it or not.

Twenty-three

The following Monday afternoon, Joe, Gabby and Miranda went to the Catholic church and had a meeting in the priest's office.

Once everyone was settled, Father Gerry encouraged Miranda to trust him with her secrets.

'Miranda, it is very important that you tell me everything you heard and saw in these ceremonies. I need to know the strength of this congregation and the level of their commitment to Satanic worship.'

Miranda's voice was hardly more than a whisper as she explained all the things she had seen and done. 'The services are conducted quite similarly to a church service, except everyone wears black robes, and the priest wears a chasuble with the Sigel of Baphomet on the front. This is an inverted pentacle with the goat's head inside, which is the image of Satan. Their prayers are to Lucifer instead of God.

'A naked woman lies on the ground with her legs spread open as they pray to Lucifer, who has many names: the Morning Star, Prince of the Earth, Angel of the Bottomless Pit or the

Demon of Lust. Any of these were spoken in divine supplication. The black mass always has someone dressed as a nun wearing the full habit, and during the ceremony, she urinates in a font. The priest then consecrates this to Lucifer, and then will dip a chunk of black bread in her offering. This is shaken over the five points of the pentacle and then rubbed through the breasts and vaginal area of the naked woman. Finally, the priest will rub it on his own genitals before consuming a small part and sharing it with the congregation.'

Gabby just stared in horror at Miranda, unable to take in what she'd just said. Joe looked like he was having similar difficulty.

Father Gerry asked if they had made any human sacrifices, and Miranda nodded tearfully, then told him what had happened to Rowan. Other cultists had confessed that the priests regularly sexually abused children from as early as four years old, and in some covens, they even impregnated women in the order to use the infants as human sacrifices. This was considered the purest offering of all as the infant is a pure, innocent soul.

'Father Gerry, their evil powers have no boundaries, and they can control people and objects with their minds. This is a secret society, a group of madmen who have no respect for life or anything other than their own carnal lust and following the orders of 'the Morning Star'.

'They will not forget what happened that day at my house. I know too much and Gabby is already considered an enemy. They hate her for some reason and are hell bent on hurting her. They will not rest but seek us out and do everything they can to destroy us.' She looked around the room with wide eyes full of fear.

Father Gerry nodded and rubbed his chin, then spoke gravely. 'There is an expression that you must look fully into darkness before you can be enlightened by the light. So I am not going to pretend or tell you that these people are harmless because they're not. They meant to kill both of you, and I agree with Miranda that they will try again.

'Darkness is opposite to light, and these elements will not tolerate any opposition. For some reason, Gabrielle, they see you as a threat and will not hesitate to strike again.' He looked intently at each one as if to take their measure.

A shiver ran up their spines to hear Father Gerry speak of such an evil organisation. Miranda took Gabby's hand and squeezed it in comfort. 'I am so sorry that I have dragged you into my mess, Gabby,' she whispered.

'None of this is a coincidence, Miranda. We were meant to meet and work together, so never blame yourself. Father Gerry, is there anything we can do to fight back or are we just at their mercy?' Gabby asked in desperation.

'Unfortunately, this is a worldwide organisation that has infiltrated all levels of government and has many influential leaders as members. You would be surprised who is involved, from high court judges to doctors, police commissioners, politicians, bankers. These seemingly upright citizens by day become evildoers by night. Their members are from all walks of life but they mostly court important people as they will have the greatest influence for their ambitions.'

Gabby's shoulders slumped. 'So we are to become causalities of their crusade?'

'Well, not entirely. You have already proven that you have more strength than they first believed; however, they won't make that mistake again. Firstly, I think it would be a good idea to warn your friends what threats they face by being associated with you. Everyone needs to be prepared for the worst, should it happen, and we don't want any innocent bystanders unnecessarily wounded.'

'I have no fear of these fiends, Father Gerry. I am only concerned that those I love will be targeted.'

'Well, Gabby, there is a great likelihood that there will be other attacks, especially now that you have killed or injured one of their elite. Miranda, do you have any names or know the occupations of the other members in this coven?'

Miranda just shook her head and spoke quietly. 'All meetings were very secretive. We only got notification in our letter boxes, and you never ever saw anyone actually put them in there. After your induction ceremony, you were given special religious names so you never referred to anyone by their real names. My religious name was Blood Rose and Rowan's was Trickster,' she explained.

Father Gerry just sighed and stared off into space.

'What troubles you, friend?' Old Joe asked him

'A long time ago I was part of a small team chosen by the church in Rome to infiltrate these organisations. We were young, the most devout and dedicated priests that they gathered from all around the world. It was a spiritual war, a battle similar to what Gabby endured and fought against that afternoon. The highest cult masters can spirit travel, as these girls found out. They leave their body behind and enter the world in a different way. They look real, and feel real, but it is just a projection. Their actual body is left in another physical place. The strongest of these priests can maintain their astral travel for as long as they want to. When Gabby used a greater force to destroy this man–demon, she realised that he was not there in a physical sense at all.

'Even with them facing significant losses, we couldn't stop the tide. Their numbers were growing faster than we could recruit priests strong enough to hinder their advance. Eventually the program was abandoned, and even the most devout Catholics are completely unaware that this faction of the church ever existed.'

Joe added his insight to Father Gerry's account. 'Behind the façade of a civilised world there are old enemies who never rest.

Day and night they conspire to exert their influence over mankind. I am not a religious man but I have lived for far too long to deny their existence.'

'Father Gerry, if these adversaries are so powerful that we can't counter their advance, how do I look after those I love?' Gabby implored.

'There are no guarantees, Gabby. If they stay close to you, then they will also be exposed to the same danger.' He didn't want to devalue her concerns.

'Well, I don't want to see any more pain or suffering, and I think we need to get the rest of our friends in here so that they can choose if they still want to be a part of our future plans.' Gabby looked at the three of them before making calls to invite the rest of their Greater Good team to come to the church as soon as possible.

They waited for Ben, Elisabeth, Paul and Michael to arrive. Once they were all ensconced in the room, Miranda and Father Gerry filled the rest in on the previous conversation.

There was silence as each of them processed this most unusual tale. Elisabeth was first to break the mood. She asked Miranda a host of questions about the legal ramifications of what accounted to murder and how these people weren't charged in a court of law.

Miranda replied that even judges were a part of the occult and that there were always ways to obviate the course of justice.

'Surely, somebody can come forward as a witness to bring the murderers to account,' Elisabeth argued.

'If a witness did come forward, they would soon disappear without a trace,' Miranda countered her argument.

Michael seemed more concerned with how great a hostility they were facing. 'Miranda, how many people are a part of this cult? Are we talking about ten or fifty, and how likely are they to strike at us?' He was doing the math in his head.

'Michael, my group was just a small part of a huge underworld that is in every part of the world. I would say it's an international threat more than a local Victorian concern.' Miranda shrugged her shoulders to show she didn't know how many enemies they were dealing with.

Paul seemed more concerned about Gabby than his own safety. 'Gabby, I don't want to see you hurt again,' he muttered.

Ben spoke his promise with body language more than words. He just stood and went to Gabby's side and pressed his shoulder into hers to show his love and support.

'Ben, Elisabeth, Michael and Paul, I love you all. I don't want any of you to get hurt or suffer because of an association with me. There is no dishonour at all if you don't want to continue to work together. We will not judge you or think any worse for your decision.' Gabby's eyes solemnly spoke to each of them.

This was no trifling affair. Everyone present had seen how close to death Gabby was just a few weeks ago, and it was the same adversary that was now a threat to everyone here.

'Count me in. I'm here for the long haul, and nothing and nobody is going to scare me away from what I plan to do with my life.' Ben smiled grimly to reinforce his statement.

Gabby nodded her acceptance of his decision and let the quiet settle again.

Paul re-pledged his continued support. 'Without this group of people, I'm nothing, so I would rather continue to the end, supporting you, Gabby, at whatever cost that may be.' He looked seriously around the circle.

Michael and Elisabeth both spoke up at once, then Michael stopped to let her continue.

'Well, I have listened and weighed up the risks, and I am not going to be bullied out of what I believe. So I'm not going anywhere.' She smiled at Michael to encourage him to have his say.

'Elisabeth has spoken for me too,' he replied simply.

'It's settled then. We stick together until the end.' Gabby looked with trepidation at her truly loyal friends, hoping that the end would be a ripe old age for each of them.

Joe reached over and hugged her close. 'I want to throw my support behind all of you, so know that I will always be here for anyone in this group. You have all become a second family to me. I promise to stand shoulder to shoulder with you against this new threat, and if we unite, I believe we should withstand whatever diabolical plan they hatch.'

Gabby hugged him back fiercely. Whatever would she do without this rock in her life? Always it was Joe she turned to, from trivial to life-threatening situations.

'There is another otherworldly encounter I think we should share, just so that you know an attack could happen in the most ordinary of places.' Joe then asked Gabby to explain to the group what had happened the night the Titans first arrived. They had never shared that experience before as it seemed too weird, but in light of recent events, Joe thought it best that Father Gerry knew this had also happened to Gabby years earlier.

After her voice trailed away, Father Gerry interjected. 'Well, I think that you would have had trouble with this evil even if Miranda wasn't in your life. It's obvious that you are a target who they want eliminated, one way or another. And we need to find out why. The fact that you were able to crush one of their own with your bare hands is something we need to explore.' Father Gerry's frown had almost as many wrinkles as Old Joe's.

Gabby had no answers and couldn't explain to the priest and her friends where this power had come from.

Turning to the concerned priest, she voiced out loud what all the others had on their minds. 'Father Gerry, I don't have any answers for you, so what now?'

'Now is being cautious, now is always looking out for each other, now is being aware of this unseen menace and never, not ever, underestimating their evil intentions.' His deep voice reverberated through the small office.

A heavy silence weighed upon them until Joe broke the spell of doom with some much-needed brevity.

'Let's go home and eat something.' He offered a small slice of normality on such a strange night.

Father Gerry cautioned them all one last time before they left his office. 'Do not think that they have forgotten you because all seems quiet. Another thing to remember is this: Please don't mention any of this to anyone outside this circle. I can't emphasise enough that everyone who knows of their existence is at risk. We need to minimise their targets as much as we can.'

They all sombrely nodded their acquiescence and said their farewells.

The warm cavern suddenly felt too hot, and the demon stalked stiffly around his chamber to consider the disturbing report he had just received. Sut was so furious that even his marvellous chair couldn't calm his temper.

'Jinn, where the hell are you? Come at once,' he demanded through the cavernous cave.

Jinn hurried into the warm space to stand before his leader. He sensed the belligerent mood so hunched his shoulders and kept his eyes lowered to the dusty ground. 'Sut, my leader, what perturbs you?' he asked timidly.

'Your wicked plan has come to naught and instead the virtuous one has injured one of our faithful. She used her powers!' Sut screeched this final comment at Jinn.

'Fallon used her celestial powers?' Jinn whispered in surprise.

'Yes, you moron, she used her powers, and now both realms are in uproar. The council will be scouring the earth trying to find her conspirer, a messenger known as Josiel, to punish her for disobeying their orders.' Sut began to pace out his angst.

'Punish her how?' Jinn asked with intrigue.

'Probably put her in chains or even clamp her wings if they're really pissed,' Sut revealed.

'Clamping her wings seems harsh. Maybe we're still more alike than I thought,' Jinn mused.

Sut wasn't listening. He had bigger worries. 'Now this will impact us and our plans. The last thing we need is a bunch of scout angels moving through our realm.' He fumed at the thought.

'What does this have to do with us anyway?' Jinn uttered in confusion.

'You fool, it means with their heightened presence here, they may just stumble over our truth,' Sut said between gritted, sharpened teeth.

'I still don't understand. What is our truth?' Jinn countered, knowing he was on unsteady ground.

'No matter, you foolish, lowly demon. You are not in the confidence of our great leader, the Prince of the Earth. Instead, you continue to fail at the tasks assigned to you.' Sut stalked back to his shimmering seat to contemplate this new dilemma.

'I promise this errant messenger will rue the day she chose to live among humanity and the fallen. Even with her powers, she is one amongst many and will fall as brutally as we dared to hope.' Jinn pleaded for Sut to believe in him.

'All I can say is you had better make her suffer and bring me her blood as promised or you will be thrown into the pits to live out your eternity,' Sut threatened menacingly.

That night, long after everyone had either left or retired, Gabby lay on her bed looking at the ceiling. She dared not close her eyes for fear of the visions that would flood forth, some mesmerising and others quite frightening.

In desperation, she opened her underwear drawer and began to rummage through bras and lacy underwear, her actions so hasty the contents spilled out over the timber floor.

Finally, her fingers brushed against the familiar cold red metal and she drew out the pieces she had secreted away at different times in her life.

The first red metal piece had been the treasure she had retrieved from the seabed at San Remo Beach, an act that had almost taken her life. Here it sat in the palm of her hand, the coolness somehow soothing on her feverish skin. Then she picked up the second piece that Dr Scarlett Jones had pressed into her hand that night at the hospital.

It was almost identical, like a matching piece, and for such a long time, Gabby rolled one over the other in her hand, trying to find a link or something that made the two pieces fit back together.

In frustration, she threw them down on her bedspread, and as they landed tangled in the covers, a miracle happened. Somehow as they struck each other at a certain angle, they fused together as one piece once again. What looked like two identical pieces were actually the two halves of metallic red star.

The star began to shine as brightly as a burning sun and strangely, she could see blood bubbling inside

In wonder, Gabby picked up the splendorous jewel, and as it touched her skin, a fire began to burn within. The star glimmered in her hands with a life of its own, and Gabby's entire body began to hum with a new force coming from deep within. An aeon of memories flashed through her mind, restoring her awareness of her true being. Rising from her bed, she was now filled with the certainty of who she was and who she had been.

No longer fearful of the memories of a past life or lives, Gabby understood the path that she, as Fallon, had taken after that innocent soul in the orb had died. It was a path that had led to her being ostracised from her own kind, and explained why this life was full of vipers and perils as payment for her act of selfless love.

There was one memory that stood out amongst all others. She saw it standing there majestically, the Blood Tree, thrumming with that celestial tune that always drew her in like a siren. Gabby whispered reverently, 'I'm back, my old friend. I can feel your power and wisdom flowing through me again. I'm going to need you now more than ever.'

Knowing her remarkable backstory, Gabby couldn't sit still, especially not with this new force bubbling like champagne through her veins. Restlessly, she paced about the room, suddenly feeling confined in the small space. She paused halfway between her bed and the bedroom door and stared at the wall in front of her.

Remembering how Fallon could move through matter, Gabby walked forward to tentatively place her hand upon the wall, and to her incredulity, her flesh disappeared into the wood. She felt no pain and no sense of displacement, only the thought of going from here to there.

Gabby or Fallon, whatever her name may be, knew she was no longer a victim. And on this night, the hunted became the hunter.

END OF BOOK ONE

ACKNOWLEDGEMENTS

Thank you to my amazing editor and independent publisher, Dr Juliette Lachemeier at The Erudite Pen, who has made this rough diamond into a bright star. To my book cover designer Judith San Nicolas for creating such an eye-catching, unique design. To my much-loved family, husband Fred Casella, my sons, Evan, Aaron and Ben, to their partners, Claudia, Makala and Loccy. To my sisters Gale Poyner and Leandra Watson for being my sounding board. Thank you to my beta readers, Mary Casella, Marcia Fry, Tairiau Bridgart, Nola Thorburn, Jenna D'Addona, Lucinda Drake, Janine Currie, Melanie Zappulla and Felise Johnston. Thank you to Darren Davis for retrieving my manuscript from the Kensai Airport lost property. You have all been invaluable in supporting my writing dream so that it could become a published reality.

ABOUT THE AUTHOR

Lyndell Casella grew up in Far North Queensland, Australia. She always remembers the thrill of learning to read. Words sparked her imagination and together they became a doorway into another world – an enchanted world. This infatuation with stories led to the desire to write her own story, her very own arrangement of words that would also transport readers into other worlds.

As a child, Lyndell's mind always thirsted for fanciful flights into exciting adventures. She was constantly reading and devouring every word her eyes could discover. As an adult, she became busy with life, and those imaginary flights of fancy took a back seat. However, her childhood wish to create and write her own adventures lay dormant like a seed buried deep beneath a winter snow. It only stirred and began to swell after a heartbreaking period in her life.

This heartbreak caused her to look closely at life and death. Was there still a consciousness when physical life ceased? This questioning ignited something deep within, and she 'saw' her own arrangement of words for this trilogy, strung out like a string of pearls, gleaming and beautiful to the eye. *The Blood Tree* is the first book in The Greater Good Trilogy, her gleaming string of pearl-words.

Enjoyed the book? You can follow the author at:

Email: lyndell.casella@gmail.com

Facebook: facebook.com/lyndellcasella.author

Website: lyndellcasella.com

If you liked the book, please leave a review on Amazon, Goodreads or with the author directly. Reviews are invaluable in supporting an author's hard work and are greatly appreciated.